She lunged forward, slamming him against the brick wall at his back, her forearm against his throat. "Who are you?" she snarled.

Stunned, he didn't resist her. Clearly, she had some serious self-defense training, which only furthered his certainty that this was a woman who believed herself to be in mortal danger.

"I told you," he rasped past her forearm. "I'm Marcus Tate."

"That's your name. Who are you?"

"I don't understand—"

"How did you follow me without me spotting you? How do you know I look in shop windows to check my six? For that matter, why are you here? Why did you think you could take down some bad guy who might be following me?"

Aah. He didn't usually talk about his job, and certainly not with civilians. But this situation was not usual in any way. "I'm a soldier," he gasped.

Dear Reader,

Greetings! I'm so delighted you're here and that we get to spend a little time together! I've written a story for you that I hope will sweep you away into the high Rockies of Montana and bring you a bit of excitement and escape.

I can't tell you how excited I am to get the opportunity to combine three of my all-time favorite series in one book! In *Her SEAL Bodyguard*, we meet Marcus Tate, who is another of my yummy SEAL heroes. I mean, who doesn't love a big, dangerous guy devoted to keeping you feeling safe and loved? We also get to know Medusa Gia Rykhof as she stars in her own suspenseful story. (For those of you new to the Medusas, they're an all-female Special Forces team who can keep up with the boys step for step, but also relish being women.) And third, we get to go back to Sunny Creek, Montana, and the Clearwater Valley where I've written lots of other fun stories.

I do have to confess I went into this book with a goal in mind of keeping this story fun and a bit lighter than I usually write. I tend to lean in hard to the suspense, danger and heavy tension, but I think we've all had plenty of that the past few years in our real lives. My hope was to deliver a pulse-pounding adventure and also to make you smile now and then, too.

So, sit back, pour yourself your favorite relaxation beverage, prop your feet up and get ready to enjoy a fun ride as Gia and her SEAL bodyguard, Marcus, sweep you away to romance, suspense and happily-ever-after...

Hugs and happy reading,

Cindy

HER SEAL BODYGUARD

Cindy Dees

ISBN-13: 978-1-335-75971-9

Her SEAL Bodyguard

For questions and comments about the quality of this book, please contact us at CustomerService@Harlequin.com.

Harlequin Enterprises ULC
22 Adelaide St. West, 41st Floor
Toronto, Ontario M5H 4E3, Canada
www.Harlequin.com

Printed in U.S.A.

New York Times and *USA TODAY* bestselling author **Cindy Dees** is the author of more than fifty novels. She draws upon her experience as a US Air Force pilot to write romantic suspense. She's a two-time winner of the prestigious RITA® Award for romance fiction, a two-time winner of the RT Reviewers' Choice Best Book Award for Romantic Suspense and an *RT Book Reviews* Career Achievement Award nominee. She loves to hear from readers at www.cindydees.com.

Books by Cindy Dees

Harlequin Romantic Suspense

Runaway Ranch

Navy SEAL's Deadly Secret
The Cowboy's Deadly Reunion
Her SEAL Bodyguard

Colton 911: Chicago

Colton 911: Desperate Ransom

Mission Medusa

Special Forces: The Recruit
Special Forces: The Spy
Special Forces: The Operator

Code: Warrior SEALs

Undercover with a SEAL
Her Secret Spy
Her Mission with a SEAL
Navy SEAL Cop

Visit the Author Profile page at Harlequin.com for more titles.

Chapter 1

Gia Rykhof's fingers danced on the roller ball mouse beside her computer monitor as she made tiny, continuous adjustments to the video image on her screen. It was dark and grainy, but then, it was being shot from a highly classified surveillance drone cruising at 60,000 feet altitude over the spec ops mission on her monitor.

The special operations team she was providing real-time intelligence assessments to was clearing out the compound of a notorious warlord halfway around the world from where she sat tonight, just outside of Washington, DC. Sometimes the global nature of modern military technology startled even her.

She spoke into her headset. "Alpha Four, you've got two hostiles hiding behind the chicken coop at your ten o'clock, distance thirty yards. They're armed and appear to be waiting for you to approach."

"Roger, Eagle Eyes," one of the operators breathed.

She watched in the red-tinted darkness of the ops center as two operators peeled off from the pack and ran over to the front side of a narrow, stucco chicken coop. The pair crouched beside it and placed a shaped charge on the wall about waist high. They ran back to the team and, at a hand signal from their leader, blew a hole through the chicken coop that threw the two hostiles some fifty feet back to slam into the compound's stone wall. Both hostiles lay on the ground, unmoving.

She rolled her view to the right of where the team was advancing. "Alpha Four, I've got six heat signatures in the building at your three o'clock. Four are child-sized. Two adults. The building beyond it at your two o'clock had five adult heat signatures sixty seconds ago, but they are no longer present. Either the targets went outside and managed to drop off my screen, or they went underground."

A single click in her ear was all the acknowledgment she got, but it was enough. She watched as the team leader fanned out a dozen of his men to the right toward the second building. Another team of four guys entered the first building with the kids and, presumably, two women. She lost visual on the four operators but picked them up on the infrared monitor to her left as they entered the building. They met no resistance inside.

Not so, the men outside. A sharp firefight ensued, and she was kept hopping, calling out positions of the hostiles as they darted from building to building for cover. The warlord's compound had some fifteen buildings in it, and every one had to be taken, cleared, secured and then advanced past.

Gia's neck was stiff and her shoulders were aching by

the time the team finally declared the compound clear. Alpha Four's team leader assigned about a quarter of his men to guard prisoners and make one last sweep of the compound. He and the rest of his guys headed into the house where the hostiles had disappeared from. They would head underground and try to track down the warlord, who had escaped the initial assault.

"Thanks for the help, Eagle Eyes," Alpha Four's leader transmitted.

She clicked her mike button once. "Good hunting," she wished the team as, one by one, they disappeared from her infrared feed when they went down into whatever tunnels lay beneath the compound.

She took advantage of the end of active combat to lean back and stretch her arms over her head. She wished she could've been there on the ground with the team tonight, but her own Special Forces team, the Medusas, was on leave for a month of R & R, and then would go into a training rotation after that. They'd be deployed again in about six months when they were all rested, fit and honed to an even sharper edge than ever.

A flu outbreak had taken the visual intel analysts at this station out of commission, and she'd been asked if she would delay her vacation for a week to come up here and fill in until the usual real-time intel analysts were out of bed and back at work.

A movement on her screen made her yank her arms down and lean forward intently. Nobody should be moving where those shadows had just slid along a wall at the edge of the compound. Had the warlord somehow managed to hide in one of the buildings and was he now trying to sneak out the back gate?

It would be a huge mistake. A Humvee with a machine gun mounted on it and three marines inside was standing off from the gate about a hundred feet, with orders to kill anyone who fled the compound.

She zoomed in the camera hovering miles over the compound and checked her infrared feed. The heat signatures of four men carrying a large object between them lit up. It looked like a wooden crate of some kind. The small infrared designator beacons that marked them as friendly forces to other operators—and, incidentally, to her—blinked on her screen. Those weren't hostiles escaping. Those were American Special Operators taking something out of the compound.

She frowned. She'd heard the entire mission briefing, and nobody had mentioned finding and pulling out a package of any kind. Packages could be people or objects, or even information. They were any valuable thing that a mission was designed to capture, move or retrieve.

Whatever was in that crate was heavy. Really heavy. Four Special Operators were staggering a little under the load of it, which would put the weight at close to a thousand pounds. The crate was around the size of a small desk. But what was in it?

People? Bodies? Gold? Or, more practically, weapons? Ammunition? A bomb? Her money was on it being metal, at least in part, to be that heavy.

She was reaching for her mike button to warn the marines outside that four friendlies were coming out through the gate, but just as she keyed her mike, the gunner swung his weapon up and away from the friendlies. He, too, must have spotted the flashing infrared beacons that indicated them as friendly operators.

The four men carried the crate over to the Humvee and set it down. Then, as a guy leaned in each of the open windows of the vehicle, the gunner ducked down inside, no doubt to hear whatever the Special Operators were saying.

The camera glitched for a moment, and when the picture came back, the four men were finishing horsing the big crate into the back of the Humvee. She watched in confusion as the vehicle drove away from the compound. What was up with that? The op wasn't over. Why had the marines in that vehicle abandoned their position?

Had new orders been given that she was unaware of? But as the real-time intel provider, she heard everything on all the radio channels and had been read in on the same mission briefing the operators on the ground had—

The door behind her opened and a slash of bright white light from the hallway outside blinded her.

"Hey! You just wrecked my night vision!" she protested. "You're supposed to close the outer door before you open the inner door."

A large black shape strode toward her as she blinked furiously, unable to even make out the guy's face. "I need your computer," he said gruffly.

"I beg your pardon?"

"Get out of your seat. I need your computer."

"I'm in the middle of supporting a live operation—"

She might be half-blind, but she wasn't so blind that she couldn't see the handgun the man pulled out of a shoulder holster under his suit coat and pointed at her.

"Sheesh. All right, already," she muttered as she stood up. She took off her headphones and laid them on the desk on the assumption that this jerk had new orders for the team and needed to relay them.

But the man didn't pick up the headphones. In fact, he didn't even sit down. He opened the cabinet under the workstation and yanked out the entire computer tower. He grabbed the bundle of wires plugged into the back of the machine and pulled them all out with a single, violent jerk.

"What are you doing?" she demanded. She started to move forward, but the man swung his pistol up fast.

She raised her hands and took a few steps backward. Her eyes were adjusting to the white light pouring in from the open door, and she memorized everything she could about the man. About six foot three. Muscular. Mostly bald. Remaining hair was cut very short and was gray. Oval face. Pale eyes, blue or maybe gray. Nose slightly crooked as if it had been broken. Wide mouth. Thin lips. Dimple in his chin. Long earlobes. Calloused and scarred hands—

"I was never here, and you never saw that mission," the man growled as he tucked her computer tower under his left arm, keeping the pistol trained on her with his right hand. "Say nothing to anyone about anything you saw tonight or about my having been here, or else you'll meet with an unfortunate accident very soon. Got it?"

She nodded slowly, never taking her gaze off him. Small scar under his left eye, about an inch long, right along the bottom of his eye socket. Five-o'clock shadow of white whiskers.

The man backed away from her, passed through the doorway he'd come in and closed the door. She rushed after him, but the door was locked. Irritated, she ran back to her desk, fumbled in her purse, retrieving her pistol and the key to this room's lock. She raced to the door, quickly unlocked it and charged out into the hallway.

Empty. The man and her computer tower were gone.

She ran down the hallway and burst outside through the fire exit. Loud alarms clanged behind her as she tore around the corner of the building to the parking lot.

Silence. No car was moving, no taillights retreating in the distance. She swore under her breath. She hadn't been fast enough. He'd gotten away. She did a quick circle of the building anyway, gripping the small pistol she kept in her purse as she scanned the woods around the single-story building.

No movement. If the guy had gotten away on foot, he was already too deep in the trees for her to spot him.

She ran back inside and closed up the building once more, checking each of the exits to be sure they were locked and the building secured. Thankfully, the deafening alarm went silent as she pulled the fire exit shut. Returning to the intel center, she called the facility commander, waiting impatiently for him to show up and decide how to proceed.

While she waited, she moved over to one of the other workstations and pulled up the security camera feeds for the building. At least she could try to isolate a good picture of the intruder to show to the security police and the guy in charge of this place when he got here.

She went through the feed of the main hallway leading back to this room. The intruder didn't show up anytime in the past hour. She rewound all the way back to when she'd arrived here some three hours ago and watched herself walk down the empty, antiseptic hall, unlock the door to this facility and step inside. She fast-forwarded through the rest of the footage between then and now, and there was no sign of the intruder.

She watched the feed of the rear hallway that led to the fire exit but didn't expect to see him there, either. After all, the loud door alarm hadn't gone off when he'd disappeared, but it surely had when she burst outside. She watched herself emerge from the surveillance facility and run down the hall.

She watched the footage from the exterior security cameras around the building, but still, there was no sign of the intruder. How in the heck had he gotten into and out of the building without being caught on camera?

For that matter, who in the heck was he, and how had he gotten into this facility at all? It took a specially encoded key with a computer chip in it to open any of the doors. And why had he gone straight for her computer? What was on it that was so important?

She looked over at her workstation. The jumble of unplugged cables lay on the floor, and the computer tower was definitely gone.

Pulling out her cell phone, she called her boss, Major Gunnar Torsten, commander of the Medusas and in charge of training and equipping the all-female Special Forces team.

"Hey, Gia. Have you been cut loose to start your leave?" he asked cheerfully.

"Not exactly. I think I was just robbed—or rather, this surveillance facility was just robbed—by a ghost. A ghost who threatened to kill me..."

Chapter 2

"Rachel. Rachel."

Oh, shoot. That was who she now was. Gia's head jerked up. Her middle name was Rachel, and she would've thought she'd be better at answering to it, but nope. She still had to remind herself every few minutes that she was Rachel, not Gia, and Boyd, not Rykhof.

Rachel Boyd. Rachel Boyd. Rachel Boyd.

Nobody'd warned her that assuming a fake identity would be this hard.

"Rachel!" a female voice called louder from behind her.

She turned around, smiling apologetically at Annabelle Sutter and saying, "Sorry. I couldn't hear you over the water." Not that the creek chuckling past—Sunny Creek, to be precise—was all that loud. It flowed out of Crystal Lake a mile east of here and was wide and shallow with a gravel bottom at this spot, its water clear and cold, with plenty of overhanging boughs and little tide pools perfect for trout to lurk in. Which was, of course, why the fly-fishing lesson was taking place here.

Annabelle tromped over to her through the water, looking ridiculous in a giant pair of rubber pants that came up to her armpits and were held up with suspenders.

"Do I look as funny as you in these waders?" Gia asked.

"Totally," Annabelle laughed. "I feel as if I'm about six years old and trying to walk in my father's boots."

"I know, right?"

Jackson Sutter, Annabelle's husband and today's fly-fishing instructor, called out, "Everyone gather over here."

Thankfully, "here" was only a few steps away, about hip deep in the cold water. The sun glittered off the riffles of water and flies buzzed lazily in the dappled sunlight near the shore. The air was warm, and it felt wonderful in contrast to the icy chill soaking through Gia's rubber waders.

Jackson said to the half dozen people gathered around him, "Now that you've all clumped around the river and scared away the fish, this is a perfect time to practice our fly casting. I'll explain and demonstrate. Then all of you can give it a try."

Gia watched carefully as Jackson demonstrated pulling about twenty-five feet of heavy fly line off his reel with his left hand and casting the featherlight hook and fly with his right hand. The shining strand of nylon line sailed out behind him in a candy-cane arc that was sheer art to behold. Backward and then forward the line flew, finally settling lightly to the water. Jackson reeled in his fly slow then fast, in fits and starts, mimicking the movement of an actual fly across the surface of the water.

When the fly was reeled all the way in, he started over, backcasting, then casting forward, letting the line sail out in another perfect, shimmering arc. He gave them a few tips about where to put their thumbs on the fishing rod, how to keep their wrists stiff and how to move the rod in a straight line.

Then he said, "Okay. All of you spread out and give it a try."

Gia slogged upriver several dozen yards, following a big, muscular guy who'd been mostly silent and had only given his name as Marcus back at the fishing lodge. His hair was dark brown and shone with red highlights in the bright sun. She had no idea what her hair was doing because her brunette locks were dyed a color her Medusa teammates had called honey blond. They'd even dyed her eyebrows sandy brown. It definitely felt weird looking in a mirror and seeing a blonde staring back.

The good news was that if she barely recognized herself, hopefully the guys trying to kill her also wouldn't recognize her.

"Okay, everybody," Jackson called. "Unspool twenty or twenty-five feet of line and give it a try. Don't forget to look back over your shoulder to see when the line is completely unfurled so you know when to make your forward cast."

Easy-peasy, right? She accelerated her arm back and then snapped it forward. Her lure and line plopped in a tangle about ten feet in front of her. Huh. She reeled in her line partway, undid a knot in it and started over. Thumb. Wrist. Look back. Cast.

She flung her rod and line forward.

"Ouch!" the big man upstream of her yelped.

She looked down the length of her rod and heavy white line. It ended squarely in the middle of the man's muscular back.

"Aw, crap," she muttered. Then louder, "Don't move. I think I've hooked you."

"Ya think?" the man replied dryly.

Of course, she had to make a complete idiot of herself in front of the hottest guy in the whole river. Although, there was a certain ironic humor in the notion that she'd caught herself a man. Literally.

She slogged toward him as fast as she could shove her legs through the water, reeling in line as she went.

"Are you actually reeling me in?" he demanded, looking over his shoulder at her approach.

"I've already had to undo one big knot in the line. I figured you wouldn't want to have to stand around with my hook in your back while I untangled my line."

He scowled but said nothing.

She reached his cotton-clad back and leaned in close to have a look. "I'm gonna have to cut your shirt to see what's up with the hook."

"Aw, man. I love this shirt," he muttered.

"I'll get you a new one," she replied tartly. "Stand still. I have to see how bad the hook is buried in your skin." She pulled out her handy-dandy pocketknife and unfolded the tiny scissors. She enlarged the small tear in his shirt where the fly and hook had poked through it.

She pulled the fabric away from his tanned skin and the long, thick bulge of a muscle running parallel to his spine. She put her finger next to the fly and noted that the muscle was rock-hard. This guy was in seriously good shape.

"Don't move," she murmured. "I'm going to cut away the feathers from the hook to see what's going on."

She snipped at the little bit of fluff and feather, disappointed to have to ruin the first fly she'd ever tied. It had been pretty, if she said so herself. If she were a trout, she was sure she'd have found it irresistibly tasty-looking.

Snip. Snip. Snip.

The feathers fell away and she leaned in close to examine the small hook. She exhaled hard in relief. "Only the tip of the hook is poking into your skin. The barb didn't embed itself in your back. All I have to do is pull it out like this—" she tugged the sharp little hook out of his back, and a thin trickle of blood ran down his skin "—and voilà. You're off my hook. You're free to swim away, Mr. Very Large Trout."

He turned around to glare at her. "A trout? Seriously?"

"Well, you do look more like a shark than a trout," she allowed.

"Thank you, I think," he grumbled.

In fact, he was quite a handsome shark. His bronzed features were rugged without being rough, and his eyes were a blue so dark they almost looked black. He radiated aggressive health and quiet, but total, confidence. One hundred percent her type.

Too bad she couldn't even contemplate starting a relationship. Not in her current mess. The last thing she needed to do was drag some nice civilian guy into her danger. It was hard enough looking out for herself. She didn't want or need to be responsible for keeping another person safe, too.

But at least she could enjoy looking at this man and chatting with him for a few minutes. After all, she wasn't dead, yet.

"Rachel Boyd. And I'm really sorry about hooking you."

One corner of his mouth turned up in an adorably crooked smile. "Marcus. Marcus Tate. I have to give you props for an original come-on. Can't say as any woman has ever gone fishing for me quite like this."

She felt her face heating up. "I've got a first-aid kit. I should probably sterilize that wound and put a bandage on it so you don't catch…I don't know…trout plague."

"You have a first-aid kit on you here, in the middle of the river?" he echoed, sounding startled.

In point of fact, she was wearing her military utility vest, which was a nylon mesh affair covered in small snap-shut pockets that would hold all the doodads, small gadgets and spare ammunition that were her tools of the trade. Today it was minus the ammunition, det cord and grenades she would usually carry into combat. But she hadn't removed her first-aid kit, power bars, knife and a few other handy essentials. And it did look a lot like a fishing vest, if she said so herself.

To Marcus, she shrugged. "I like to be prepared. You never know when you'll need to dig a fish hook out of a hot guy's back—" She broke off, horrified. "I'm sorry. That was inappropriate—"

His dark blue eyes glinted for a moment in what she hoped was humor. Then he murmured, "No offense taken. If you've got the stuff handy, I guess I will take a little alcohol and a bandage. Wouldn't want to catch trout plague, after all, and start growing fins and gills."

She rolled her eyes at him as he smirked at her. "Turn around, then."

He presented his back once more, and this time she took note of the width of his shoulders and the lack of any inner tube around his hard, lean waist. Real regret that she absolutely couldn't pursue any kind of relationship with this man coursed through her. He really was a thing of beauty to look at and seemed reasonably nice.

Over his shoulder, he said, "Did you know that vest you're wearing is military surplus and not a fishing vest? That's a utility vest soldiers would wear to haul around spare ammo and the little stuff that comes in handy in combat."

"No kidding?" she murmured, rolling her eyes at his back.

She had to admit, this guy was friendlier than most of the operators she hung out with at work. He seemed generally pleasant and able to converse comfortably with normal human beings. Not that she was normal by any stretch. But in this setting, given that he knew nothing about her, she probably seemed pretty normal to him. Except for having put a fish hook in his back, of course.

She dug out her first-aid kit, tore open an antiseptic packet, pulled out the alcohol-soaked towelette and reached for his shirt. Instead of working through the narrow hole in its fabric, she lifted his whole shirt up to reveal a good chunk of his—

Holy moly. Now, that's a back. It was covered in muscle, with no sign of any body fat to disguise his incredibly well-developed musculature. This guy didn't just work out; he worked out like a beast to get a back like that. Even the small stabilizer muscles running down the edges of his ribs were wildly developed. He must do the same kind of functional movement exercises Special Operators did.

Realizing with a start that she was just standing there staring at his back, she lurched into motion, dabbing at his back with the alcohol wipe. She cleaned not only the tiny puncture wound in his back, but also the trail of blood leading down toward the first bulge of his impressive glutes. *Gulp.*

Fumbling a little, she managed to open a paper-wrapped bandage and stick it across what amounted to a boo-boo once the blood was cleared away. With no small regret, she pulled his shirt back down. She barely refrained from running her fingers over that amazing caboose.

Do not fondle the hot guy. It would be creepy and stalkerish. But, dang, her fingers tingled with curiosity. Was he as hard and toned there as he was everywhere else?

Crumpling the wrappers and stuffing them back in the zipper pocket with her first-aid kit, she croaked, "There you go. Good as new."

He turned around to face her. "Thanks."

"I'm the one who should be thanking you."

"For what?" he asked.

"For not freaking out and, I don't know, suing me."

He snorted. "Honey, I've had a lot worse things stuck in my hide than a teeny little fish hook."

Startled, she blurted, "Like what?"

His dark blue eyes clouded over and took on a distinctly guarded look. "You know. Shots and stuff. Vaccines."

Right. Vaccines. That was totally not what he was thinking of when he'd made that comment. She frowned. If he'd been one of the Special Operators who trained the Medusas, she'd have guessed he'd been in a few knife fights in his day, or maybe in close-quarters combat with bayonets.

"Tell you what," he said, startling her out of her speculation. "You stay here, and I'll move upstream—completely out of range of your deadly casting. And maybe you could point your rod across the river instead of throwing it at me?"

"I promise you. I was not intentionally casting in your direction. I looked back over my shoulder like Jackson said to, but I forgot to look around to the front before I cast my line forward."

"Let me see you cast," he said. "I'll stand here on your left where you won't hook me again."

Frowning, she readied her fly line self-consciously. She could do this. It was just like training back at the secret military base in Louisiana where she and her Medusa sisters trained. She was accustomed to instructors watching, judging and correcting her every movement.

Focusing on her rod and line, she blocked Marcus out of her thoughts. *Up and back, then snap forward.*

Her line did the plop-and-knot thing again. She swore under her breath. She hated failing in front of other people.

"Ah. I see your problem. You're trying to brute-force the line," Marcus said.

"How's that?"

"You're flinging your whole arm around as if you can force the line to go where you want it to. Pretend you've got a paintbrush sopping with paint in your hand, and you want to throw it at a spot about twenty feet behind you and a few feet over your head. But you don't want to fling paint across the whole ceiling in the process."

She frowned, finished untangling her line and reeled it back in.

"Play along with me," he continued. "Imagine that sopping paintbrush. If you fling it and your arm back hard from your waist all the way back to the spot behind your head, paint will fly in a big arc over your head, right?"

"I guess so."

"But if you lift the brush up and back slowly and only accelerate at the end, flicking the brush directly at a spot high in the corner behind you, you'd only send a splash of paint where you wanted it to go, right?"

The light bulb lit in her brain. Up and back slow, gradually faster, and then a hard backward flick to throw the paint at that one spot high behind her. She gave it a try, and her line sailed back in the same gorgeous candy-cane arc that Jackson's had.

"Perfect!" Marcus exclaimed. "Now do the same thing going forward. Slow, then faster, then flick the paint toward a spot out in front of you and over your head. Slow, faster, flick. Slow, faster, flick."

She tried the technique. Her line sailed back, and just when it had flown out behind her in a straight line, she moved her arm forward, accelerated gently, then flicked her pole, moving her arm from the elbow instead of trying to force the line forward with her shoulder.

Her fly line flew out in front of her and settled across the surface of the water perfectly.

"You did that like a pro!" Marcus exclaimed.

"I had a good teacher. That paint analogy really did the trick. Thanks." She smiled up at him a little.

He replied, smiling back, "You're a fast learner. And

you've got the shoulder and forearm strength to accelerate smoothly and give the line a good flick."

"I might just catch a fish one of these days instead of you."

"You'll be an expert fisherman—fisherwoman?—in no time."

"Thanks again, and I'm really sorry about sinking my hook into you."

He shot her another one of those endearing crooked smiles and shook his head a little. Then he turned and waded away from her, seeming not to notice the rather strong current pushing against him. She waited until he was at least a hundred feet away from her to attempt casting again, and she was careful to aim her line across the river and nowhere near him.

Eventually, her arm tired, and as she reeled in her line and stowed her rod over her shoulder, she noticed that Marcus was casting with his left hand. For all of his expert instruction earlier, he was casting rather stiffly and awkwardly himself. Frowning, she watched him cast again.

Of course, he glanced in her direction just then and caught her frowning at him. "What?" he called. "Are you hung up on a log underwater or something?"

"No. I was just watching you cast. Is your shoulder hurt?"

He looked startled for a moment. "Yes and no."

"How can it be both?"

"My right shoulder is hurt, which is why I'm trying to learn to cast left-handed. My left shoulder is fine."

"Ah."

He waded over to her, rotating his left arm around to loosen up his shoulder. "You have a good eye for detail to have noticed I'm casting with my off arm," he commented.

She shrugged. Being observant was critical to her work as a real-time intel analyst. It could mean the difference between life and death. A faint indent in the ground might indicate a buried explosive device, a slight movement or sound might indicate the presence of a hostile enemy.

"Looks like Annabelle's laying out a picnic," Marcus said. "Trust me. You don't ever want to pass up an opportunity to enjoy her home cooking."

"Good to know." She followed him toward the riverbank, which was a vertical, thigh-high wall here. He stepped up onto the grass above the steep bank easily and turned around to offer her a hand up. Startled, she grabbed his hand, and he hauled her up the bank with a casual flex of his left arm.

Yikes. Talk about strong!

She bent down to shed her waders and carried the wet rubber and her fishing pole over to a heavy-duty pickup truck where Jackson was collecting rods and waders.

"You looked good out there," Jackson commented to her as she handed over her gear.

"Marcus gets all the credit for that. He gave me a few additional pointers."

From behind her, Marcus added dryly, "It was purely self-defense."

She rolled her eyes as Marcus related to Jackson how she'd hooked him with her fly.

Jackson grinned. "Hell of a way to catch a man, if I do say so myself."

As the two men laughed behind her, she marched

over to the picnic table, her face hot, to where a magnificent picnic was laid out.

"Help yourself," Annabelle said to her with a smile. "Or, more accurately, grab some grub now before the men get here and snarf it all down."

Gia filled a plate with fried chicken, potato salad, baked beans, fresh strawberries and garlic bread, then moved off under a graceful maple tree to sit down. She leaned against the trunk, facing the river, and took a moment to enjoy the beauty of the spot and the peacefulness of the afternoon. She'd had little of either in the past few weeks. Ever since she'd witnessed…whatever it was she'd witnessed…and people had, indeed, started trying to kill her.

She'd replayed that video feed in her head a thousand times. The darkness. The men staggering along with that crate between them. The way they'd leaned into the Humvee. And then the man bursting into the surveillance facility. His face, his voice, the way he'd carried himself—

"Mind if I sit beside you?"

She looked up at Marcus looming over her, and her heart leaped in her chest and did a little twist of joy. *Stop it, Gia.* "Not at all."

"What did Sunny Creek do to piss you off?" he asked as he sat down easily beside her.

"I beg your pardon?"

"You were scowling pretty hard at the creek."

"Oh. Sorry. I was thinking about a work thing." *Do not speak of the incident. Do not hint at remembering anything to anyone.* Major Torsten's admonition flashed through her head and her mental defenses slammed into place. "Nothing important. Just remembering something I have to do."

"It's a pretty day. There's time enough to think about work later," he said mildly.

"You make an excellent point," she conceded.

Marcus shrugged and dug into his food.

She appreciated that he didn't seem to need to fill every lull in the conversation with noise. She ate in silence beside him, savoring the fried chicken and ripe, sweet strawberries. As her plate and his both emptied, she finally commented, "You weren't wrong about Annabelle's food being fantastic."

Marcus nodded. "She and two other women are opening up a café over in Apple Pie Creek, by the new ski resort."

"They're going to make a fortune if they all cook as well as she does."

He nodded in agreement. He leaned back on his left elbow and she was startled at how intimate it felt having him sprawled in the grass beside her like this. He was a tall man, and every inch of him was sleek and muscular. It was like sitting beside a panther that was lounging in the grass after feasting on a big kill.

The silence between them was rapidly taking on a charge of…something…that made her breath hitch and her belly do flips. Yep. This was one silence that positively demanded noise to break it. And fast, before she threw herself at this man.

"Must be nice to live in a pretty place like this full-time," she blurted, hoping her desperation to distract herself wasn't audible in her breathless voice. "This is the kind of place I could see myself settling down in, someday."

He glanced up at her, his eyes intent. Up close like this, they were the exact same color as the deep ocean, miles from the nearest shore. He said quietly, "I'm just visiting for a few months."

Her internal alarm bells clanged wildly. He wasn't one of the men who'd been carrying that crate, was he? One of the people trying to kill her because of something she'd seen and didn't understand?

"Oh?" she asked lightly, fighting to control her racing pulse and jerky breathing. "What brings you to an out-of-the-way place like this?"

"An old friend. He and I go way back, and when he heard I messed up my shoulder and needed to rehab it, he called and suggested I come hang with him here for a while."

"That's nice of your friend."

"He's good people."

"Do I know him?" she asked, fighting not to panic and bolt.

"Brett Morgan. His family owns Runaway Ranch."

Everyone in Sunny Creek knew who the Morgans were. She'd only been here two weeks and even she knew the name. They owned a ranch outside of Sunny Creek. The way she'd heard it, the place was quite a spread.

Marcus continued, "He and I were in the military together."

Holy crap. This guy was military? Had he, indeed, been one of the Special Operators who'd covertly taken that box out of the compound?

Her smile felt brittle and fake as she rose to her feet. "Well, I think I'm going to pack up and call it a day. Thanks again for the fishing lesson."

Chapter 3

Marcus frowned after Rachel as she all but ran away from him. What had he said or done that suddenly caused her to bolt as if he'd just announced he had the plague? Granted, he could be an intimidating guy—at least, when he was in work mode. But, today, he thought he'd been relaxed and easygoing around her. Heck, he hadn't even gotten tense when she'd snagged him in the back with a fish hook. Why did she leave like that, then?

He didn't like the feeling of scaring off a woman he would've liked to have gotten to know better. Those finely cut shoulders and that lean, lithe frame of hers didn't come from sitting around doing nothing all day long. He hadn't found out how she worked out to be that fit, nor what activities she enjoyed that used all that glowing health of hers.

Instead, her golden-brown eyes had gone wide for no

apparent reason, her pupils had dilated hard in alarm, and she'd fled as if he were the Big Bad Wolf and he'd just taken off his granny disguise.

Not wanting to scare her further, he rose to his feet and followed behind her slowly enough that she had a chance to throw away her paper plate and plastic utensils and practically run for her car before he reached the trash can.

He noted how she glanced around the parking lot furtively, her eyes roving constantly, as if she expected somebody to jump out from behind a vehicle or bush and attack her any second. Frankly, her jumpiness put his instincts on high alert, too. He glided past the picnic table quickly, keeping her in sight all the way to her car.

He watched alertly for danger as she climbed in and backed up fast enough to spurt gravel out from under her tires. Perplexed, he frowned after as she peeled out of the parking lot inordinately fast.

Jackson said tersely from beside him, "Everything okay?"

Spoken like a military man with the same finely honed instincts he had. "As far as I can tell," he murmured, frowning.

Brett Morgan had mentioned over breakfast this morning that Jackson Sutter was retired army. 75th Ranger Regiment—one of the army's elite special operations outfits.

Marcus asked, "Do you know Rachel Boyd very well?"

"No. She's brand-new to the area. I can ask my wife about her. They talked a bit."

"That's okay. I'm probably overreacting. She seemed tense about something."

In point of fact, she appeared to be scared out of her mind. But it felt like a bit of an overstatement to express something like that aloud. Especially in this peaceful little corner of nowhere.

Who are you, Rachel Boyd, and what's your story?

He'd never met a mystery he wasn't bound and determined to solve, and she was no exception. Climbing into his truck, he headed back thoughtfully toward Runaway Ranch. Rachel's arms had been lean but muscular, and the major vein running down the middle of her biceps had even been visible. Very few women had that kind of muscle mass or that little body fat. She wasn't bulky enough to be a bodybuilder, which meant that was functional muscle she was sporting. Maybe she was just into weight lifting or CrossFit.

An unpleasant thought made him scowl at the road in front of him. Or maybe she was a scared woman working out frantically so she could defend herself.

No doubt about it, a mystery swirled around the enigmatic, and athletic, blonde.

Brett had asked him to swing by the hardware store on his way home to pick up some heavy-duty staples, so he pointed his truck at downtown Sunny Creek. If you could call a few square blocks of quaint mom-and-pop shops and cafés a "downtown."

He spied an open parking space on Main Street several doors down from the hardware store and took it. As he walked toward his destination, he spied a familiar blonde hurrying along the other side of the street. It was as if his curiosity had summoned her to his presence once more.

Acting out of years of training and long habit, he slipped into the vestibule of the nearest shop—a bookstore, as it turned out—and watched Rachel hustle along the sidewalk. Her shoulders were hunched up around her ears, and he caught her glancing in the glass window of a storefront, checking behind herself for a follower without actually turning around to look.

Only trained operatives—and terrified women, he supposed—generally pulled a maneuver like that. What on earth had her so spooked? Alarmed now, he let her move another thirty feet or so ahead of him, and then he unobtrusively stepped out onto the sidewalk to follow her, paralleling her from across the street.

He wasn't interested in where she was going so much as making sure she got there safely. She obviously thought someone meant her harm and was worried that person was nearby. A violent ex, perhaps?

She scurried past a half dozen shops and then swerved abruptly into a beauty salon. He snorted at the name painted on the glass. Sharon-Dippity. *Cute.*

He strolled past the salon, still across the street at a safe distance, waiting for a semitruck to pass by so he could see inside. Rachel was talking with somebody and laughing. Her shoulders had come down from around her ears, and her facial expression was open and relaxed.

Whew. She obviously felt safer now. His work was done. He turned around and headed back toward the hardware store. Who could make a strong, capable woman like that look scared for her life?

Ah, well. It wasn't his problem. But still. He didn't like seeing any woman with that haunted look in her eyes. His mother had raised him to like and respect women, thank you very much.

He popped into the hardware store and found the staples Brett needed. He carried them to the checkout counter and asked the young guy behind the register, "Do you know a woman named Rachel Boyd?"

"New girl down at Sharon-Dippity? Lives over in

the Sunny Acres apartment complex? Hot blonde with a great a—"

He cut the guy off sharply. "Yeah. Her." He didn't need to listen to this jerk's opinion of Rachel's posterior. He'd already clocked that she had a fantastic caboose. Truth be told, she had a fantastic everything. She was slim without being skinny, muscular without being overbulky, and her skin was smooth and glowed like satin.

"Who doesn't know her?" the checkout guy said, smirking. "She's an eyeful, man. Every single dude in town has noticed her. Heck, probably some of the married guys are eyeing her, too."

An errant urge to bury his fist in this guy's smirk flowed through him, startling him mightily. He said with forced calm, "Do you know anything about her? Why she's here? If there's anyone bothering her?"

"Couldn't tell ya. But, day-umm, that a—"

He snatched up his bag of staples and whirled, leaving the store before the guy could say something that would force him to defend Ms. Boyd's honor. Ideally with his fists.

Nope. Not gonna pick any fights in this town or any other town. Men like him with their lethal training never ever could turn it loose on unsuspecting civilians. At least, not without a whole lot of cause and a whole lot of warning.

He climbed into his truck and tossed the bag on the seat beside him. Sheesh. He barely knew the woman. There was no reason for him to get all defensive because some twerp talked about her being hot. But an image came to mind of those soft brown eyes of hers swimming with pain, confusion and a king-size dollop of fear.

Fine. He didn't like it when women, children or animals were scared. He always felt an impulse to protect them. It was just the way he was wired, and Rachel Boyd had triggered his guard-dog instinct. That was all.

So. She worked at Sharon-Dippity, did she?

He was not pulling out his cell phone to find out what time the place closed up. Nope. And he wasn't planning to come back to town to conveniently hang around on Main Street when she left the salon and headed for her car. Double nope. She did not need him stalking her, and he was not going to overreact like that, no matter what his gut was shouting at him about her being in danger.

And yet here he was at nine o'clock as night fell, watching Rachel and another woman—presumably Sharon of Dippity fame—closing up the shop and heading outside in the gathering darkness. Sharon turned right out of the store and Rachel turned left, retracing her steps from earlier back toward her car, a beat-up little sedan that was more rust than red paint. Marcus stuck to the shadows, keeping pace several dozen yards behind her and across the street.

She sped up her steps as if she sensed danger, then slowed back down as if she'd talked herself out of panicking. Faster. Then slower. She was walking erratically enough to trigger his internal warning system, and he looked up and down the street, seeing nobody that should be setting off alarms in her head. Was she just being paranoid? Or had he missed something that she hadn't?

He moved even more cautiously, gliding from shadow to shadow, recessed store entrance to recessed store entrance, his head on a swivel, his gaze probing every possible spot along the street where an assailant might hide.

Nothing. He didn't spot a soul out here. It was just Rachel and him.

He watched in relief as she approached her car.

But then she surprised him and walked on past it, lengthening her stride until he had to actually work to keep up with her. What on earth was she doing?

Without warning, she ducked into an alley and disappeared.

No, no, no! She shouldn't go into a dark, deserted alley by herself where some dude could jump her. Nobody would see her being assaulted or hear her cry for help!

He broke into a run, racing to the mouth of the alley. He flattened himself against the wall beside the opening and then slowly peeked around the corner. Dammit. The alley was deserted. Man, she was fast.

He spun into the dark tunnel of brick and charged down it. Where did she go? Was she all right? Was she in terrible trouble? Why hadn't she shouted for help? He ran on the balls of his feet, not so much because he cared about being silent but because he was listening with all his might for a scream, a muffled cry, even a scuffle of someone struggling ahead of him.

But all he heard were the light, fast sounds of his feet on the broken asphalt. That, and the lighter, faster sound of his tense breathing.

He reached the end of the alley and had to force himself to stop and exercise a modicum of caution. He chose the most heavily shadowed side of the alley and eased around the corner—

Something hard and unbelievably fast slammed into his solar plexus, just at the base of his sternum, and he doubled over, gasping in pain, the breath knocked out of him. He heard running footsteps and tried to look up, but his vision swam. He couldn't breathe. At all.

Her attacker was getting away! No help for it—he had to find a way to move. Simultaneously grunting and exhaling hard to expel the pain, he forced his unwilling body into motion.

He dragged himself upright using the wall beside him for support and took off in a shambling run. The dark figure in front of him was moving fast, and he had to put on a full—painful, gasping—sprint to close the gap between them.

He was sucking wind hard by the time he finally caught up with the fleeing assailant a couple of blocks from the alley exit.

Just as he was about to reach out and grab the guy, the attacker shocked him by screeching to a halt, spinning around and throwing a vicious roundhouse kick at his face. It took every ounce of his formidable strength and quickness to avoid getting his nose broken. As it was, the bottom of the guy's shoe grazed his cheek painfully.

Enough was enough. He was bigger and taller than the attacker, and he charged the guy, who turned to flee again. Marcus closed his arms around the jerk from behind and yanked him back hard against his chest. He flung his own head up to avoid getting cracked hard in the chin as the attacker threw his head back violently.

He felt a foot hook around his right ankle and barely managed to shift his weight off that foot before the attacker would have tripped him and sent him to the ground. He tightened his arms around the attacker as hard as he could, hoping to rob the guy of oxygen and subdue him at least a little.

The guy went still in his arms.

And that was when Marcus noticed something.

Something completely unexpected and incongruous.

The attacker's chest was soft. Squishy, even. In fact, two mounds of mashed flesh pressed against his forearm.

Breasts.

Holy crap on a cracker. The attacker had breasts.

Woman. He was holding a *woman* in his arms.

Oh, God. That meant this was not a man who'd been attacking Rachel Boyd—

"Let go of me," Rachel gasped.

He let go of her so fast she stumbled and nearly fell in front of him. "Aw, hell. I'm so sorry," he blurted. "I thought you were attacking Rachel. I mean, I thought you were a man. I didn't realize—" He broke off. "You were so fast. And strong. And fought like a man… Good grief. I can't believe you… I didn't realize it was you… I'm such an idiot…"

"Yes. You are," Rachel said in disgust in front of him.

His gaze snapped up to hers. She stood about six feet away from him, with her fists planted on her hips. If it was possible for a human being to glare a hole through another human being, he was Swiss cheese at the moment.

"I'm sorry, Rachel. I thought you were in trouble. You passed your car and bolted down that alley, and I thought someone was chasing you. So I followed him—well, you, as it turned out."

"I get the idea," she muttered.

He shook his head, appalled at the magnitude of his mistake. "Look. If you want to call the police, press charges, I totally get it. I'm sure I scared you half to death."

"You did. But I don't see a need to involve law enforcement in this. You obviously mistook me for someone else."

He frowned at her. "But you are scared about someone following you, aren't you? I didn't misread that in you, did I?" He'd been an operator for a long time, and he knew body language. Surely he hadn't read her that colossally wrong?

"Am I right?" he pressed when she didn't answer him.

"You seem to have answered your own question. I didn't see any need to do it again," she snapped.

"Who are you scared of? Who's stalking you?" he asked gently.

"What makes you think anyone's stalking me?"

He frowned. "The erratic way you walk. The way you check behind yourself in shop windows. The way you hunch your shoulders. Everything about you shouts of you worrying about being followed, and being scared of whoever you think is after you."

She lunged forward, slamming him against the brick wall at his back, her forearm against his throat. "Who are you?" she snarled.

Stunned, he didn't resist her. Clearly, Rachel had some serious self-defense training, which only furthered his certainty that this was a woman who believed herself to be in mortal danger.

"I told you," he rasped past her forearm. "I'm Marcus Tate."

"That's your name. Who *are* you?"

"I don't understand—"

"How did you follow me without me spotting you? How do you know I look in shop windows to check my six? For that matter, why are you here? Why did you think you could take down some bad guy who might be following me?"

Ah. He didn't usually talk about his job, and certainly not with civilians. But this situation was not usual in any way. "I'm a soldier," he gasped.

All of a sudden, the pressure from her arm was so heavy he couldn't breathe, and he abruptly feared she might actually rupture his larynx. Urgently needing to breathe, he reached up in reflex and pinched the pressure point in her hand between her thumb and fingers.

She yelped and jumped back from him, settling into a fighting stance with her hands in front of her and her weight lightly balanced on the balls of her feet.

"I mean you no harm, I swear," he said desperately. "You were just cutting off all my air."

"Who. Are. You," she bit out.

"Lieutenant Marcus Tate, US Navy SEAL."

She hissed in sharply at that. Welp, she knew who the SEALs were. More to the point, she wasn't thrilled he was one. Which was weird as heck. Most people would be jumping up and down for joy that a SEAL had their back.

He continued doggedly. "I messed up my shoulder a couple of months ago. Had surgery on it a few weeks ago, and I'm here in Sunny Creek to rehab it. I'm staying with my old teammate Brett Morgan at Runaway Ranch. He'll vouch for me and everything I've just told you."

Speaking of which, his shoulder was screaming in protest at all the exertion he'd just put it through.

"If you don't mind," he said carefully, "I'd like to walk back to my truck and get some ice for my shoulder. It hurts like a sonofa—" He broke off. "It hurts a lot."

"You can walk in front of me. I'll follow behind you," she said grimly.

Fair enough. He turned and walked back the way they'd come, retracing his steps through the alley. But his shoulders twitched like mad at having an angry, violent woman trailing along behind him like this. Not that he blamed her for one second for being angry or violent after his egregious mistake.

"Get in your truck," she said clearly from behind him.

He pulled out his key fob, considering how effective a weapon it would be if he spun and threw it at her face as hard as he could. Of course, he would land himself right back in his surgeon's office repairing his not-yet-healed shoulder if he pulled a stupid stunt like throwing something. He opened his door and climbed inside his truck.

"Who's going to watch you to make sure you get back to your car safely?" he asked through the open window.

"I can take care of myself," she snapped.

"That's not what your body language says."

She merely glared at him. He backed out of the parking space and drove up beside her, keeping pace with her as she walked down the sidewalk with quick, jerky strides. "Sure I can't offer you a ride to your car?"

"I'm sure," she replied.

He shrugged. "Fine. I'll walk you back to your car like this, then."

"Go away."

"Nope."

"You're embarrassing me."

He glanced around the deserted street. "No one's out here to see us."

"I can walk by myself," she declared.

"I'm sure you can," he replied evenly.

"Has anyone ever told you you're a pain in the butt?" she snapped.

"Yep. And stubborn, too," he replied cheerfully.

She stopped. "This is my car. Are you gonna pull forward so I can get out of my parking space?"

He put his truck in Reverse. He'd just started to roll

backward when she said in alarm, "By the way, I'm not letting you follow me home. If you try, I'll drive to the police station and have you arrested."

He huffed. "I swear on my mother's grave—well, she's still alive, so her future grave—that I mean you no harm. I'm only looking out for your safety."

"Go away. You hear me? Leave me alone."

He sighed. He couldn't blame her for feeling that way. After all, he'd made a giant ass of himself and scared her silly. "Fine. But if you ever need anything, anyone bothers you or even looks at you sideways, you call me. I don't care if it's the wind making you nervous. You call. Okay?" He rattled off his cell phone number and repeated it for good measure as she opened her car door.

She pulled out her cell phone.

"Are you saving my number?" he asked.

"No. I'm calling the police."

"All right, already. I'm going. I'm sorry I scared you. Really."

He drove away from her, hating every second of not following her safely home. But he believed her threat to have him arrested, and frankly, he probably deserved to spend the night in jail for his massive stupidity.

Shaking his head, he wished Rachel well and headed back toward the ranch.

Chapter 4

The next morning, Gia peeked out her living room window at the uninspiring view of a strip of grass and the parking lot of her apartment complex. It was a nice enough place with some trees, friendly neighbors and a manager who kept all the public spaces spotless. But it wasn't home.

Which was exceedingly strange for her. Homesickness was not a thing she was afflicted with. Ever. She enjoyed roaming the world, going from hot spot to hot spot. Her career, her life were the opposite of sitting at home and putting down roots, in fact.

But she missed her teammates. The five Medusas—a team of female Special Forces operatives—were closer than most sisters and usually shared every aspect of their lives with one another. It felt unnatural to be so cut off from them like this. But she loved them one and all and had no wish to get any of them killed.

The first attempt on her life had been simple—a large SUV with blacked-out windows had tried to run her off a road and into a river. Thankfully, the Medusas had been trained in both defensive and offensive driving, and she'd been able to counter the SUV driver's attempt to kill her. That, and her car was big and fast, with a muscular engine. She'd been able to outrace the SUV to a more populated area with no deep water along the road.

The second attempt to kill her had been scarier. Two of her Medusa teammates, Rebel McQueen and Lynx Everly, had been having a girls' night and slumber party at her house. Only the fact that the gas valve behind the stove hissed just loudly enough to wake her, so she could smell the gas quickly filling the house, had saved them all from suffocating to death.

Or perhaps the bad guys had intended to toss a match in the window and incinerate all three of them. Either way, she'd had to throw open her bedroom window, inhale a gasping lungful of air and race around the rest of the bungalow rousing her friends, throwing windows and doors open, and then helping Rebel and Lynx stagger outside until they, too, caught their breath.

The police had declared it an accident that the gas valve behind her stove had somehow broken off the wall and been spewing gas fumes into her home. Which was poppycock, of course. Someone had broken into her house and snapped the valve right off the end of the pipe.

But since the local police didn't find any evidence of a break-in and couldn't figure out exactly how the valve broke off, they chalked it up to the age of the house and bad luck—or exceedingly good luck, as it were—that Gia woke up in time to save everyone's lives.

None of the Medusas bought the accident theory. They'd wanted to close ranks around her and protect her from any more attempts on her life. But she had no intention of endangering her five sisters in arms. She was better off drawing her would-be killers away from her teammates and figuring out on her own who they were and why they wanted her dead.

She was half tempted to let the bad guys catch her so she could tell them she had no idea what she'd seen on the video feed that night and that they could chill the heck out. But she suspected they a) wouldn't believe her, and b) would promptly kill her.

Which left her hiding in this quaint little town in west-of-nowhere Montana, hoping the bad guys would tire of trying to find and kill her and would go back to whatever classified or criminal activities they usually engaged in. As plans went, it wasn't a great one, but it was better than sticking around her home and getting killed.

Anyone who could get in and out of her house undetected and tamper with the gas valve, while three Special Operators slept in it, was good. Very good. Plenty good enough to kill her sooner or later. It was only a matter of time and a bit of bad luck on her part until one of their attempts on her life succeeded.

With a sigh, she eased the window curtain back into place and got dressed for work. Who knew her part-time job years ago as a teen working in a spa would come in so handy? She'd been able to land a job at Sharon-Dippity giving facials and doing mani-pedis for the summer while the regular girl was out on maternity leave.

She grabbed a protein bar on her way out the door and bought a cup of coffee on the way to work. As she walked into the salon, the first customer was already seated in Sharon's beauty chair, getting color and highlights in her hair. Folded tinfoil squares stuck up all over the woman's head.

"Good morning, Rachel!" the irrepressibly cheery salon owner called out to her.

"Hey, Sharon," she replied, more subdued. The caffeine hadn't hit her yet, and she was only barely human until it did.

"Have you met Miranda Morgan?" Sharon bubbled. "Miranda, this is Rachel. She's filling in for Angela while she's on bed rest…"

Gia was spared having to say hello as Sharon took off gossiping about all the problems Angela had had with her pregnancy. Gia listened idly as the two women agreed that it would all be worth it when Angela had a healthy baby in a few weeks.

Babies. Not a topic that came up often—or ever, really—at Medusa Ops. All the women there were totally focused on their military careers. They were unanimous that they could have babies later, but they needed to be operators while they were at the top of their games, when their bodies were at the absolute peak of physical strength and stamina.

Male operators could back off to about 80 percent of their maximum performance during downtimes between deployments, but the women had to stay at the absolute peak of their form all the time. The Medusas had to push their bodies so hard to meet the standards for special operations that they had no leeway at all to slack off. It was just too hard to get back to that peak performance, otherwise.

The first Medusas had been in their late twenties and early thirties. They'd run in the field for between three and five years and then started settling down and having families. The second Medusa team was tragically lost a few years back, and nobody talked about it. To this day, she had no idea how they'd died.

Most of Gia's teammates had come into the Medusa program in their midtwenties in an effort to get a few more years out of them before they got injured out of the job or just wore out.

She'd been recruited at age twenty-five and was twenty-eight now. She figured she had another seven or eight years in her body, barring any major injuries, and then she would call it quits and let the next generation of badass women step up to the plate.

"You're quiet over there," Sharon said, breaking into her thoughts.

Gia shrugged. "I was thinking about babies."

"Want one of your own?" Sharon asked.

Gia's gaze jerked up in horror. "Good grief, no! I was thinking about how I'm not ready for one yet."

"Well, first you need to find a nice young man, anyway," Sharon said. Gia watched in her mirror as Sharon looked down at the matriarch of the Morgan clan. "Are any of your boys in the market to meet a sweet, attractive young woman? I can vouch for Rachel. She's a love and a hard worker."

"Sorry, no," Miranda said. "The only boys of mine in town right now are Brett and Wes. Brett's engaged to Anna, and I expect Wes will pop the question to Jessica any day now."

"Oh, I'm so glad to hear that! I really like that Jessica. Beautiful girl. So tall and striking with all that wavy blond hair of hers..."

Gia sighed in relief as the topic moved past trying to set her up with some dude from around here. Not that she had a thing against cowboys or guys from small-town Montana. But she wasn't planning to stick around long enough to have a serious relationship. And she wasn't into quickie flings or one-night stands.

But she'd relaxed too soon. Miranda commented, "You know, a military friend of Brett's is staying out at the ranch with us. Name's Marcus. He's a lovely man, and he's single. Maybe I could introduce Rachel to him—"

"No!" Gia blurted.

Miranda and Sharon both stared at her.

"I mean, thank you, but I'm fine with being single for now." Sheesh. She went back to swabbing down her cuticle trimmers, nail clippers and files, with alcohol.

So. Marcus Tate hadn't been lying about being a SEAL buddy of Brett Morgan's. But that still didn't make him innocent. It was entirely possible he'd been one of the helmeted, goggled Special Operators she'd seen come out of that compound.

Unfortunately, the theft of her computer tower meant there was no record of the compound raid, and she couldn't play it back to try to find any identifying features that would have told her which of the operators in Alpha Platoon had surreptitiously made off with that crate.

Major Torsten had requested a meeting with the

leader of Alpha team when they came back stateside, to find out if any last-minute side missions had been added into their mission parameters, but the team had been held up in the Middle East, dealing with some emergency there before they came home.

The shop filled up with women as the morning progressed. It was Friday, and there was a big dance at Sunny Creek High School on Saturday night—some sort of fundraiser for the school's extracurricular programs. Women would be getting gussied up for the shindig all of today and tomorrow.

Gia dodged the inevitable questions from her clients as to whether she was going to the dance or not, mostly making noncommittal noises and bland comments about waiting to see how tired she was tomorrow after work.

Just before noon, the bell over the salon door rang. Gia wouldn't have taken notice, except for the instant hush that spread over the whole place. She looked up... and stared.

Marcus—of trout plague fame and attempted assault infamy—stood in the doorway, looking around awkwardly. And darned if that man didn't have a big bouquet of flowers in his hand, wrapped in pretty paper.

Please don't be here for me. Please don't be here for me—

He looked right at her and made his way around the beauty chairs, wash sink and hair dryers, making a beeline straight for her.

He's here for me.

Not only did her face heat up, but her entire head felt as if it had burst into flames of embarrassment.

"Hey, Rachel," he said in a low voice.

"Marcus." A pause. "Are you looking for someone?"

"Yeah. You."

Oh, Lord. Her entire body was on fire now. She noted that even her forearms had turned bright pink.

"Here." He held out the flowers to her.

She put down the nail file and accepted what turned out to be a gigantic bouquet of summer flowers in yellows, reds, oranges and purples. It was actually beautiful. "What's this for?" she asked him in puzzlement.

"To apologize for last night."

She frowned, vividly aware that every pair of eyes in the joint was locked onto the two of them in avid curiosity. "I told you it was fine. I'm not mad."

"Still. I owe an apology," he said implacably.

She had to give the guy credit. He'd entered a den of estrogen so thick that most men wouldn't even dare try to swim through it. And the flowers really were pretty. And thoughtful.

"Fine," she sighed. "I accept your apology. And thank you for the flowers. They're lovely."

"I didn't know what your favorite color of flower was, so I got all the colors."

"Good thing white isn't my favorite," she commented. Her gaze snapped up to his. "I'm sorry. That was rude. These really are nice."

Sharon called out, "I've got a vase in the back if you need to put those in water, Rachel."

"Uh, thanks," she mumbled. She stood up, unsure of what to do about the very large man shifting his weight from one foot to the other in front of her. Shouldn't he be leaving, now that he'd delivered his apology and she'd accepted it?

She headed for the storeroom/break room in the back

of the store and felt Marcus following along behind her. What was he doing?

"Um, it's employees only back here," she muttered.

"I'm not big on rules like that," he replied, jumping in front of her to open the door for her.

She slipped past him, and sure enough, he followed along behind her, shutting the door and depriving all the prying eyes behind them of any further show. For that, at least, she was grateful.

She made a production of searching the shelves for the vase and found it tucked away behind the mousse and frizz-control products. She carried vase and flowers over to the big laundry sink in the corner and settled the flowers in water. She forgot for a moment about the man behind her as she arranged the flowers attractively.

"That's nice," he commented, startling her.

She turned around fast, demanding, "Why are you here?"

"Suspicious much?" he retorted.

"You'd better believe I am. You followed me, tried to tackle me, and now you're showing up at my workplace."

"I'm not a stalker, if that's what you think," he bit out.

"Then I repeat—why are you here?"

He shoved a hand through his thick hair, and then winced, dropping his right arm quickly. At least he didn't seem to be lying about the bum right shoulder. She waited expectantly for an answer.

Finally, he said low, "I'm worried about you. You acted so weird yesterday when you left the creek, and then you acted so scared last night. Something's going on with you, and I'm the kind of guy with the skills to help."

"I can take care of myself," she ground out.

"I believe that. You strike me as an unusually capable, self-reliant, strong woman. But what if you can't handle whoever's got you so tense? I repeat—I can help."

"If I need help, I'll keep you in mind," she said stiffly.

He sighed. "Why are you so defensive around me? What have I done to make you so distrustful? I'm a soldier and a decent, honorable guy."

She stared at him through narrowed eyes. What if she was overreacting? What if he really had nothing to do with her problem? Then she was being a giant jerk to him.

Major Torsten's admonition early in her initial Medusa training floated through her mind. *You owe nothing to people who make you uncomfortable. Don't apologize, don't ignore your gut instincts. If someone makes you nervous, get away from him and never worry about seeming rude. It's perfectly fine for women to be rude if they're worried by or suspicious of anyone. Better that than assaulted or dead.*

She checked in with her gut to see what her intuition had to say about Marcus specifically. Her internal warning system was entirely quiet. Not even a hint of warning passed through her belly.

She sighed. "Look. It's possible that you're exactly who you say you are. But I can't afford to take that chance."

"Why not?" he asked. The poor guy sounded mighty frustrated.

"Do you tell every person you meet on the street about the stuff you do in your job?" she asked.

"Of course not. Most of what I do is classified."

"So it's okay for you to have secrets and things you keep private, but it's not okay for me to do the same?"

"But the two are not the same. One is a government mission. The other is something that's scaring a woman who's all alone."

She shrugged. "I have secrets I don't care to talk about. That's just the way it is."

It was his turn to stare hard and long at her. He surprised her, though, when he said, "Okay. Fair enough. I won't talk about my work, and you don't have to talk about whatever's scaring you so bad. Maybe one day you'll trust me enough to tell me about it. But until then, I can live with you keeping it to yourself."

She laughed. "Gee. Thanks. I wasn't aware I needed your permission, but I guess I'm glad I have it."

He huffed. "How is it you always manage to take the things I say exactly the way I don't mean them?"

"It's a gift," she replied lightly.

He grinned reluctantly. "Can I at least take you out to lunch to complete my grand apology?"

"That's not necessary—"

He interrupted lightly. "I didn't ask if it was necessary. I asked if you would eat with me."

This man did not take no for an answer. But she sensed that his intentions were good.

"I shouldn't," she replied. "I'm only here for the summer." It was a lame excuse, but it was all she had.

"Great. So am I. Can we at least be friends while we're both here?"

"Why are you so determined to spend time with me?" she demanded.

"You're interesting."

"Try again."

"Have you looked in a mirror?" he demanded back.

"Yeah. I have. I'm pretty average as women go."

"Except for the part where you're blind if that's what you see when you look in a mirror," he shot back.

"But I'm not girlie like other women. I don't wear much makeup or do my hair. I like to work out, and I don't do regular girl things."

"Good for you, then, that I'm not much into girlie girls."

It was her turn to huff at him in frustration.

He said reasonably, "Look. Worst case, you and I are going to have to walk back out through that salon. Every woman in the place saw me bring you a bouquet of flowers and apologize. They're going to think you're a terrible person if you turn down my lunch offer."

She frowned. "A) I don't care what they think. B) How will they know I turned you down?"

"Oh, if you say no, I'm totally going out there all sad and hangdog to ask them what I did wrong."

She stared at him, aghast. "You wouldn't."

"Try me."

It was blackmail, straight up, but it was effective blackmail. She had no desire to spend the next month getting harassed by every customer in the salon about why she'd been so mean to that nice man visiting the Morgans.

Irritated to death at having been neatly outmaneuvered, she bit out, "Fine. Lunch. And then you'll leave me alone and quit showing up with flowers at the place I work?"

"Deal."

Suspicion bloomed in her gut immediately. He'd agreed to that *way* too readily. Yep, that was a full-on shit-eating grin he was wearing.

"C'mon," he said cheerfully. "It's lunchtime now. There's this great little joint over in Apple Pie Creek that makes the best burger in the whole Clearwater Valley." He turned and headed for the salon.

A frisson of amusement inserted itself into her general annoyance at his pushiness. She had to give the guy credit. Not too many people managed to get her to do anything she didn't want to do.

They walked out into the salon, and Marcus went over to Sharon, who simpered as he flashed her a charming smile. He said winningly, "Would you mind terribly if I took Rachel out for lunch? I promise to make it fast because I know you're busy. But I really need to finish apologizing to her."

"Why, of course, young man. You go right ahead," Sharon gushed.

A glint of triumph shone in his eyes for just a moment as he looked back over his shoulder at her.

While the women tittered behind them, already gossiping up a storm about the two of them, Marcus held the street door for her and she stepped past him. Glaring.

He smelled good.

Darn it, why did he have to go and do that? In the field, operators could go for days or even weeks without a proper bath, and she'd developed a real appreciation for men who didn't smell like stale sweat or ripe armpits.

As he followed her out the door, he rested his hand lightly in the middle of her back for a moment. It was a brief touch to guide her in the direction of his truck, but her whole body reacted, tingling with awareness of that exact spot at her waist.

Yikes! She had casual contact with men all the time in her job and never reacted like that. She could still feel the spot where he'd touched her as they headed down the sidewalk. And she was breathing funny all of a sudden.

Frowning, she counted out a couple of sets of breathing in, holding her breath, breathing out, and holding her breath again. She resumed breathing normally but still felt a little breathless. Weird.

He stopped in front of his truck and she turned toward it. "How did you get Sharon to let me go?" she asked curiously. "The salon is swamped today."

"It was my irresistible charm and a dash of honesty," he answered breezily.

She expected it had more to do with his impressive biceps and the sex appeal that oozed from him, but she bit back any snarky comments. After all, the guy was being pleasant and had asked her out to lunch. And, clearly, he didn't need a boost in his self-esteem!

He helped her up into his truck, which was entirely unnecessary, but polite nonetheless. This time she was braced for the touch of his hand as he grasped hers, and didn't hyperventilate. But that tingling thing happened again. Frowning, she watched him walk around the truck and climb into the driver's side.

He backed out into the street and pointed his truck toward the east end of the Clearwater Valley, where Apple Pie Creek flowed into Crystal Lake. Sunny Creek was at the west end of the valley, where its namesake creek flowed out of the lake.

"So, tell me about yourself, Rachel Boyd."

The name was two weeks old and was a fake. She had no history to go with it. There hadn't been time to build an entire legend to go with the alias. And once she'd arrived in Sunny Creek, nobody had been interested enough in her to dig for any detailed backstory, so she hadn't bothered to build one. A mistake she was bitterly regretting just now.

She did, however, know better than to make up a bunch of lies on the fly. There would be no way to remember them all, and she was bound to weave in some inconsistency that this ultra-observant man would catch.

"Not much to tell," she mumbled. "I work at the salon and am saving up my money to head west."

"Where west?"

"I don't know. Wherever I land, I suppose." *Please, God, let that be vague enough.*

"What do you do when you're not working at the salon?" he asked.

"Fly-fish and sleep," she shot back. "Tell me about you."

He shrugged, never taking his eyes off the road. "I'm from Michigan originally. Went to U of M. That's why my buddies all call me Blue."

"As in 'maize and'?"

He nodded. "Folks back home joke that my blood runs maize and blue."

"That's a football thing, right?"

"And now I know two more things about you," he

replied, grinning. "You don't know squat about football, and you're not from the Midwest."

"Correct on both counts," she commented.

"Where's home for you, then?" Marcus asked.

"California. Upstate." She hoped that was vague enough. She had an aunt and uncle who lived not far from Big Sur, and Gia had loved visits to their home every few years. Home was actually Arizona. But she was familiar enough with Northern California to pretend to be from there. "How about you? Where in Michigan?"

"West coast," he replied. "By Lake Michigan."

As she recalled, Lake Michigan ran along the entire western side of the Lower Peninsula. He was being nearly as cryptic as she was. Which she supposed she should expect from a SEAL.

"Are you still in the military?" she asked.

"Remains to be seen."

"Isn't that kind of a yes-or-no question, like *are you pregnant?* You either are or you aren't."

He glanced over at her. "I'm in the military for now. What remains to be seen is if my shoulder will rehab well enough for me to return to active duty or not."

"Aren't there other jobs you can do in the military besides the one that messed up your shoulder? I mean, don't they have guys who sit at desks all day and push paper?" She knew full well the spec ops community had a large team of support staff, many of whom were former operators.

He shrugged. "I'm not fond of pushing paper."

"Yeah, but couldn't you help out the rest of your group—or whatever they're called?"

"I suppose I could. But can you imagine how hard it would be to have been the guy doing the job for all these years and suddenly having to be the guy sitting back watching the rest of your team go forth and do cool stuff?"

Actually, she completely could imagine that, and it would suck. In some ways, she already did that as a real-time video-intelligence analyst. The good news was she got out from behind her desk and got to be the person doing the cool stuff plenty often.

But being a full-time support staffer would probably be almost as bad as it would be to sit back and watch someone kill one's teammates…and have it be her fault.

Chapter 5

Gia noted that the town of Apple Pie Creek was larger than Sunny Creek, and traffic was a lot heavier. But then, Apple Pie Creek was much closer to the new ski resort set to open this winter for skiing and already open for summer activities like hiking, mountain biking and dryland bobsledding.

They found a parking spot about a block from the Not Bad Diner and strolled toward it, passing an array of cute boutiques. Thankfully, he kept his electric hands to himself and she had no more random tingling incidents.

Were it not for the man with her, she might have been tempted to duck into a few of the cute stores to check them out. But long experience around male Special Operators had taught her to be wary of doing anything that might be construed as girlie at the risk of enduring merciless ribbing from them.

Marcus opened the diner door for her, and they stepped into a noisy, crowded space. She was almost disappointed that he didn't put his hand on her back again—

Sheesh. Since when did she obsess about getting touched?

As they looked around, a couple got up from a booth by the front window and Marcus headed for it.

Nope, nope, nope. She hated the idea of sitting there, practically on display to anyone who might pass by. "Couldn't we wait for something in the back room—" she started.

But the door opened just then and a crowd of loud teens piled into the diner and immediately headed for the back room.

"Never mind," she mumbled, sliding into the seat across from Marcus.

He passed her a menu and she browsed it, keeping her face down and her head turned away from the window.

She settled on a grilled chicken sandwich and homemade potato chips. Marcus ordered chicken fried steak with mashed potatoes and green beans. Ah, how she missed her daily workouts with the Medusas. She could easily put away a lunch like that and not think twice about her weight.

It was important in her line of work to make sure her muscle-to-weight ratio stayed constant—or changed in favor of her being able to do more to throw her body around obstacles, climb and lift heavy objects.

"What sorts of things are you doing to rehab your shoulder?" she asked Marcus.

"Mostly work around the ranch. Repetitive stuff like

weight lifting wouldn't be good for it at this stage of recovery."

"Sounds invigorating," she commented, sipping at the water the waitress delivered.

"It's harder than it looks. Ranchers are surprisingly tough. How about you? What do you do to work out?"

"I watch fitness videos on the internet and do them in my living room. Sometimes I go for a jog, and I like to get out and hike on weekends."

"You got arms like that doing workout videos in your living room?" He stared at her biceps.

Emphatically not. The Medusas worked out like dogs and did daily workouts even a SEAL like him would be impressed by. For women to keep up with the boys, they had to go beyond being excellent athletes to being superb physical specimens.

A person passing by bumped Marcus's elbow as he was picking up his water glass and jostled him enough to slosh water on the table. She reached for napkins and passed several over to him just as he was reaching for the napkin holder. Their hands collided, palm to palm, and she dropped the napkins.

Marcus's hand grabbed hers so fast she didn't have time to jerk her hand back. She tried to pull her hand free, but he absently resisted her tugging and instead pried her now-fisted fingers open to examine her palm. The pad of his thumb rubbed over the hard shooter's callus she had at the base of her right thumb.

Crap, crap, crap. There was only one way to get a callus like that, and they both knew what it was. She'd shot thousands and thousands of rounds of ammunition out of every size, shape, make and model of firearm over the past several years, on a weekly, if not daily, basis.

She glanced up at him, and he was staring back at her intently. She didn't even try to lie to him. "Yes. I shoot guns, sometimes. Target shooting, mostly. Haven't been able to find a decent firing range around here, though."

He appeared to believe her, for he nodded and said evenly, "There's a spot out back on Runaway Ranch that the boys use for target practice. If you'd like to go shooting out there sometime, give me a holler."

"I will," she replied, thanking her lucky stars she'd dodged that bullet.

Thankfully, their food came and saved her from any more awkward conversation about her experience with firearms. She usually was quite talkative and outgoing, but having to keep track of her fake identity made spontaneous chitchat exceedingly dangerous. She generally opted to say nothing rather than get herself into trouble.

Over their delicious food, they chatted about harmless things like the weather, living in a small town and stuff to do at the new resort. Gia found herself relaxing with Marcus. He was intelligent and observant, and also witty with a wry sense of humor.

She felt at ease with him, perhaps because he was a Special Operator. The rhythms of his speech and how he carried himself were familiar to her—comforting, even. Being around him felt like a little breath of home. By the end of the meal, he had her laughing aloud at stories from his early days in the military.

She hadn't realized how lonely she'd been these past few weeks until just now. It was good, really good, to sit and talk with someone she shared so much in common with. Even if he didn't know just how deep their similarities ran.

The check came and he snagged it before she could even think about reaching for it. "My apology-tour meal, remember?" he said.

She shrugged. "But next time it's on me."

"You can't imagine how glad I am to hear that," he replied lightly. "Now, if only you'll agree to put my cell phone number in your phone so you can reach me to invite me out…or call for help, anytime, day or night."

"Fine. What's your number?" She entered his number into her phone and then texted him quickly so he would have her number, as well.

They drove back to Sunny Creek, and he stopped in front of the salon.

"Thank you for letting me properly apologize to you," he said formally.

"My pleasure," she said automatically.

"I hope we can do this again."

"Me, too." Darn it. The words were out of her mouth before she could stop them.

He smiled broadly and came around the truck to open her door for her. She half expected him to bow like some sort of old-fashioned gentleman of yore. Shaking her head, she turned away from him to face the salon.

She should've known that the second she set foot inside, she would get the third degree. But she was in a good mood and obliged Sharon and the clients by sharing a few highlights of her lunch with Marcus.

Sharon asked, "Did he invite you to go to the dance with him?"

"Certainly not! We barely know each other."

"Sounds as if he'd like to get to know you better, and

it sure sounds as if you'd like to get to know him better," her boss observed.

Gia worked through facials and manicures mechanically over the next several hours. If they'd been back in Louisiana, where she lived, and Marcus was stationed nearby for a couple of years, she might, indeed, want to get to know him better. But as it was, it seemed like a waste of her time and his to start a relationship they couldn't possibly develop past the next few months.

Quitting time came, and as they locked up the store at nine o'clock, Sharon commented, "You need to get out more, Rachel. You're young and pretty. You should have fun. Meet some men your age."

"But I don't know how long I'll be in town."

"Pishposh. Don't waste your youth worrying about being serious in every relationship. Kick up your heels a little. Enjoy life. Have a fling or two. You take everything so seriously. You need to relax. Act your age for once."

"G'night, Sharon," she called, turning away from her well-meaning boss.

As she walked toward her car, she chewed on Sharon's advice. Maybe she should take the woman up on her suggestion. It wasn't often that she got to escape the grind of training and responsibility of being a Medusa. If she was stuck hiding for a few months and pretending to be a normal person, maybe she should allow herself some normal pleasures.

She was almost back to her car when she finally noticed a man walking along the opposite side of the street, much as Marcus had last night. If Marcus was tailing her again, so help her, she was gonna strangle him.

She turned abruptly into the open door of a coffee

shop that was open for another half hour and peered back at the street behind her. She caught just a glimpse of a tall shadow turning down a side street. It was tall enough for Marcus, but she couldn't make out any more detail than that. But at least whoever it was wasn't following her anymore.

She asked the barista if she could use the rear exit, and the startled teen nodded, pointing toward the storeroom.

"Thanks," Gia murmured. She slipped through the space and out into a narrow alley, down which she took off running. It was dark and empty except for the occasional trash can. When she got to the end of it, she would loop back to her car, walking toward whoever might be tailing her.

But as she slowed near the end of the alley, a tall, muscular shape slipped fast around the corner into the alley, ahead of her.

She froze. Sometimes, even if a person was standing in plain sight, if they were perfectly still, they wouldn't be seen by other people. Human eyes, like most predator eyes, were wired to notice movement long before they took note of shape and color.

But as her eyes adapted to the dark, she took in more and more details about him. He was tall, but leaner in build than Marcus. His hair was shaggy, and he wore a beard. He also wore a crappy surplus army jacket and jeans, but on his feet, he wore top-of-the-line running shoes that looked new.

The man held his position with his back to her. He peered around the corner from time to time, obviously lying in wait for her. Each time he stuck his head around the corner, she took a few silent steps backward, gradually putting another dozen yards between her and whoever the heck he was.

Was she fast enough to outrun him if she turned and took off now? If he was a Special Operator, maybe not. He had close to a foot on her in height, and most of it was in his legs. His stride would make him impossible to get away from. She needed a distraction.

The next time he peered around the corner, she bent and picked up a rock that fit nicely in her fist, not too big, but with enough heft to really fly. She managed only one step backward before he pulled back into the alley.

She waited in an agony of suspense for him to lean out again to check the street. But, finally, he did it. She cocked her arm and threw the stone for all she was worth. It sailed up and over the man's head, clattering to the ground in the continuation of the alley across the street.

The man bolted forward toward the sound, and she spun and took off running for all she was worth. She didn't bother to check the coffee shop exit. It would be locked from this side anyway. Instead, she sprinted to the far end of the alley. Footsteps pounded behind her. The good news was they were distant and didn't seem to be gaining on her much. She hit the end of the alley and turned right, away from her car.

She raced to the next corner and turned left, praying the guy behind her hadn't seen which way she went. She ran as fast as she could to the next corner and bolted right. She kept running, not stopping or slowing, until she was lost on a residential street somewhere north of her car and well away from the shopping district.

Finally, she dodged into a yard and hid in a bunch

of tall bushes beside a house whose windows were all darkened. Breathing hard, she listened for the sound of footsteps.

Nothing. It was silent except for crickets tentatively resuming chirping around her and a few night birds.

She stayed in that bush for upwards of an hour. Most people would probably consider that overkill, but extreme patience was one of the virtues that separated Special Forces operators from normal people.

At last, she crept out of the bushes and headed behind the house. She went around the bungalow's detached garage and crouched facing the rear of another house. She couldn't go back to her car. Once the guy lost her, he would've returned to that area and would be staking it out. At least, that was what she would do.

She highly doubted a town this small had any kind of rideshare service, but she pulled out her cell phone and checked for one nonetheless. No joy. She looked on the internet for some kind of local taxi service and struck out there, too.

She could walk home, but she really hated the idea of being out here in the streets and having to evade all the way back to her apartment a couple of miles from here. She knew how to do it, but it would take most of the night. Plus, it was entirely possible the man would choose to stake out her home rather than her car, if he knew where she lived. Which he might.

She closed her eyes for a moment of frustration and dialed Marcus's number.

"Hey, beautiful," he answered cheerfully. "Have you picked out where our next date is going to happen?"

"Our lunch was not a date. It was an apology," she replied very quietly. "And I'm not calling to ask you out."

His voice changed completely as he said seriously, "What's up?"

"I kind of got separated from my car, and I could use a ride." She grimaced and continued, "You said to call anytime, and I'm in a bit of a bind."

"Say no more. Where are you?"

She didn't know, actually. "Just a sec," she muttered, pulling up a GPS map that would pinpoint her current location. She rattled off the address of the home now in front of her.

"I'll find it," he said, sounding as if he was walking rapidly. "I'll be there in about fifteen minutes. Will you be safe until then?"

"Of course," she replied. "I've told you before. I can take care of myself."

"Hang in there. And call the police if any tangos—bad guys—pop up."

She knew what a tango was, but she wasn't about to tell him that.

He continued, "Police will arrive on target sooner than me and can R&C the area faster than me."

"Okay." She hung up the phone, shaking her head. It was a good thing she spoke Special Forces lingo. "R&C" was short for "reconnoiter and clear." Not that she had any intention of calling the police. They would ask a lot of questions, and more to the point, they would enter her name in a report, which would find its way into a computer, and from there into a database. Nope. She wouldn't be involving the police at all.

She circled wide of the backyard, which might contain a noisy dog, and crouched behind the evergreen bushes beside this new house.

It was closer to ten minutes later when Marcus's

truck turned the corner down the street. Aw. He must have driven like a bat out of hell to get here that fast. That was sweet of him.

She stood up, brushed any twigs or leaves off herself and walked out of the bushes with as much dignity as she could muster. Marcus was just pulling up to the curb as she reached the sidewalk, and she opened the door and stepped in. He pulled away practically before the door was latched. He had stopped less than five seconds in all. It was a combat pickup any operator would've been proud of.

"How exactly did you end up here on the complete opposite side of town from your car and your house?"

"How do you know where I live?"

"Guy at the hardware store told me. Everyone knows everyone else in this town."

Her impulse was to groan at the complete lack of anonymity around here. But that sword swung both ways. A Special Operator or two looking to kill her would stand out like sore thumbs in this town.

"Where to?"

She contemplated the wisdom of returning to her place. Low to downright stupid. She could head back to her car, but the wreck she'd purchased for this operation had the gumption of a couple of goats and couldn't outrun a fast man on foot. If the guy from the alley was waiting for her by it, he would have no trouble catching her and killing her.

"I honestly don't know," she admitted. "Is there a motel around here? Maybe over by the new ski resort?"

Marcus's knuckles visibly tightened on the steering wheel. She could all but hear the wheels turning in his head over why she hadn't asked to go home or back to her car. Finally, he bit out, "You're coming with me."

"No. I'm not! The last thing I want to do is drag you into my problems!"

"I already told you, I'm prepared to help you out with your problems."

"Marcus. That's really generous of you. Noble, even. Truly. And I appreciate it. But I'm not involving you in my life. It wouldn't be a good idea for either one of us."

"How about you let me be the judge of that?" he retorted.

"How about I not?"

His face was set in implacable lines, but he said no more.

It took her a minute to register that the truck was not heading back toward the main valley but rather was heading toward its west rim…where only ranches and forestland were.

She crossed her arms and huffed in annoyance. It wasn't as if she could dive across the interior of the truck and wrest control of the vehicle out of his hands. If he wanted to take her out to Runaway Ranch, there wasn't much she could do about it. And, truth be told, it was a good idea. Whoever that man had been back in town, he wasn't likely to find her if she was tucked away on a giant ranch outside of town. At least, not until someone gossiped about her staying out there. Then, in a matter of hours, everybody in Sunny Creek would know exactly where to find her.

But for tonight, she would be safe.

Chapter 6

Marcus unlocked the door to the one-bedroom cabin and went in first, scanning the space quickly. He moved into the bedroom and attached bathroom and returned to the living-dining-kitchen room to find Gia waiting expectantly.

"No bogeyman hiding in the closet?" she asked lightly.

"Nope. All clear."

If he wasn't mistaken, her shoulders relaxed fractionally. Good. Maybe she would relax enough out here to tell him what the heck was going on with her and who she was so afraid of.

On impulse, he stepped forward and wrapped her in a hug. She was stiff against him for a moment but then relaxed and accepted the hug. Her hands even came to rest on his waist.

For just an instant, she shuddered a little against him.

It was the one and only sign of weakness she'd shown him in the whole time he'd known her. He was relieved to know she was actually human under that I-can-handle-anything exterior of hers.

She was as athletic, but still soft and warm in the right places, and he reminded himself sternly that this was a platonic hug to comfort a woman who'd asked him for help.

"You're safe now," he murmured, verbalizing the silent message of their hug.

"Well, at least for tonight," she amended.

He turned her loose and stepped back a little. He felt her absence from his arms as a keen physical loss. Odd. She was standing right there. But, apparently, his subconscious believed she belonged in his arms. He gave his head a little shake to clear it of any bizarrely possessive notions about this woman.

"Hungry?" he asked. "You just got off work, right?"

"Yes, and correct."

He nodded and moved over to the kitchenette to start pulling out food. It wasn't fancy, but he had some nice smoked venison sausage, a couple of cans of baked beans, and an apple pie Miranda Morgan had brought down to his cabin earlier today.

He browned the sausage and added beans to the cast-iron skillet to heat up, all the while watching his guest out of the corner of his eye. She wandered around the cozy space, running her fingertips along the edge of the hand-carved mantel, looking into the bedroom, and returning to the fireplace to stoke up the coals and stack wood on them to renew last night's fire.

Two things leaped out at him immediately about her. One, she stayed away from the windows and out of any sight lines of someone outside looking in. And she did it so naturally it was almost an unconscious move for her. Two, she built a fire so quickly and efficiently that he could've mistaken her for someone who did the task every day.

She didn't waste wood nor did she need more than a bare handful of kindling to light the wood. She blew with just the right amount of air and force to get the coals to flare with heat and light off her kindling. Not a single match was necessary. Just that small pile of embers she'd found in the ashes. He couldn't have done it better himself.

He opened the cupboard and pulled out a pair of tin plates with high rims, and he pulled out utensils and tin cups.

"I have water, coffee, tea or beer to drink," he offered.

"Water, please."

Coming up. This cabin had a big rainwater cistern mounted behind it, and he turned on the gravity-fed faucet and filled her cup with fresh cold water. He, too, opted for water. He wanted his mind clear to talk with her, or—more accurately—to badger her into telling him what was going on with her.

"Food's hot," he announced.

She rose gracefully from the raised hearth and came over to the tiny table.

"It's nothing fancy, but it'll stick to your ribs," he commented.

"And it's high in protein, to boot," she added.

He moved swiftly to the chair nearest her and pulled it out, holding it expectantly. Surprise lit her gaze for a moment. Then she moved over to the chair, sank into it and let him push it in a bit.

He waited until she took her first bite of food before digging in himself. The sausage was spicy and the sweetness of the beans was the perfect contrast. He'd learned a long time ago to savor any meal that wasn't freeze-dried or foraged on the move in a combat zone. Rachel seemed to enjoy the simple food nearly as much as he did.

He let her get nearly through her meal before asking quietly, "So. Now that I've rescued you and fed you, are you going to tell me what's going on?"

She laid down her spoon and sat back, cupping the tin mug in both hands. She stared down into the water it held as if attempting to scry the future. He waited her out. One thing he had plenty of after two decades in special operations was patience.

At length, she sighed. But when she spoke, her words were 100 percent not what he'd been expecting. "Where were you four weeks ago?"

"I don't understand."

"I mean, as in physically, where were you located?"

"In a hospital in Washington, DC. My shoulder surgery was four weeks ago yesterday."

"Would you mind if I take a look at the surgery scar to verify that?"

Startled, he blinked at her for a minute. "You know what a four-week-old scar looks like?"

"Yes. I do."

Bemused, he stood up, grabbed the hem of his cotton T-shirt and stripped it off over his head.

From inside the cotton, he heard her sharp intake of breath. Whether that was in response to his ripped physique or the impressive collection of scars he'd accumulated over the years, he couldn't tell. By the time he yanked the shirt over his head and he could see her again, her face was back to its usual cautious stillness.

He half turned and leaned down to present his right shoulder to her. "Laparoscopic scars are here and here." He pointed out two fresh pink lines of scarring on his skin, one on the front of his shoulder and one on the back, each less than an inch long.

"Thank you."

As he turned his T-shirt right side out, he commented, "Aren't you going to ask me about any of my other scars?"

She leaned back and pursed her mouth. "I gather from the number of them that you're not a very good Special Operator. A good one wouldn't have that many scars, would he?"

She delivered the words as dry as the desert. For a moment his jaw dropped, but then he caught the glint of humor in her dark gaze and let out a crack of laughter. He pulled his T-shirt on and sat back down in the chair.

"The number of scars I have are a testament to the number of ops I've run on and how dangerous many of them were."

"If you say so," she replied skeptically.

He pushed his empty plate back and planted his elbows on the table. "Any other questions for me?"

"Yes. What SEAL team are you on, and can you prove to me that you're on it?"

"Team Four." He frowned. "As for proving it, we don't exactly carry around membership cards—" He stood up abruptly. "Wait. I've got something."

He left the main room swiftly and headed for the chest of drawers in the corner of the bedroom. He emerged carrying a beat-up T-shirt in a wad. He dropped it on the table in front of her. She unfolded it to reveal the Team

Four emblem—a rather tough-looking seal of the aquatic animal persuasion. It was holding a KA-BAR knife and leaning on a depiction of the earth. The Team Four motto was emblazoned on a red ribbon beneath them.

Rachel murmured, "What does *Mal Ad Osteo* mean?"

He grinned. "What else? *Bad to the bone.*"

She rolled her eyes. "Do you have any more proof than a crappy T-shirt you could've ordered online?"

"Hey! I've sweat blood and tears in that shirt." He thought for a moment and then reached into his jeans pocket. "How about this?" He flipped his Team Four drinking coin on the table. It was a brass slug about two inches in diameter. On one side was stamped the SEAL trident emblem, and on the other was the Team Four insignia, an exact replica of his T-shirt but enameled on raised brass.

She picked up the coin and turned it over. Silently, she held it out to him. "Okay. I believe you."

"Do you even know what this is?" he asked, picking up his coin and slipping it back in his pocket.

"It's a drinking coin. And the way I hear it, guys on the teams are pretty stingy about handing them out to anyone who's not actually one of them."

"Where did you hear that?" he asked lightly.

"Around."

"C'mon, Rachel. This secretive act is getting old. Someone's trying to hurt you or worse, and you could use a friend. I'm offering to be that person, but you're really starting to piss me off with this whole refusal-to-trust-me thing."

Her gaze slid away from his guiltily. She knew he was right. This was it. Either she ponied up and told him what the hell was going on, or he was washing his hands of her once and for all.

She let out a long, slow breath that sounded like half sigh and half resignation. "I had to be sure of you."

"Sure of what about me?"

"That you're not one of the Special Forces guys trying to kill me."

"The…what?" he said blankly.

"I'm in the military," she said bluntly. "Air Force."

Well, that sure as shootin' explained a few things, like her aggressively good conditioning, her trained self-defense skills and her ability to build a killer fire practically without thought.

"I'm a real-time intel analyst," she continued. "And four weeks ago, I witnessed…something…on a spec ops mission I was providing drone overwatch for. Shortly thereafter, someone started trying to kill me."

"Where are you stationed?" he shot at her, hoping to catch her off guard.

"I was on temporary assignment on the East Coast when this all started."

One corner of his mouth turned up sardonically. The evasiveness of that answer was worthy of a SEAL.

"Then what brings you to Montana? Unless you're a missile operator, there's not much military activity in this neck of the woods."

"Exactly. I took some leave and picked someplace as far off the beaten track as I could find to lie low for a while."

He leaned back, studying her intently. He didn't pick up any deception in what she was telling him. Of course, she wasn't telling him a whole lot about her particular situation. “Who are these spec ops types who are after you?”

“If I knew, I’d be taking direct action to confront them.”

He frowned. “If you were working with them, surely you know who they are.”

“My boss has a call-in to the unit’s commander to ask what exactly it was that I witnessed and if he has any knowledge of it.”

“Please tell me it wasn’t a SEAL operation you were observing.”

She shook her head. “Nope. Not SEALs. You guys have your own real-time intel people.”

Thank goodness it wasn’t his brothers in arms that she’d crossed. “Did you witness a war crime?” he asked reluctantly. He hated the idea of anyone in the same military as him doing something illegal or dishonorable.

“I don’t know what I saw!” she burst out. The frustration packed into her words was palpable. “I don’t know who I saw or what was so secret about what I saw that someone feels a need to kill me to silence me!”

“Okay. Well, how about we figure it out together? I know a whole lot about special operations. If you describe what you saw to me, maybe I can tell you what the operators were doing.”

She threw him a withering look. “I know what I’m looking at when I watch a spec ops mission. It’s my job to know what the guys on the ground are doing.”

“Were you able to see any identifying features on these people you saw doing something bad?”

“No. They were in full tactical, night operations gear.”

He winced. That meant they’d have been wearing helmets, goggles and bulky gear, all of which would’ve made the soldiers impossible to identify. She wouldn't even be able to tell hair or skin color because the whole thing would've been photographed in lime-green low-light optics or red infrared optics.

"What unit was it? I can put out some feelers to see if there are rumors of any hanky-panky going on in that group."

She shook her head. "I appreciate the offer, but I've already put out feelers. Either nobody knows anything or nobody's talking."

He huffed. "Operators won't talk outside of the community to nonoperators, even if they're active-duty military and even if they provide support for the spec ops community. You're either one of us, or you aren't."

She opened her mouth and looked as if she was about to respond hotly to that, but then she subsided all at once. She opened her mouth again and said evenly, "Someone in the community already reached out on my behalf. The unit is downrange on another op and won't be coming up for air for a few more weeks. Until then, no one's saying anything."

He leaned back in his chair, balancing on two legs and frowning. "If the whole unit is downrange, why are you so nervous now?"

"Classified."

His chair legs thumped to the floor. "Don't give me that crap. I've got a higher security clearance than just about anybody in the entire armed forces."

It was her turn to scowl at him. "Sharing of classified information includes not only the recipient having the clearance to hear it but also having a need to know."

He bit out, "If I'm going to be protecting you, I need to know."

“I don’t need protection!”

“From where I’m sitting, darlin’, you sure as hell do.”

“Why?” she shot back. “Because I’m some helpless little girl who can’t lift one weak li’l finger to take care of herself?”

“No. Because if someone in the special operations community wants you dead, you’re in grave danger and actually very likely to die without swift and skilled intervention to protect you.”

“Yeah,” she said dryly, “I got that memo.”

He ground out, “Does that mean you’re going to stop being suicidally stubborn and will let me protect you until this…whatever it is…is sorted out?”

Chapter 7

Gia stared across the table at Marcus in frustration fully as great as the frustration showing on his face. An urge to accept his offer—to have a second operator on high alert nearby, to have someone skilled who could watch her back—was very tempting, indeed.

She sighed. "Here's the thing. I left my own military unit because I didn't want to get any of my teammates hurt. Why would I enlist you to help me and drag you into danger when my whole purpose is to avoid getting anyone else caught in the cross fire?"

"Because I'm volunteering and because I'm a lot less likely to die than you are."

She opened her mouth to disagree, but then shut it again. She might have admitted she was military to him, but she sure as heck wasn't about to reveal she was a Medusa. The very existence of an all-female Special

Forces team was one of the most closely held secrets in the entire US military arsenal.

A great deal of the Medusas' effectiveness relied on nobody—*nobody*—knowing they existed. No foreign enemy looked for women operators to come at them, and it was that blindness to women as threats that gave the Medusas one of their biggest edges in the field. It was literally a matter of life and death not to reveal who she worked with.

Marcus was speaking again. "...am going to assume whatever you saw was not an official part of the operation or else you'd have been briefed in, or at worst, what you saw wouldn't have been illegal or secret enough to merit killing you to silence you. If it were part of the op, you'd have been ordered to sign a nondisclosure statement after being briefed that you'd seen something above the level of your security clearance to know."

She nodded. "That is standard procedure in those cases."

He continued, "Not all members of a large spec ops team deploy on any given mission. Part of the team will be in training rotations, usually stateside, part may be overseas gearing up to go into the field. They'll have support personnel with each portion of the team. If someone back here in the States tried to hurt you—"

She interrupted. "To kill me."

Marcus's eyebrows sailed up, but he continued on with his line of reasoning. "If someone back here tried to kill you, they're in league with someone on the team who is downrange and operating in the field now. Which means you've stumbled upon a large criminal conspiracy. You are, indeed, in mortal danger if a whole group of Special Operators want you dead."

He was not wrong. That was exactly where her own logic had led her. "Hence my caution in not trusting you right off the bat."

He nodded slowly. "I get it now. But I promise you, I'm a straight arrow. I would never use my rank or position in the military to do anything illegal."

"I think we all say that to ourselves. But when the opportunity arises under our noses, I wonder how many folks cave in to greed or power or lust or whatever it is they cave in to."

He shook his head sharply. "Nope. I've opened up chests full of cash, confiscated millions in drugs, taken priceless art off walls—but I've never been tempted once to pocket some of it for the Marcus Tate retirement fund."

She shrugged. "Okay, so you're a Boy Scout. Can you say that of all the guys you run with in the SEAL community?"

He was silent, and she pressed the point. "Or are some of them a little too eager to kill people and blow stuff up? Do they get a little too jazzed at the idea of lining their own pockets after they get off active duty? Aren't there guys who leave the SEAL teams as soon as they can and jump into mercenary work for hundreds of thousands of dollars per year in compensation?"

He scrunched up his face, unhappy with her argument. "You're not wrong. We've got some guys like that. Is that what you saw? Did some guys take something they weren't supposed to?"

He was getting way too close to the truth for comfort, and she merely shrugged. "Like I said before, I have no idea what it was that I saw. But whatever it was, someone got *real* tense that I had eyes on whatever happened."

"Why don't you just ask for a review of the mission videos by the inspector general or someone like that?"

Dang it. He was too knowledgeable about spec ops missions and had zeroed in on the crux of the problem with unerring accuracy. She shrugged. "There aren't any mission videos."

"Why the hell not?" he exclaimed. "All that stuff is kept for exactly this reason—to clear operators of wrongdoing when accused."

"Or to prove their wrongdoing when caught," she added.

"What happened to the tapes?" he demanded. "Did you mess up?"

"No!"

"Then what?"

She closed her eyes in frustration and thought fast. She could talk to him purely in her role as an intel analyst, and she never had to bring up her work with the Medusas.

"The tapes were stolen."

"Stolen?" He stared at her. "Don't you guys work in secured facilities?"

"We do."

"Then..." He trailed off leadingly.

"A person, a man, came into the facility where I was working and removed the tapes from my workstation shortly after the incident occurred. He took the whole computer tower, hard drive and all."

"Holy crap. Who was he?"

"I have no idea. And before you ask, the surveillance cameras at the facility didn't capture a single image of him coming or going. And, yes, I realize that means he's probably a Special Operator. A very good one."

"Well, hell. You really are in a pickle, aren't you?"

She sent him a withering look. "Ya think?"

"Good thing you put that fish hook in me and caught yourself some top-notch protection."

"Puh-lease. That was an accident."

He grinned. "You sure about that? Or maybe your arm strayed in my direction because of how strong and capable I looked."

He'd looked strong and capable, all right, but that hadn't had anything to do with any distraction she might have felt that day. It had been his good looks and charm that distracted the heck out of her. Not that she was about to admit it to him. She, of all people, knew just how healthy—wildly inflated, even—the egos of male operators could be.

She stood up and carried the plates and cups over to the sink and commenced washing them. She watched out of the corner of her eye as Marcus moved over to the front window of the cabin and plastered himself to one side of it, partially behind the long curtains. He peered outside into the darkness for a long time.

Of course, she knew he was taking that long both to let his eyes adjust to the low-light conditions outside and to scan for movement of any kind out there that might give away someone who shouldn't be lurking nearby.

She finished drying the last plate and putting it away in the cupboard, then turned off the kitchen light. Moving quietly in the now-dark cabin, she eased over beside him to peer outside. "See anything out there?"

"Nope. All's quiet."

She shifted her weight to look around him and accidentally ended up with her left arm pressed up against his side. Or did he move just enough to bring them into physical contact? Either way, her mind jumped around in random bursts, and that darned tingling thing happened again. She *had* to stop touching this guy until she got her reaction to him under control.

Except just then he put his arm lightly around her shoulders and drew her in front of him so they could look out the window together from the best vantage point. He was tall enough that he could look over her right shoulder with ease. His left hand held the curtain back, and his right hand rested lightly on her waist. It was something she might have done if she were standing here with one of her Medusa teammates scanning outside together.

It was a totally innocent touch. But her body burned from his hand outward, and her entire being focused on the spot at her right waist where his palm rested against the waistband of her jeans. A parade could've marched past the front door just then and she wouldn't have noticed it.

His body heat warmed her from neck to toes, vividly announcing that he had her back. An errant urge to lean back against him, to let him be her strength for a minute, nearly overcame her. The past month had been extremely tense and she would love to set down the load of her worry, even for a short time.

Of course, she was trained to endure incredible stress for long periods of time and not to buckle under it. But that didn't mean it was easy or pleasant to do. Now and then, even the toughest of operators wished for a little breathing room. And, unbeknownst to Marcus, he was giving her that now.

She exhaled slowly and inhaled deeply. That might've been the first full breath she'd drawn in weeks. It felt good. Really good. She exhaled again, releasing everything weighing on her mind. Calm flowed over her. Or rather, it flowed from Marcus and into her. And she let it.

As the physical heat built between their bodies, something else began to build, as well. A connection. They had so much in common, and now they had a common cause. It was different from being on a mission with her teammates, because his purpose was to protect her. She was the package and not the operator this time. And that made all the difference.

Marcus shifted his weight behind her, and truth be told, she sidled away from him, afraid he might slide his arm around her waist or in some way ruin the moment. Also, it wasn't as if she was seeing a darned thing outside anyway. She moved away from him and his seductive, disturbing touch. Or, more accurately, her disturbing reaction to his all-too-wonderful touch.

She sank down into the well-broken-in cushions of the beat-up sofa in front of the fireplace. Marcus surprised her by sitting down on the hearth directly in front of her, their knees only inches apart. He planted his elbows on his knees and stared into her eyes. She noted absently that he put more weight on his left arm than his right. His shoulder was still bothering him more than he let on.

He spoke quietly. "Thank you for trusting me enough to tell me what's going on."

She shrugged, a little abashed.

"I really need you to start at the beginning and tell me everything, so I'll know what I'm up against."

"It's not your problem!"

"And yet I've made it my problem. Could we please quit arguing about that already?"

She huffed, and he huffed back. She stared stubbornly at him, and he stared back just as stubbornly. She shifted her weight as if to rise, and he leaned forward fast and planted his hands on top of her legs just above her knees. He pressed down with the effortless, breathtaking strength all operators had, pinning her in place whether she liked it or not.

Sure, she knew a move to throw off his hands, twist his thumbs and stand up anyway, but she had no intention of showing her tactical cards to him like that.

"Talk to me, Rachel."

Thinking fast, she mumbled, "There's not much to tell. I went to work. I watched a mission go down on a live video feed from a surveillance drone. The objective was secured, the operation winding down, when I saw some operators doing something I couldn't really make out. A few minutes later, a man came into the facility, took my computer tower at gunpoint and disappeared. Oh, and he told me I would have a very unfortunate accident if I told anyone what I'd seen that night or about him."

"Then what happened?"

"After I unlocked the room he'd locked me into, I chased after him. He was gone. No sign of him. I called the facility commander and my boss, and about a week after that, a blacked-out SUV tried to run me off a road into a river. Then, about a week after that, my house developed a mysterious gas leak in the middle of the night that nearly killed me and a couple of friends who

I work with. And that was when I asked to take all my stored-up leave and came here."

"To hide."

"Right. Until my boss can figure out what happened on that mission and who came into the facility to take the video."

"Is your boss any good at getting to the bottom of stuff like this? Are military police involved? What's the air force equivalent of NCIS?"

"The OSI. Office of Special Investigations," she supplied.

"Are they investigating?" he demanded.

She shrugged. "Above my pay grade to know. I just reported the break-in and theft."

"And nobody provided any security for you after two attempts on your life?" Marcus asked incredulously.

"Nobody witnessed the first one, and the police declared the second one an accident."

He snorted. "Did your gut tell you they were attempts on your life?"

"Absolutely."

"Then they were. Most civilians put far too little stock in their intuitions. In my line of work, we're taught to listen to our guts and always believe the little voice in our heads, especially when it's warning us that something is wrong."

She had the exact same training but merely nodded at his words.

"What did the man who stole your computer look like?" Marcus asked.

She'd given the description so many times she could recite it by rote. But every time she did so, a clear image of the man flashed into her mind's eye. Particularly the cold, flat gleam of his pale eyes in the red light of the surveillance facility.

"Tall, around six foot three. Muscular build. Mostly bald with extremely short gray hair. Caucasian, but tanned. Pale eyes, maybe blue or gray. Small, horizontal scar under his left eye. Nose slightly crooked as if it was broken before. Wide mouth. Thin lips. Dimple in his chin. Long earlobes. Calloused and scarred hands."

"Dang. That's quite the detailed description. I can practically see him in my mind's eye!"

"Photo intelligence analyst here. Detail is my specialty."

"Good point." Marcus shook his head. "Okay, so Baldy busts into the watcher facility and does what?"

"First thing he did was blow my night vision and half blind me by opening the outer door without warning. He moved over to my workstation and went for the computer tower. When I made a move to interfere, he pulled a handgun on me."

"What did the weapon look like?"

"It looked like a .460 Magnum."

"You could tell what kind of gun it was?" Marcus blurted.

"You're not the only person in the world whose job it is to recognize handguns," she retorted.

"Okay. Color me impressed." He paused, then added ruefully, "I gotta say, I'm a little turned on by a woman who can identify a handgun make and model on sight."

She rolled her eyes at him but couldn't help smiling a little.

Marcus gave himself a little shake. "Okay. So he points a Magnum at you, and you did what?"

"Duh. I put my hands up in the air and backed away from him slowly."

It was Marcus's turn to smile. "Which is probably why you're alive right now to tell me this story."

"He grabbed the whole computer tower, yanked out all the wires and left as fast as he arrived. He locked the door behind himself when he left. I grabbed my purse, dug out the key and let myself out—" she omitted pulling out her own SIG Sauer P229 handgun "—and chased after him. I went outside the facility, but there was no sign of him. No vehicle driving away, no movement in the woods. I went back inside, locked the place down and called my boss and the facility commander."

"Baldy sounds spec ops trained. He moved in fast, shocked you into cooperating and got out fast, leaving no trace of himself behind."

She merely nodded, failing to add aloud that the guy had moved like an operator, with the rolling heel-to-toe stride they were all taught, or that his gaze had never been still, or that he'd held the Magnum as if it was an extension of his arm.

Marcus leaned back, his shoulders resting on the river rock surround rising beside the fireplace. "What are you planning to do if Baldy or his buddies find you here in Montana?"

"Draw them out and kill them." Dammit. The answer had popped out of her mouth before she thought to stop it.

Marcus had the decency not to laugh, but amusement glinted in his eyes. "You and what army?"

She shrugged. "If they don't expect me to fight back, I could surprise them. Take them off guard."

"Honey, men like that are never off guard."

This, she knew all too well. But then, she was never off guard, either—unless she let her mouth get ahead of her brain and she blurted out something a bit too revealing. At least she seemed to have distracted Marcus from the obvious question of why she thought she could take on multiple Special Operators and live, let alone win.

Marcus stood up. "In the morning, I'm going to make a few phone calls."

"I'd rather you didn't. Nobody knows I'm here, and I'd prefer to keep it that way."

"I swear I'm only going to call a couple of guys I would trust with my life. They're longtime teammates of mine and absolutely honest, stand-up guys. And they're SEALs. You said the operation you were working wasn't a SEAL mission, so there's no way my buddies could possibly be the ones you saw, right?"

"Right," she agreed unhappily. But she still didn't like the idea of him calling anyone.

"Also, I'm going to let Brett and Wes Morgan know what's going on. They're good people, and they're both recently retired military officers. Brett was a SEAL, and Wes was a marine. It'll be good to have them on board and keeping an eye on you."

She winced. "Great. So instead of killing my friends, we're going to kill yours."

"Nobody's dying on my watch," he bit out. "At least, not among the good guys."

"You can't promise that, and you know it. Besides, the more people who know about me, the more chance there is of someone saying something that gets back to one of the bad guys or to Baldy himself."

Marcus said gently, "I promise not to say anything about why you're in trouble to Wes and Brett. In my calls, I'm just going to ask around about what operations were running a month ago and in what places."

"I know that information. The op took place in Zagastan, and it was a joint task force. Alpha Platoon, stationed at a forward operating base over there, ran the op."

"Great! Then I'll ask around about the reputation of that unit. See if there's any scuttlebutt floating around about them pulling any extracurricular shenanigans."

One thing that was true across all branches of the military: gossip got around about *everything*. Secrets were a near impossibility within specific military communities, the special operations bunch being a major one.

"Can we talk about it in the morning before you make any calls?" she asked.

He turned away from her and efficiently shoveled ashes up and over most of the fire, banking it for the night. He put a screen stand across the front of the fireplace before he turned around to face her.

"We can talk, but you won't change my mind. The resources of a team are always better than those of a single operator. In my line of work, lone wolves have a way of dying early and alone."

She sighed. Major Torsten had said something in a similar vein to her just before she left for Montana. He'd wanted to surround her with the entire Medusa team until the whole mess was sorted out, but she wasn't having any part of it.

In fact, he'd made her promise to come to this sleepy little town before he'd agreed to sign her leave orders, and she was beginning to suspect she knew why. She would bet her next paycheck that Gunnar Torsten and

Brett Morgan were old teammates from their SEAL days. Her boss had sent her straight to his good buddy to keep an eye on her.

Jerk. Although, she thought it of her boss fondly. It was decent of him to make sure she had reliable backup close by.

“I’ll take the sofa,” Marcus said, startling her out of her thoughts.

“That’s ridiculous. I’m not putting you out of your bed.”

“Yes, but if Baldy decides to bust in here to kill you, he’ll have to go through me first,” Marcus argued.

“But what if Baldy isn’t an idiot and decides to break in through the bedroom window instead? Then you should sleep in the bedroom to stop him there, and I’d be safer out here.”

“Watch it, Rachel. According to that logic, we should both sleep in the bed together. That way, I’ll be right beside you to protect you no matter which direction he comes from.”

Her gaze snapped up to his, and she caught the wry glint of humor in his eyes. “The couch it is, for you,” she declared.

Marcus grinned broadly. “So glad you saw it my way. Lemme grab a blanket and a pillow, and I’ll leave you to your rest.”

As if she was going to get a wink of sleep tonight with him just on the other side of the bedroom door. Not bloody likely.

Chapter 8

Marcus didn't catch a wink of sleep all night. Not with Rachel sleeping just on the other side of the bedroom door. It had been a pitched fight to keep his hands off her earlier when they'd been looking out the window.

There was something about her that just drew him to her. She was so familiar, somehow. As if he'd known her for years and not days.

He spent hours thinking about what she'd said and he came to a single conclusion. She'd witnessed some of the members of Alpha Platoon doing something really, really illegal. His money was on them having stolen something extremely valuable. It would have to be, to get several operators to go in together on a theft and to have someone back home involved, as well.

It was incredibly dangerous for Special Operators to risk their careers on stealing something, so whatever they took would have to be able to fund the rest of their lives—comfortably—for them to take the chance. Then there was the ethical dilemma of any operator crossing the line into crime with their skills. They were all specifically chosen for their ability to control their lawless impulses. To have multiple operators cross that line meant the temptation had been spectacular.

He suspected they would try to smuggle whatever they'd stolen back into the United States. Why else have somebody in on the theft back here in the States? Why not just keep the money, or drugs, or whatever they'd stolen, for themselves? Why cut in someone back here, too, unless the thieves needed Baldy to help them in some way?

He must've dozed off in the early hours of the morning as the first gray light of dawn was creeping around the heavy curtains, for he woke up with a jolt sometime later. He smelled bacon. And coffee.

He smiled and sat up on the sofa, glancing over his shoulder toward the tiny kitchen tucked in the back corner of the space. Rachel was at the stove, flipping pancakes. She wore her jeans from last night and his SEAL Team Four T-shirt. It hung large on her slim frame and looked good on her. Really good.

He'd seen the wives of some of his teammates run around in their husbands' team shirts, and he'd always thought it was one of the sexiest things he'd ever seen. He stood by that observation now that it was his shirt on an attractive woman. Rachel's golden hair was pulled up in a high ponytail that made her look young and cute, and her skin glowed with dewy health.

"Good morning, Rachel," he murmured.

She must've been deep in thought because she didn't

look up immediately. When she did, her gaze jerked over toward him a beat late, as if she hadn't heard him use her name. "Uh, hi," she mumbled. "I hope you don't mind that I raided your kitchen for something to eat."

"Are you kidding? This place smells great." He refrained from mentioning how amazing she looked. He got the distinct impression she wasn't the kind of woman who would appreciate him pointing out that she was barefoot in his kitchen. She had way too big an independent streak for that, and frankly, he liked it in her.

He ducked into his bedroom to shower and dress, and he was just emerging, his hair damp and face freshly shaved, when she said, "Good timing. Breakfast is served."

He moved swiftly to reach her chair just as she did. With an arch smile over it at her, he pulled it out and held it for her.

She just shook her head. "Thank you."

"You're welcome."

"Was it your mother who was the stickler for manners or someone else?" she grumbled.

"It was my mom. And my dad, who worshipped her. And my grandmother. My whole family, actually."

"Anyone in your family besides you in the military?"

"Oh, yeah. My grandfather served in Korea, and my dad served on an aircraft carrier in Vietnam. My younger brother is a surface warfare officer on a destroyer in the Pacific, as we speak, and my baby brother is in his senior year at the Naval Academy."

"Wow."

"How about you?" he asked. "Any other military types in your family?"

"Nope. I'm the black sheep of my family for joining

the military. My whole clan is deeply pacifist. I keep trying to convince them that idealists like them need pragmatists like me to protect them."

He picked up his knife and fork. "And how's that going?"

"Not well. But I persist. Mostly, we agree to disagree, and politics are strictly off-limits at all holiday gatherings."

"Fair."

They dug into the tall stacks of pancakes on their plates and ate in silence. As he pushed back his empty plate a few minutes later, he sighed in pleasure. "That was tasty. Thanks for making it."

She shrugged. "I wanted to thank you for helping me out last night and taking me in. It was the least I could do."

He shrugged back. "My mom always said I was a natural-born Boy Scout."

"I'll bet you were an actual Boy Scout, weren't you?"

"Pinned on Eagle Scout when I was seventeen."

"Figures," she muttered. "That metaphorical white hat looks permanently attached to your skull."

He grinned. "It is." She started to get up and he waved her back into her seat. "Sit. You cooked. I'll clean up."

She subsided and he carried their plates over to the sink. As he quickly washed up, he asked her, "What's on your agenda for today?"

"I have to go into the salon to work."

He frowned. "Given your current situation, don't you think maybe you should call in sick?"

She shook her head. "Sharon will be slammed because of the dance tonight at the high school. She desperately needs me there today."

"How long will you be there?"

"All day. We open at ten and close at six."

His internal warning antennae wiggled furiously at the idea of turning her loose in a public space for eight hours by herself. Now that someone was in town following her, it was only a matter of time before an entire kill team showed up to take her out. He would hate to see a bunch of sweet old ladies shot up in a beauty salon.

He sighed. "I guess I'm spending the day at Sharon-Dippity with you, then."

"Wha—what?" she stammered.

"You don't think I'm letting you go into your known place of work all by yourself, do you? Obviously, Baldy knows where you work. He was lurking outside the salon last night, wasn't he?"

"Well, yeah."

"Then I'm going with you. No way can you keep a sharp lookout for him outside and do your job at the same time. You do…whatever you do there…and I'll stand watch for your guy."

"He's not *my* guy," she snapped.

"You know what I mean. How soon do we need to leave for Sharon-Dippity?"

"Do you understand we're talking about an entire day at a beauty salon? Full of women? You won't survive an hour!"

"Why, Ms. Boyd, that sounds like you just issued a challenge to me."

She scowled at him and opened her mouth to say something, undoubtedly snarky, but he cut her off, saying smoothly, "Challenge accepted."

"No. No way," she declared.

"I suppose I could just stake the place out all day, but my reaction time if your hostile from last night shows up would be compromised. It would be better if I were right there with you. And I'd hate to see Sharon and her clients get caught up in the cross fire of a gunfight."

Rachel's eyes widened in horror for a moment before they narrowed in calculation. What she was calculating, he couldn't fathom. But in a moment, she said, "Fine. You can come to the salon. But for God's sake, keep your weapon concealed."

"Of course. But we are in rural Montana. Handguns, shotguns and rifles are a way of life around here. Nobody would be surprised or bothered if I wore a holster in plain sight."

"Just stay out of the way, will you?"

Easier said than done, as it turned out. He was a large man in a space wholly dedicated to women fussing over their looks. When he and Rachel arrived a few minutes before ten, Sharon already had the place open, and it was already half-full of women. He stepped inside beside Rachel and scanned the space quickly for any signs of hostiles. Unless the kill team after her was a bunch of blue-haired women in their seventies and eighties, Rachel was good to go.

"Hi, Rachel," Sharon called from behind a woman getting red goop smeared all over her hair in what looked like some sort of bizarre ritual.

"Hey, Sharon," Rachel called back, heading for a table off to one side that already had a lady sitting at it expectantly.

He moved over beside the woman at Rachel's manicure table and nodded down at her politely as she stared up at him in something akin to shock.

As Rachel sat down at the table and reached for the customer's hands, Sharon strolled over toward him. "Hi… Marcus, right?"

"Yes, ma'am. Marcus Tate. It's a pleasure to officially meet you, Sharon. Rachel's said a lot of nice things about you. And thanks for letting me take her out to lunch yesterday."

"Aw, she's so sweet." Sharon turned to Rachel. "So. Is this bring-your-boyfriend-to-work day, and I didn't get the memo?"

Rachel's gaze jerked up to him and then over to her boss in alarm.

He intervened smoothly. "I'm here because I lost a bet. I might have said something about working in a salon not being hard, and Rachel challenged me to work here for a day with her."

He felt as much as heard the collective sigh of amused understanding behind him and heard a few titters of laughter.

Sharon, directly in front of him, grinned broadly. "Well, then, I'm happy to put you to work, young man. You can start by sweeping the hair from around the chairs over there. When you're done with that, you can help me prepare some hair color."

The sweeping wasn't bad, although he was shocked at how much hair a few women could shed in a few haircuts.

Sharon pointed at various tubes of color concentrate that he was supposed to dilute in a hydrogen peroxide paste and stir thoroughly.

"What is this stuff?" he blurted as his eyes watered

and his sinuses *completely* cleared. "Are you sure it's not a chemical weapon?"

The women laughed and Sharon said, "Aw, it's just a little peroxide and bleach."

"I'm pretty sure this stuff should be classified as hazardous waste," he declared, handing the plastic tub of sludge to Sharon.

"This is nothing. You should see the stuff we use to straighten curly hair. It'll strip paint."

He threw up his hands as if to ward off evil.

Sharon said, "Good grief, Marcus. Look at your nails! You need a manicure, my dear boy. First break Rachel has, you let her fix those for you."

He would've refused on the spot, but a wave of laughter passed through the dozen women customers. No way was he about to admit that they were right and he was afraid of a little manicure. Eyes narrowing, he said gamely, "Okay. Will do. What next, boss?"

Sharon grinned. "If you're asking, station two could use a mopping. Erica's infamously messy with her bleach products."

He went into the storeroom, hunted down a bucket and mop, and filled the former with hot water from the sink and added soap. He hauled it all out front and mopped down the floor. He hauled the dirty water into the back, poured it out, and as he emerged into the main room, Sharon called out to him.

"Marcus, the Wiltons are arriving. Could you run outside and help Tasha with her grandmother? Poor Opal broke her hips a few months back and she's not getting around very well yet."

He hustled outside to a car parked in the handicapped access space where a young woman was bending over an elderly woman in the passenger seat of the vehicle, trying to help her to her feet.

He took the opportunity to glance up and down Main Street as he approached the car. No sign of Baldy. But then, if the guy was half as good as Rachel said he was, he wouldn't spot any sign of the dude out here anyway.

"If you'll allow me?" he said smoothly to the granddaughter.

The young woman looked up gratefully and stepped back. He leaned down and scooped the elderly woman out of the seat and into his arms. "If you'll grab her walker, I'll take her inside. That way we don't have to mess with the cobblestones, the curb or the door threshold."

"And who might you be?" the silver-haired, birdlike woman in his arms asked cheerfully.

"I'm Marcus. I'm helping out at the salon for the day."

"Well, my heavens. I haven't had this much fun since my husband was still alive and used to carry me up to our bedroom to make whoopee."

He stumbled, startled, in the act of turning sideways to carry Mrs. Wilton into the salon. The elderly woman laughed gaily and reached up to lay a soft, dry hand on his cheek. "I may be old, but I'm not dead, Marcus. And you're very handsome."

Smiling sheepishly, he set her down gently, steadying her as her granddaughter put the walker in front of her and Mrs. Wilton transferred her hands to the metal contraption.

A general hello went up from the assembled women to Opal and Tasha while he moved over to Rachel's side.

"All clear outside," he muttered under his breath to her.

Rachel, who'd just finished with a customer and was cleaning her manicure station, gestured for him to sit down in front of her. Frowning, he did so.

"Thanks for the update," she muttered back. She reached for his hands and he stifled an impulse to yank them back into his lap.

Rachel stuffed his fingers into twin cups of what felt like warm, soapy water and then looked up at him, grinning ear to ear. "Having fun?"

"I had no idea little old ladies were so frisky. I've had my rear end patted, groped, squeezed and pinched, and I haven't been here one hour."

Her eyes glinted with amusement. "You are a good-looking guy. And you do have a nice, um, posterior region."

"Thanks." She'd noticed his physique, had she? He'd sure as shootin' noticed hers.

She lifted one of his hands out of the warm water. "Relax your fingers," she murmured.

He frowned and let his right hand go limp in hers. She tsked as she examined his palm and turned his hand over to stare disapprovingly at his fingernails.

"I'm working on a ranch," he said defensively. "And in my real life I'm a soldier. What do you expect of my hands?"

She just shook her head and went to work, trimming his cuticles with a wicked-looking little pair of clippers. Nervous, he held perfectly still and waited for her to slip and slice off a chunk of his finger. But her quick, efficient snips never even hurt, let alone drew blood. When she finished with his cuticles, she filed his nails—which felt weird and unpleasant—and then started going back and forth across his nails with what looked like a rectangular sponge.

"What are you doing?" he asked.

"Buffing your nails. I mean, I could polish them, if you'd like. You could pick out a color from the rack of polishes—" She gestured at the hundreds of tiny, brilliantly colored bottles in every color of the rainbow sitting on a specially designed shelf behind her head. "Or I could give you a clear-coat polish—"

"No, thank you. No polish for me."

A burst of laughter erupted behind him. He glanced in the mirror behind Rachel and realized every woman in the place was alertly watching his and Rachel's interaction. Lord, these women were nosy. And observant.

Scowling, he lowered his gaze to his hands. Rachel turned his left hand loose and went to work buffing the nails on his right hand.

"Well, hell. My nails really do look better," he mumbled, staring at his left hand.

"Gee. Thanks. It is my job, after all," she retorted tartly.

He glanced up at her in chagrin. "I never thought about taking care of my nails before. But this looks… nice."

A smile hovered at the corners of her mouth. She said in an undertone, "I'm glad you like your manicure." She pulled out a tube of hand lotion and squeezed out a glob on the back of his hand. She commenced massaging in the lotion, her fingers strong but soft.

Dang, that felt good. She worked in particular at the base of his thumb, which was perennially sore from shooting handguns for hours and hours every week. It was as if she knew exactly where his hands and wrists held their aches and pains.

She finished massaging his right hand and went to work on his left hand. An urge to groan in pleasure nearly overcame him. And then his mind wandered to what her hands would feel like all over his body, and his pleasure morphed into acute discomfort. Which was entirely his own fault.

Do not think about Rachel naked in my bed. Do not think about it.

Aw. Hell. Now it was all he could think of. The thought of sex with a woman as athletic as her was tantalizing. With most women, he had to be so aware of how fragile they were and be extra careful not to hurt them. Obviously, he would be cautious and not hurt Rachel, either, but he suspected she could give as good as she got in bed—

"You okay there, Sparky? You're turning red. You're not embarrassed at liking a manicure, are you?"

He glanced up at Rachel guiltily. "No, it's just warm in here."

"Maybe he's having a hot flash," Opal Wilton called out from across the room. For some reason, that comment drew a big laugh, especially from the older women in the salon.

He leaned closer to Rachel and asked under his breath, "What's the big deal with hot flashes?"

"They're the bane of existence of most women when they head into menopause," she whispered back.

"Ah. Well, I'm not having one."

Her mouth twitched with amusement. "Good to know."

She finished his manicure with a small nod. "You survived your first—and probably last—manicure. Congratulations, big guy."

He spoke quietly again, for her ears only. “That was actually kind of fantastic. I wouldn’t mind having you do that again. But maybe without the audience next time.”

“I’m here all summer. You can book an appointment anytime.”

“Do you make house calls?”

Her gaze snapped up to his. She met his gaze with a boldness that shocked and delighted him. “For the right price, I might.”

He nodded slowly, his gaze never leaving hers. “Good to know.”

“Marcus!” Sharon called from across the salon. “Can you assist Marybelle?”

He turned and saw a young woman wrestling a stroller through the front door. A toddler sat in the partially collapsing conveyance, and the kid looked mad. He didn’t blame the two-year-old. He wouldn’t want to be strapped into a malfunctioning stroller, either.

Marcus picked up the front wheels of the contraption easily and lifted them over the door’s threshold.

The mom said to Sharon, “I’m so sorry I had to bring Aiden along. My babysitter canceled at the last minute.”

Sharon waved a breezy hand. “No problem. Marcus can entertain him.”

Marcus gaped, appalled. He didn’t do babies. At all.

As if on cue, the kid let out a squall. The mother unbuckled him as the kid’s face turned red and the squall became a scream. He watched in dismay as the woman lifted the wriggling mass of red face, slobber and diaper… and shoved the child at him.

He grabbed the toddler around the waist, holding him

awkwardly at arm's length. Aiden fell silent, staring at Marcus solemnly as Marcus stared back.

"He likes you!" Sharon cooed.

Marcus suspected it was more a matter of the kid being undecided over whether to scream or poop.

He turned, child still held out in front of him, toward Rachel, who was grinning in unholy amusement. He mouthed one word to her. "Help."

She threw up both hands and took a quick step backward. "Nope. I'm working. You've got the baby."

As he opened his mouth to point out that she had no client at the moment, Aiden's mother slipped into the chair at the manicure station. Rachel took great pleasure in reaching for Marybelle's hand and smiling up at him innocently.

Scowling at Rachel, he turned his stare back to Aiden. "I guess it's just you and me."

Experimentally, he tucked his forearm under the baby's butt and let the kid sit on his arm, leaning against his chest. Aiden half turned in his arms to watch the goings-on in the salon.

Marcus murmured to the child, "Ladies sure go through a lot to look nice, don't they? Next time you see a woman with great hair and nails, be impressed, kid."

Laughter passed through the crowd of women.

For the next hour, he carried Aiden around with him, fetching tubes of hair color from the storeroom one-handed, sweeping up hair one-handed and getting bottles of water for the customers. And everywhere he went, women cooed at the two of them. Who knew a baby was such a chick magnet? He'd heard a cute dog was a surefire female attractor, but this kid was pure gold.

Just his luck, though. The one woman in the room he

wanted to be attracted to him seemed fully as put off by little kids as he was. He tried several times to foist Aiden off on her, but she wanted no part of babysitting the little rug rat.

Without warning, Aiden stiffened against him and stared up at him while frowning intently, just as a suspicious odor began to rise from the toddler's diaper. Alarmed, he carried the child swiftly to his mother.

"I will babysit, but I don't do diapers," he declared, thrusting the kid at his mom.

"Scared, are you?" Marybelle asked him, grinning.

"Nope. Just completely unequipped with either the proper training or any desire to deal with diapers."

He looked away as Aiden's mother quickly laid out a changing pad, stripped the kid, cleaned him up and taped a new diaper on him. As she pulled the toddler's pants back up and handed him back to Marcus, she murmured, "Mark my words. You'll change your tune when it's your own baby."

"Nope. Not me."

Every woman in the salon laughed heartily, and he looked around, confused. "What?" he blurted.

Sharon ended up fielding the question. "You can say whatever you want now. But your wife will make sure you pull your weight as a parent and do your fair share of poopy diapers."

Frowning, he turned away. Or he could assign himself to a nice long deployment halfway around the world and not come home until the kids were potty-trained and talking in complete sentences.

Rachel strolled up to him, amused. "I recognize that 'no power on earth is gonna make me' look. Never fear.

When it's your kid, you'll be so besotted with him or her that you won't even mind their stinky poo."

"I'll have to see that to believe it." He waved a hand in front of his nose. "I can still smell that Aiden bomb. Kid's a toxic waste machine."

Rachel's grin widened.

He scowled. "I don't see you fawning all over this kid."

"Thankfully, my biological clock isn't ticking too hard yet. I won't consider starting a family until my career is winding down."

He met her gaze in understanding. Nobody here knew she was active-duty military. And, yes, that would make being a parent hard. He'd watched plenty of his teammates miss the births of babies and not be there for their kids' early years, and although he might joke about it, separations had been rough on all concerned.

Blessedly, Aiden's mom was only in for a manicure and a hair wash and blowout—who knew that those were a thing?—and she fetched her spawn shortly thereafter.

For the barest instant after he turned Aiden over and helped Marybelle maneuver the stroller out the door, he missed the kid. Maybe someday he'd like to have a few of those of his own.

Huh. Where had *that* thought come from? He'd barely thought about marriage, let alone settling down and starting a family. It must be all those fumes he'd inhaled mixing hair dye. He was high. Why else would he contemplate hitching himself to a pooping toddler for years?

Around lunchtime he ordered a big pile of pizzas for the salon staff. Sharon tried to reimburse him for the food, but he would hear nothing of it. He declared it part of the penalty of losing the bet and refused to take the money Sharon held out to him after he paid the delivery driver.

When Rachel finally caught a break long about midafternoon, he carried over a couple of slices of cold pizza to her table on a paper towel and sat down across from her with a couple of slices of his own.

He murmured, “This isn’t exactly a romantic meal for two, but it’ll fill your stomach and it doesn’t taste like worms or grass.”

Rachel laughed with rich appreciation, almost as if she’d had to dine on bugs and weeds before and knew exactly of what he spoke. “Thanks for doing this for me. You’re going above and beyond the call of duty to put up with all these women on my behalf.”

“It has been an education, to be sure. I had no idea of the suffering women endure to look good.”

“It’s tough being female. We have to be twice as good at everything to get half as far as men.”

“Surely it’s not that bad anymore.”

She shot him what could only be called a death stare.

He threw up his hands in surrender. “All right. I’ll take your word for it and be grateful to my dad for giving me a Y chromosome.”

“Lucky bastard,” she muttered.

“What has being female prevented you from doing in your life?” he asked, picking up a second slice of pizza.

She gnawed on a piece of crust, clearly thinking. “I haven’t let it prevent me from doing anything I’ve wanted to, but being female has made any number of things immeasurably harder for me to accomplish.”

He opened his mouth to ask for examples, but she anticipated him and cut him off.

"Athletic things and jobs in the military being the most obvious ones. And lots of annoying little stuff like being able to speak up in a classroom or meeting and not get talked over by some guy. Or being able to walk home at night alone and not worry about being mugged. Or being able to go to a bar or party by myself and not have to be with other women to look out for one another and make sure none of us get drugged or assaulted."

He grimaced. "My ribs are still sore where you hit me in the alley. I don't think you need any man to protect you."

She shrugged. "Not anymore. But I had to go out of my way to get the training to defend myself. And let me tell you, it wasn't easy training."

He snorted. "You forget what my job is. I've been through worse training than you can ever imagine."

She snorted back as if she knew full well what he'd endured to become a SEAL. It was one thing to read about it or see TV shows depicting it. It was another thing altogether to go through it. He added, "BUD/S is ten times worse than any movie you've ever seen showing it."

She reached for her second piece of pizza. "Okay, Mr. Big Bad SEAL. Top this—childbirth."

He closed his eyes in chagrin.

"Let's see you push a cantaloupe out of your hoohah…and voluntarily have sex ever again. I would remind you that you folded and ran when faced with one poopy diaper."

He laughed helplessly. "I yield the argument to you, ma'am. Women are, indeed, the tougher gender."

She sat back triumphantly.

He muttered under his breath, "But I'd like to see you

go on a patrol in hostile territory that's crawling with insurgents who'd love nothing more than to torture you for a few months before they get around to killing you."

"Anytime," she muttered back. "Anytime."

"Did I mention the venomous snakes and poisonous bugs all over the place? Or having to pee in a bottle and not shower for a week?"

She shrugged. "Sounds like a walk in the park."

His gaze narrowed in challenge, and hers narrowed right back. Which privately amused the hell out of him. She had spunk. He had to give her that. But just because she was in the military didn't mean she had the faintest idea what a Special Operator like him did.

Even if she watched Special Operators on camera all the time, she didn't observe the grueling hikes in and out of target zones, the constant danger of hiding in enemy territory, the grinding weight of hauling in all of their own gear, ammunition and food.

Not to mention, when she watched the hour or two of actually executing a mission, that was nothing like being on the ground taking incoming fire and fighting for one's life. He'd like to see how she fared under that kind of pressure. She would change her tune fast enough about women being tougher than men—

"I've got an idea," he said suddenly.

"What's that?"

"There's a big dance tonight, right?" he asked.

She nodded. "Hence the salon full of women getting gussied up."

"What do you want to bet that Baldy will stake out the big shindig to see if you show up there?"

"That would make sense," she answered cautiously.

"You and me. Let's stake out the dance ourselves and

see if we can spot the guy. Do you think you'd recognize him if you saw him again?"

"Maybe. I mostly saw him in silhouette in very low-light conditions. I might recognize his profile or the way he moves, though."

"If you think you're so tough," he said in a low voice, "let's see you operate in my world for a change."

"Okay," she said jauntily. "After all, how hard can it be to sit in a bush and watch a bunch of folks through binoculars?"

"Really?" he bit out. "You're going to challenge me? With my skill set?"

She smiled archly. "Challenge accepted."

Oh, she was going to regret saying that. She had no idea what she was in for. They weren't going to drive into the parking lot and stroll into the bushes. Oh, no. They were going to approach the high school from the dense forest and rough, steep terrain behind it. In the dark. Carrying tactical gear. He would run her into the ground. She would cry uncle in two minutes flat. Well, given how fit she was, maybe ten minutes. But she wouldn't make it a mile with him.

Oh, yeah. This was going to be fun.

Chapter 9

It was all Gia could do to keep her expression innocent and open as she watched Marcus silently plotting his revenge upon her for subjecting him to this day at the salon. He was obviously relishing the notion of dragging her up and down the mountains at night and putting her into the most uncomfortable situations he could come up with on short notice.

She couldn't wait to see what he tried to put her through.

As Sharon and the other hairdressers put the final touches on the last hairdos of the day, she finished up the last few manicures. Marcus was suspiciously happy to mop the whole salon while she cleaned her manicure tools one last time and the other women put their equipment away. Oh, man. He was seriously pleased with whatever he'd cooked up for her tonight.

Marcus smiled winningly at Sharon and asked if he and Rachel could leave by the back door since it was closer to where he'd parked, and Sharon was so dazzled she didn't even bother to ask where his truck was. The woman just let them out into the alley and locked the door behind them with an admonition to have fun at the dance.

Oh, she was planning to. She was eager to take on whatever Marcus threw at her.

They drove back to the ranch in silence and, in the gathering dusk, turned into the driveway. They rattled over a cattle grate and passed under the wrought iron arch declaring this to be Runaway Ranch.

"Wow. This place is impressive now that I can see it," she murmured as a massive log mansion came into view around a bend in the driveway. Perfectly maintained pastures stretched away on either side of the drive, dotted with fat, happy-looking cattle grazing in knee-high grass.

He circled the truck wide of the house, taking a road along the north side of the long valley, which was rimmed by towering mountains. As he drove, he told her, "The ranch encompasses this entire valley and most of the mountainsides you can see. Brett told me it's nearly six thousand acres."

"Wow. Well, it sure is pretty."

Marcus nodded as he turned off the ranch road onto a narrow dirt driveway. In a moment, his cabin came into view.

She reached for her door handle but was startled when the automatic lock clicked into place.

"Stay there. I'll come around and open your door for you," he said as he climbed out of the truck.

Seriously? She was plenty capable of opening her own door. But hey. If he wanted to lock her in and play the gentleman, who was she to stop him? After all, she was only a weak, helpless female who couldn't keep up with a big strong manly man like him…

She had to wipe a smirk off her face as he opened her door and held out a hand to her. She laid her palm in his and let him help her down. His hand was warm and gentle. It was also smooth, compliments of the manicure she'd given him earlier.

He could thank her later for not filing off his shooter's callus, too. Any decent manicurist would've gone to town on the thing, but she'd merely rubbed a moisturizer into the area to keep it from cracking and had otherwise left it alone.

After he took a long, hard look around the valley, which she joined him in doing—all was quiet—he turned and jogged up the front steps, saying over his shoulder, "I figure we should eat before we head out tonight. You rest, maybe take a nap, while I pack some gear for us. I only have a kit for myself, but I can hit up Brett for some spare gear and a rucksack for you." Marcus added with a brief smirk, "After all, I want you to have the full SEAL experience this evening."

"Oh my. I really should lie down, then, and gather my strength."

"You do that. I'll wake you when supper's ready."

She made it to the bedroom and closed the door before she burst out in giggles, but barely. And she had to clap her hand over her mouth lest he hear her mirth.

As an operator, she'd learned never to pass up rest, for in her line of work, she never knew when the next sleep might come. She lay down on top of the quilted bedspread, pulling the blanket folded at the foot of the bed over herself. She closed her eyes and went through the relaxation exercises she'd been taught. Her muscles released, one by one, and she drifted off to sleep quickly.

A hand touched her foot sometime later and she came instantly awake, battle alert and combat ready. Operators were known for waking up violently, and it was standard practice to stay out of harm's way by touching their foot to wake one. He'd probably done it out of habit, but it was the safest way to wake her, as well.

"No threats nearby," he murmured automatically. "Supper's ready."

She was more grateful for the way he'd woken her up than he could fathom. Although she didn't usually attack anyone who startled her out of a deep sleep, it did happen sometimes, particularly when she was tense. Which had been her constant state of existence ever since her house nearly blew up with her and her teammates in it.

Supper was a pair of the juiciest, most flavorful steaks she'd ever eaten, a big salad and an entire Italian loaf of garlic bread. She ate her steak and salad fully and nibbled on the bread.

"You'd better eat up," Marcus warned her. "You're going to be starving by midnight, and the dance isn't over until two a.m."

"Then I'll pack a snack."

"You're hauling your own grub," he warned her.

"Okay, fine."

He shot her another one of those smiles that said she had no idea what she was in for. She hid her own smile behind a slice of the buttery, garlicky bread.

She insisted on washing the dishes since he'd cooked, and he disappeared into the bedroom to change into all black clothing while she did the chore.

Marcus had been busy during her nap. Two rucksacks sat by the front door, packed and ready to go. Drying off her hands as she strolled over to them, she experimentally hefted them. One weighed around thirty pounds, the other around twenty.

Ha. Kid stuff. She'd humped seventy pounds of gear, including all her own ammo and water, on various missions, some of them treks of twenty miles or more, made at night at a grueling pace.

She opened both packs, taking a quick inventory of the contents. She approved of the binoculars and bits and pieces of hiking gear he'd packed. She threw in a half dozen snack bars she'd found in a cupboard and a few extra bottles of water for both of them, and then closed the packs and set them back on the floor.

Marcus emerged from the bedroom. "I borrowed black clothes from Brett's wife for tonight. She's about your height and build."

"Great!" she said brightly. "Good thing I was wearing my running shoes yesterday. They'll be good for walking in."

Marcus's mouth twitched with humor.

She undressed quickly and braided her hair the way she always did in the field. She pulled on the black clothing, which fit fine. As she did so, Rachel the manicurist fell away and Gia the Medusa took over her body and mind. Her body felt light and fast, and her mind felt sharp.

She stepped out into the main room and gushed, "This shirt is so cute! Any chance you've got a hat for me? I'd hate to get, you know, leaves and twigs or—oh, God—bugs in my hair."

He didn't even bother to hide his smirk now.

She continued innocently, "Maybe I should wear work gloves or something so I don't scratch up my hands?"

Marcus grinned. "Sure. One hat and gloves coming up."

He dug around in a big duffel bag in the corner that she recognized from her own spec ops kit. He pulled out a floppy brimmed hat made of canvas and a pair of leather work gloves that were miles too big for her. But they would be better than nothing if the two of them ended up needing to do any heavy lifting or digging.

She pulled the hat on at a jaunty angle and grinned cheekily at him. "Ooh. Do I get to paint my face with that green makeup stuff you guys use?"

"It's called camo grease, and I suppose so."

"I want the full commando experience," she declared.

"I'm not a commando. They barge in guns blazing and kill everything that moves. SEALs rely on stealth as much as possible. We slip in, do our job and slip out undetected if we can. We only get into shoot-outs if there's no other way to get the job done."

She nodded and did her best to look at him in wide-eyed wonder. It was all she could do not to burst out laughing. She followed him as he picked up both rucksacks and headed outside. He lifted the rucksacks into the truck one at a time, using his left arm to hoist each one in turn.

This was her favorite time of day—poets called it the gloaming—when the light was dying, all color fading to black and white. A few lightning bugs blinked lazily in the clearing in front of the cabin. As darkness fell around them, its familiarity was comforting. Nighttime was the office space of Special Operators. She slid into its cover mentally and physically, embracing the invisibility it provided.

They climbed into the truck, and Marcus passed a folded paper map over to her. "This is a terrain map. I've marked the high school on it. We'll approach from the north. You can check out the route I've marked down the mountain to the school's gymnasium."

As he drove out of the ranch and headed toward town, she made a production of unfolding the map, turning it upside down and then turning it back upright. Using a flashlight, she studied the route quickly. Based on the terrain lines depicted on the map, she built an image in her mind's eye of the hillside they would descend to approach the school from the back. Mentally, she added in trees, brush and loose rocks. It would be a difficult descent even for an experienced operator.

"Are you trying to kill me?" she muttered.

"You wanted to see what it's like to do my job."

"Just don't lead me off a cliff," she retorted.

"I promise. I won't lead you off a cliff."

"No, you'll just shove me off it, right?"

Marcus grinned over at her. "You'll be more likely to shove me off one before this night is over."

"Duly noted."

He drove along the north rim of the Clearwater Valley for a bit and then turned downslope onto a road that looked like little more than an old logging trail. They slowed to a crawl, and the truck's four-wheel drive was necessary to navigate the uneven tire tracks and potholes so deep they would have swallowed a lesser vehicle.

Marcus consulted a portable GPS lying on the seat beside him, drove a bit more, consulted their position again and then turned off the engine. "We're here," he said cheerfully.

Trees pressed in on all sides and the darkness was thick and complete out here.

"Um, wow. It's really dark. Are we going to use night-vision goggles or something?"

"They're called night optical devices, more commonly referred to as NODs, and no. We're going old-school."

"What does that mean? Stumbling around blind in the dark and feeling our way down the hill with our hands?"

He grinned. "Oh, this is going to be fun."

She scowled at him as she climbed out of the truck and met him at the rear bumper. If she were just some random civilian woman, this adventure would be a little mean of him. Although, she supposed making him spend a day in a beauty salon had been no less cruel and unusual punishment for him. That, and she had all but dared him to bring her out here like this.

"Take off your hat," he murmured.

"Why?"

"I'm going to paint your face. You wanted the green makeup, right?"

Well, this was novel. She usually greased up her own face. She took off her hat and turned her face up to him expectantly.

"Close your eyes," he murmured. His fingers were gentle as he drew them down her face in an irregular vertical pull. There was something achingly intimate in how his fingertips traced the contours of her face so lightly. It felt like a lover's caress.

He went back in with a second color to fill in the gaps between the first set of lines while she fought to get control of her reaction to him. He stepped back and nodded in satisfaction.

She couldn't see herself, but she expected he'd used green and black camo grease.

"All done," he announced.

"Do I get to paint you?" she asked hopefully.

"No. I'll do my face."

"Aw, c'mon," she wheedled.

"Knowing you, I'd end up with horns and a goatee and spectacles drawn on my face rather than proper camouflage," he muttered as he loaded up his fingers with green grease and pulled them down his face. She watched with interest as he quickly filled in the gaps with black camo grease while he peered in a small handheld mirror. She couldn't count the number of times she'd done the exact same thing in the past several years.

Marcus sat down on the tailgate and commenced swinging his feet idly.

She asked, "What are you doing?" Of course, she knew exactly what he was doing—letting his eyes adapt to the low-light conditions. Or in this case, the practically-no-light conditions.

"Getting my night vision."

"Ah." She hopped up onto the tailgate beside him. She closed her eyes to help them adapt faster. She'd kept her eyes closed for most of the last part of the drive as well, so her vision was already sharpening. She made out the silhouettes of trees first. Then she started picking out details on the ground nearby. Finally, she looked around, able to see the terrain reasonably clearly.

"Ready to go?" he asked.

"Yep. Lead on." She hopped down off the tailgate.

He picked up the heavier rucksack with his good arm and slung it across his back, then slipped his right arm through the second shoulder strap carefully. She picked up hers, slipping her arms into the straps and tightening the bag down to her back until it was snug against her body and wouldn't slide around.

"Before we take off, it's standard ops to do a gear check. Turn around," he ordered.

He poked and tugged at the rucksack slung over her shoulders, then ran his hands down her arms and around her waist.

"Are you searching me for firearms or something?" she asked.

"I'm checking for loose flaps or hanging threads. Anything that could snag on a bush or twig and make a sound or leave a trail."

"Oh. Cool. Do I get to check you?"

"If you'd like." Humor laced through his voice. He turned around and presented her with his back.

She actually performed a gear check on him, but as she'd expected, his rucksack and clothing were squared away, with everything neatly stowed and no loose threads anywhere. Amused, she took her sweet time running her hands down each of his arms and around his waist. Her palms might have strayed lower, dangerously close to his tight glute muscles, before she slid her hands around the sides of his waist.

"Should I check your legs?" she asked innocently.

He cleared his voice abruptly. "Uh, no. That's fine. This isn't a real op."

She batted her eyelashes at his back and murmured, "I like pretending, though."

He made a noise that sounded suspiciously like he was choking a little. Then he collected himself and said more calmly, "We have a saying in the SEALs. 'Slow is smooth. Smooth is fast.' We're going to take our time and try to make as little noise as possible. Try to follow right behind me."

She nodded, doing her best to look naively confident. *Honey, I can follow in your exact footsteps and walk in exact time and rhythm with you, as slow or fast as you care to go, for as long and as far as you care to go.*

He headed into the brush, stepping over a fallen log and navigating around a patch of thorny brambles. At this altitude, the trees were mostly aspens and pines, neither of which were particularly messy trees that dropped a lot of branches. The forest floor was reasonably open. Little gullies from snowmelt and loose rocks were the biggest hazard up here.

"Let me know if I'm going too fast," Marcus murmured in a low voice that would only carry a few yards.

Laughing silently at his back, she mimicked his tone and replied, "Will do."

She fell into the rhythm of movement as naturally as breathing. Yet again, she was grateful for the thousands of hours of rigorous training Gunnar Torsten had put her and her teammates through. She froze anytime she felt a twig underfoot or heard a leaf start to rustle, and then she adjusted her step and tried again.

Even to her ears, she was moving well tonight. Marcus was setting a moderate pace that gave her plenty of time to move quietly. Plus, she was well rested after a month out of the field. It also didn't hurt that she was out to make a point to Marcus about the capabilities of women.

They hiked for about a half hour before Marcus held up a fist to indicate a stop. She halted immediately out of long habit. Then she realized what she'd done and lurched forward, stumbling into his back.

"Oompf," he grunted as she slammed into him.

"Why did you stop?" she demanded.

"Rest break."

She was just getting warmed up and feeling great, but she sat down obediently on a boulder.

"You holding up okay?" he asked.

She laughed a little. "What are you going to do if I say no? Give me a piggyback ride up the mountain?"

"I would if necessary."

She sighed. "I believe you. But I'm fine. I'm ready to continue whenever you are."

He laughed. "I'm just getting warmed up. By the way, I'm impressed by how quietly you move."

"What can I say? We women learn how to move quietly and not draw attention to ourselves."

He shot her a look in the dark shadows that she wasn't sure how to interpret. Sympathy, maybe? Or concern? Thing was, she wasn't lying. Far too many women moved through life fearfully and as unobtrusively as possible.

Marcus commented, "Most guys take months of practice to become as quiet as you." He was peering at her with just enough curiosity and suspicion that she felt a need to distract him. Quickly.

"Can I lead for a bit?" she asked lightly.

His eyebrows sailed up. "If you'd like."

"Great. How does this GPS thing work?" She picked up the unit he'd been checking from time to time to navigate down the mountain. She listened through a quick lesson she could've given to him, picked up the GPS and shouldered her rucksack once more.

"Do we need to feel each other up again before we head out?" she asked lightly.

She just loved that little choking noise he kept making whenever she mentioned putting her hands on him or him putting his on her.

Suppressing her grin by the slimmest of margins, she headed out, moving rather more quickly than he had, but at nothing close to her top speed. No sense giving away the full extent of her training to him. After all, she had no intention of revealing to him who she really was.

But they moved swiftly down the mountain over the next twenty minutes or so, and the valley floor came into sight between the trees.

Marcus touched her shoulder and she stopped, turning to face him.

"I'll take over from here," he breathed.

She nodded, and he moved past her, assuming the lead. He started to move laterally, paralleling the football field behind the school. They would need to move to one side of the big brick building housing the gymnasium to see people coming and going from the dance.

Marcus was in full stealth mode now as they glided through the trees, and she had to admit he was good. Very good. It took all of her skill to move as quietly and smoothly as he did.

He chose a thick stand of brush to sink down behind, and she knelt beside him. Slowly and carefully, he cut away vines and brambles until he'd created a little cave inside the bushes. He moved back and gestured for her to go in first.

She paused, whispering, "Do you have something we can lie on? The ground's all wet." She knew full well there was a plastic tarp in her rucksack since she'd inventoried its contents earlier.

"Turn around. There's a ground cloth in your pack. I'll pull it out."

They worked together to ease the black tarp open and spread it on the ground without making a lot of noise or fuss that someone below might notice. Then she crawled into the hide on her hands and knees and stretched out on her belly.

"Is there anything breakable in my pack?" she asked, her voice low.

"Nope. Why?"

"If I'm going to be here for a while, it'll be more comfortable if I put my pack under my stomach and ribs, don't you think?" It was an old operator's trick to relieve back discomfort. Also, it would allow her to prop her elbows on the ground comfortably as she held binoculars to scan the area.

"It will, indeed, be more comfortable that way," he replied, sounding surprised and tucking his own ruck under his body.

As he slid in beside her, his entire left side plastered against her right side. His body heat was a nice contrast to the cold seeping up from the ground through the tarp. And it didn't hurt that everywhere they touched, he was hard and muscular. The forest smelled intensely green around them, a combination of pinesap, crushed leaves and rain.

He passed her a set of binoculars, and she fooled around with them, pretending not to know how to prop her elbows like bipods on the ground and lean the binoculars against her face. But, eventually, she settled into a proper surveillance stance. She started with the forest on her left that arced around the parking lot. She scanned across the parking lot itself, then checked out the line of tall bushes along the wall of the gymnasium in front of them. She pivoted to her right to scan the football field and bleachers and then the woods arcing around the football field to their right. All was quiet.

"Now what?" she murmured.

"Now we wait."

"For what?"

"For you to spot the guy who chased you last night."

"But I told you. I don't know what he looked like," she whispered.

"You'd be surprised. You saw him under low-light conditions like this, and not only did you see him move, but you also caught a glimpse of his silhouette. You're more likely to recognize him like this than you would be if he walked up to you on the street in broad daylight."

"Huh. Interesting."

They settled in, and she felt his body gradually relax against hers. Tense about being this close to her, was he? Interesting. He seemed so sure of himself all the time. She did get where he was coming from, though. She lay next to hot men all the time like this, but they were colleagues. Buddies. More like annoying brothers than eligible men she would consider dating.

With Marcus, however, she felt a real spark of… something. The only reason she wasn't putting a name to it…or pursuing it…was because they were both going to go back to their operational units in a few months and never see each other again. Regret coursed through her that the timing wasn't better for the two of them.

The dance was in full swing inside, and faint strains of music drifted up to the hillside above the school. A few people straggled into the dance from the parking lot. Whether they were new arrivals or couples who had adjourned to a car for some hanky-panky before returning was impossible to tell.

The dance had started at eight o'clock, and it was approaching ten now. She figured people would start leaving in the next hour or so to get home to kids and babysitters. If she were a bad guy who'd come here to find her, she would be getting into place right about now, hunkering down like they already were to watch people leave the party.

Once the hostile spotted her leaving the dance, he would undoubtedly plan to follow her home. Maybe he expected to break into her place and kill her later tonight, or possibly to break in sometime in the next day or two and ambush her when she came home from work.

Either prospect sent a shiver down her spine. She was trained in self-defense, but of all people, she was vividly aware that there was always somebody stronger, faster and more skilled than she was. Or the guy might simply have a weapon and shoot her before she could dodge a devastating, close-range shot. If somebody wanted her dead bad enough and had enough operatives to keep sending more after her as she eliminated them one by one, someone would eventually succeed in killing her.

As she lay there, she had time to ruminate on how they had found her here in Montana so quickly. She'd traveled under a false identity, used cash on the road, changed her physical appearance, and nobody except her boss, who was fiercely loyal to his Medusas, knew where she was. How, then, had that guy been in the alley last night?

The only thing she could think of was that they'd had some sort of satellite surveillance on her and had seen her leave her home in Louisiana to drive across the country to Montana. But the power that took—the resources—was staggering.

Very few people in the military or intelligence community had the authority or raw political pull to co-opt a satellite and use it to track a single individual. Unless, of course, a satellite operator was in on the conspiracy.

What was in that crate? It had been too heavy for a person—or a corpse. A weapon or weapons, maybe? A cache of gold? Nuclear materials encased in lead? Whatever it was had to be incredibly valuable to merit tracking her across the country illegally.

She scanned methodically as her mind churned, sectioning the area in front of her into pie wedges and examining each one in order for any signs of movement or for her hostile.

Around eleven thirty, people started to leave the dance in a steady stream. She stayed busy examining each person who left the dance and also continuing to scan the hillside to their left, which seemed to be the most logical place for a bad guy to stake out the dance.

It was a little after midnight when she thought she spotted a faint movement that shouldn't be there, off to her left in the trees. She zeroed in on the spot, increasing the magnification of the binoculars to maximum gain.

It was an area of thick brush and undergrowth similar to the one she and Marcus were hunkered down in. What she wouldn't give for a good pair of infrared night optical devices right about now. She kept her stare trained on the area for several long minutes.

There. Another slight movement, as if someone was propped on their elbows and shifting their weight, maybe growing sore and uncomfortable.

Without moving, Gia breathed, "Nine o'clock. Estimated range fifty yards. Twenty feet above us in elevation. Bushes like these, one tango."

Marcus immediately swiveled his binoculars to where she directed. He murmured back, "Relative position to that twin-trunked oak leaning toward the parking lot?"

She glanced away from the bush and spotted the tree he'd described. "Come this way fifteen feet and up the hill ten feet. Bushy cedar tree fifteen feet tall, its bottom half obscured by brambles and brush."

"Got it."

They were silent and perfectly still, side by side, for several minutes. Then the person in the brush shifted once more.

"There," Marcus bit out.

"Yep. That's him."

"I'm gonna ease back and pull out my spotter's scope."

"You got a sniper rifle to go with that?" she replied in a bare breath of sound.

Marcus snorted under his breath. "I will next time."

He eased backward with admirable patience, moving only a few inches at a time, pausing before inching back a bit more. He moved with no rhythm, sometimes pausing a few seconds between moves, sometimes waiting up to thirty seconds.

She kept her gaze peeled on the other hiding spot.

Without warning, she saw the person in the hide

make a big move, swinging his whole upper body in this direction. "Freeze," she bit out, going perfectly still herself.

Marcus did so without question, his shoulders pressing against her ankles.

"Eyes on us," she breathed without even moving her lips.

She and Marcus held their positions for what she guessed to be close to five minutes. Finally, she saw the hostile swing his body back to face the parking lot.

"Clear," she reported on a bare gust of air past her throat.

"Stay here. I'm gonna go get that bastard," Marcus whispered.

"We'll go together. He's a Special Operator, and two on one is better against a guy like that."

"You're not—"

She cut him off. "No time to argue. Let's go."

She started the tedious process of backing out of the hide as well, praying that Marcus would wait for her before he circled above and behind the hostile and jumped the guy.

When she finally cleared the bush and eased upright, Marcus was still there.

Thank goodness.

He nodded tersely at her from behind the trunk of a good-sized tree, and she joined him in its lee, using the tree for cover from the hostile.

She shed her ruck, easing it silently to the ground, and while she was bent over, she pulled her KA-BAR field knife from its ankle sheath, slipped its lanyard around her wrist and brandished it comfortably in front of her. She nodded back at Marcus.

His eyes widened for a moment, taking in her relaxed stance and the lethal weapon. Then, without comment, he turned and headed out. Calling on her full abilities, she followed him, becoming one with the night and the forest. They eased from shadow to shadow, taking their time, opting for stealth over speed.

If Marcus noted her special operations training in the way she moved or the confidence with which she moved, he didn't react to it in any way. Which was just as well. She was working, and that meant she was concentrating on the objective and focusing on all the sounds, smells, sights and the slightest movements around them.

They made their way in complete silence to a spot about fifty feet above the other man's hide.

She tapped Marcus's right shoulder once, and he stopped, turning his head slowly, just enough to see her over his shoulder. She flashed him several quick hand signals, indicating that he should continue straight ahead for another dozen yards, and then they would both turn downhill and pincer the hostile between them. She signaled that he should initiate the attack.

His eyebrows shot straight up and his head turned a bit more, enough to stare hard at her.

Yeah. She was going to have some tall explaining to do after they caught this jerk and got back to her place.

C'mon, Marcus. Accept that I know what I'm doing and work with me here.

Marcus stared at her for one more moment. Then his right hand rose slowly. He tapped the side of his head and nodded slightly, indicating that they should both move out.

She eased forward, step by careful step, moving with

delicate care. In their training, the Medusas had proved to be particularly skilled at moving quietly, more so than most male operators, in fact. Their instructors guessed it was because they weighed less than most men. At any rate, she moved down the hillside in maximum silent mode.

As they neared their target, she spied a pair of combat boots sticking out of the bush. She exhaled slowly, relaxing her entire body and doing an exercise a Korean special operations instructor had taught the Medusas. He'd called it pulling in their energy auras. It involved going still from the inside out. That way, the hostile would be less likely to sense her presence behind him.

Out of the corner of her eye, she spied Marcus's big shadow easing out from behind a tree to her left. They were both about twenty feet from the hostile now.

The combat boots in front of her shifted slightly, then suddenly went perfectly still. Crap. He'd sensed something, even if he hadn't heard her or Marcus. She froze, sucking in her energy as much as possible. She was the forest. She belonged here. She was as still and quiet as a tree.

Without warning, the man in front of her surged upright and bolted forward, crashing through the brush and sprinting down the hill toward the parking lot. A couple walking out of the gym toward their car lurched as he charged toward them.

Gia took off running after the hostile, who was definitely the man from the alley. He had the same lean, whipcord strength and that long, ground-eating stride. He was wearing a black knit watch cap on his head, but she got the impression he might be bald beneath it. No sign of any hair or sideburns was visible as he tore down the hill away from them.

Dang, he was fast.

Marcus broke out of the trees a millisecond behind her. They both charged down the hill, maintaining about fifty feet laterally between them as they chased their quarry. For a short-distance sprint of, say, less than fifty yards, she could hold her own with any male operator.

The grass on the hillside smoothed out as it became a grassy slope beside the school, and she stretched out into a full sprint. As fast as she was, the guy in front of her was slightly faster. It was those long legs of his, darn it.

Marcus also stretched out in a hard run, but Gia noted vaguely that he wasn't pumping his arms evenly. His right arm was a tad weaker and less flexible than his left. It wasn't much of a handicap, but it was enough that he also couldn't close in on the fleeing man.

The hostile sprinted between rows of cars ahead of her and she watched in chagrin as he leaped into a Jeep. She put on a last burst of speed in hopes of catching a license plate number, but he peeled out and threw a painful spray of gravel at her that forced her to throw an arm up in front of her face.

By the time small, sharp pebbles quit pelting her, the Jeep was turning and accelerating away from the high school.

Marcus ran up beside her, huffing hard. "Was that him?"

"Oh, yeah," she panted.

"Did you get a license plate?"

She answered grimly, "No. But he'll change vehicles as soon as he can anyway. He's no amateur."

"Neither are you. What's up with that?"

"Later," she bit out. "I want to take a look at his hide."

"Good idea."

They moved swiftly across the parking lot and retraced their steps up into the edge of the tree line, ignoring the alarmed couple standing in the middle of the parking lot, staring at them.

The hide was efficient and devoid of gear. The hostile hadn't had a rucksack when he ran, either. He'd been pretty casual about coming up here, lying down under a bush and expecting to spot her. He would know she was a Special Operator from her prior interactions with his coconspirators and the excellent resources they seemed to have. Which meant he was supremely confident in his own operational skills.

There was an imprint of his body in the moist dirt, and she measured it quickly.

"He's about six foot two," she announced.

"I'd put him at two hundred ten pounds," Marcus replied.

"I'd put him ten pounds higher than that. The guy's all muscle."

Marcus shrugged in agreement. "He was Caucasian, light-eyed. I didn't see his hair color. Did you?"

"He was wearing a black watch cap, so I can't say for sure he was the shaggy-haired guy from the alley before."

Marcus nodded, staring at the ground. "He must've driven to the high school, grabbed a set of binoculars and hiked up here with the intent to spot you and move fast to follow or apprehend you."

She nodded grimly. "Speaking of which, are we walking back to your truck?"

"I see Wes Morgan's pickup truck in the parking lot. I'm thinking we ask him for a ride back to my truck."

Thank goodness. The whole way down the mountain, she'd been thinking about how miserable an uphill climb it was going to be. The terrain was steep and rough, with copious loose stones where there weren't vines and downed branches waiting to snag the unwary foot.

"Do you want to call Wes?" she asked. "Or just stroll into the party in full war paint?"

Marcus rolled his eyes at her as he pulled out his cell phone, and she grinned back, aware that her teeth would look weirdly white against the irregular black and green vertical stripes covering her face.

While they waited for Wes to come out, they retraced their steps to where they'd dumped the rucksacks and recovered those, along with the ground tarp. Then they headed for the parking lot.

A tall, handsome cowboy and a willowy, gorgeous blonde strolled out of the gymnasium about the same time she and Marcus arrived at the edge of the parking lot. They met the couple, who turned out to be Wes Morgan and his fiancée, at a heavy-duty truck Marcus led her to.

One of Wes's eyebrows went up when he saw them in full stealth gear and camo paint, but he merely said lightly, "Hot date tonight?"

Marcus snorted, ignored the question and opened the rear door for her. She slid across the bench seat and Marcus climbed in after her.

The blonde turned around in the passenger seat. "Hi. I'm Jessica."

"Gi—eee. Nice to meet you. I'm Rachel." Well, hell. She'd almost gone and blown her cover there. Problem was, when she was in Medusa mode, she was Gia, not Rachel.

"I've never managed to get Wes to play soldier with me. How'd you get Marcus to do it?"

She smiled broadly. "He lost a bet, and I forced him to spend a day working with me at a beauty salon. He was all over exacting a little revenge for that."

Jessica laughed gaily. "Ohmigosh. Next time he's going to work at the salon, do give me a call. I'll drive all the way to town to see that."

Marcus scowled beside her and said nothing. He, too, was in work mode and had gone mostly silent.

Wes spoke up. "So, where exactly did you leave your truck?"

Marcus passed the GPS forward and Wes studied the digital map on its face. "Got it. Those old logging roads are in pretty bad shape. Mind if I drop you off at that last turnoff before the trail you're parked on?"

"That's fine," Marcus replied. "It'll be an easy hike down the road to my truck. A whole lot easier than going up the mountain in rough terrain to it."

"Want us to stick around in case you need to get towed out?" Wes asked.

"Nah. My truck's got four-wheel drive and I've got a couple hundred pounds of sand in the back to help with rear traction. Plus, Rachel can always get out and push."

It was her turn to snort. As if. Sure, she'd pushed her share of Humvees out of mud and sand traps, but Marcus could push his own darned truck.

Wes wisely chose not to comment. In a few minutes, they entered the black forest from before, and it was even darker now that night had fallen fully. However, Gia's eyes were also completely adapted to night, so she could see much more.

The truck stopped and she and Marcus hopped out

with a word of thanks for the lift. Wes and Jessica drove off and silence fell around them.

Marcus didn't start off down the road, however. Instead, he turned aggressively to face her.

"Okay, Rachel. Start talking. What the hell was that, and who the hell are you?"

Chapter 10

Marcus stared across the cab of his truck in the dim glow of the dashboard, and Rachel stared back at him, her expression stubborn. He tossed a towel at her. "Here, wipe the greasepaint off your face. Then I'll do mine."

She refused to answer any of his questions, even when he'd threatened to abandon her out here. He'd finally given up and stomped off toward his truck, not particularly interested in whether or not she followed him.

She'd used skills tonight that *nobody* who wasn't a Special Operator knew. How on earth did she know how to move with such stealth? Or how to use her ruck to make a surveillance hide comfortable? Or how to flank a target or run that swiftly? Even the vast majority of military members—including veterans of actual combat—didn't know how to do stuff she'd casually demonstrated in the past hour.

It turned out she had followed him to the truck, not that he'd heard her back there, no more than a dozen feet behind him. Which pissed him off even more. He'd been tempted to follow through on his threat and drive away from her before she could get in the truck with him, but that would be petty.

Hence she was across the cab from him now, staring back at him implacably.

His gaze narrowed. "I know a Special Operator when I see one. You moved more quietly than me going down that mountain, and you moved fully as fast as me when we ambushed that guy. You know the hand signals. You hold a knife like you bloody well know how to use it, and you have the look in your eyes."

"What look?" she broke her mutinous silence to ask.

"The look. The cool confidence, the moving gaze that takes in everything, the self-awareness that you can take care of yourself in absolutely any situation."

"If I'm all those things, then why am I hiding in Montana and playing hairdresser while some dude stalks me?"

"I don't know. You tell me," he said with an evenness he didn't feel.

She sighed. "Look. I don't want to fight. Can we just drive home and talk about this calmly?"

"I am calm!" he exclaimed. Although, as he said the words, he realized he was anything but. Not only was he supremely irritated, he was also curious. And, furthermore, he felt duped. He didn't like feeling that way. Particularly not feeling that he'd been duped by this woman. He'd been fascinated by her since she'd sunk that stupid fish hook in his back, and the mystery of her only continued to deepen, the more he learned about her.

What he wanted was answers. He needed to make sense of this woman and put her into some understandable context in his mind. Was anything she'd told him about herself true besides the one incontrovertible fact that this woman was military trained? Hard-core military trained.

Aloud, he asked, "How do you feel about heading over to your place right now to get a few things? I'm betting Bushes Guy is busy dumping his vehicle and figuring out what the heck just happened to him."

"That's a great idea. I'd love to have some of my own clean clothes."

He drove to the apartment complex where the hardware store clerk had said she lived. As he turned into a large parking lot ringed by buildings, he murmured, "Which place?"

"That one." She pointed at one near the back of the complex.

He parked his truck and sat quietly in the dark, observing the parking lot and public areas around him. He was intrigued that Rachel also made no move to get out of the vehicle.

She was *so* freaking special operations trained. But how could that be? The few women who'd made it into the special operations world were famous among the male operators, and he'd never heard of her.

He reached for his door handle. "Pass me your keys and stay in the truck."

"Not happening. We go in together. If that guy has had the same idea we did—that I would be off balance and freaked out right now, not likely to come home alone—he could very well be inside this very minute."

"Doing what?"

"Booby-trapping the place or waiting for me to come back so he can kill me."

He thought fast. The only way he could keep her in the truck if she didn't want to cooperate with him was to tie her up or knock her out. As much as he disliked the idea, if she wanted to come along, he couldn't plausibly stop her. Plus, she could pack her own stuff inside the apartment and not have to rely on him to grab what she wanted.

"Okay. Fine. But I go first, and you do exactly what I tell you to do," he muttered.

"Deal." She held out her keys to him.

"Get out of the truck and close the door as quietly as you can. Then fall in behind me," he instructed.

When she was right on his heels, he moved swiftly into the shadow of her building. He climbed the stairs in complete silence and was vividly aware that he didn't hear Rachel make a sound, either. He had to admit, she was really good at stealth.

They reached the top of the landing and he moved to the left side of her door. He pointed to her and then to the right side. She nodded and plastered herself against the wall, squatting without him having to tell her.

He reached across the door with the keys and was surprised when she lifted the keys out of his hand and unlocked the door herself. It was, indeed, better to have the breacher on the knob side of the door do the actual unlock and open. Oh, how the questions were stacking up in his head for that conversation they were going to have later.

He glanced over at her, and she nodded to indicate she was ready. He eased the door open about halfway and spun inside low and fast, poised to dodge if anyone attacked or opened fire on him. He'd barely cleared the door frame when a blur of motion out of the corner of his eye indicated that Rachel had come in low and fast behind him, spinning to the left the same way he'd spun right.

He visually cleared the small living room as she silently closed the door behind them. He moved over to look behind the sofa as she ran, bent over low, into the kitchen. She was getting ahead of him at clearing the place, darn it. He moved swiftly across the living room to the bedroom door, which was open, and ducked inside the space.

He started as Rachel tapped his left shoulder once. She was already behind him? Dang, she was fast. He scanned the small room and bent down to check under the bed. He flashed a hand signal at Rachel to hold her position, and then he headed for the first doorway on the left.

A bathroom. He checked in the shower and opened the cabinet under the sink. It would be a tight fit for anyone under there, but he looked nonetheless.

He stepped back out into the bedroom and whirled left, entering the walk-in closet, which was mostly empty and clear of bad guys, as well.

He came back out into the bedroom and said low, "We're clear."

She merely nodded and moved past him to the closet. He watched as she grabbed a folded duffel bag off a shelf, grabbed all her clothes, hangers and all, and stuffed them in the bag. Efficient.

She slid past him with the duffel and opened the chest of drawers in the corner, grabbing the contents of the drawers with fast sweeps of her arm and dumping everything into the bag. Into the bathroom she went. One good sweep of the counter, and everything in there was packed, as well.

She joined him in the bedroom.

"You got any military gear here?" he asked.

"Negative. It's stowed elsewhere."

Smart. Surprising, but smart.

"Got everything you need?" he murmured.

"Yep," she answered. "Wanna go, or do you wanna leave behind a little surprise for our guy?"

He glanced over at her and caught the wolflike grin that flashed across her face. He grinned back. "Have you got an idea?"

"The place came with a fully stocked kitchen. Lots of pots and pans. I've always loved building towers out of my toys."

A low chuckle escaped his chest. Bushes Guy would be insulted as hell if they left behind pots and pans as booby traps to trip him up.

He liked it. A lot.

They headed for the kitchen and emptied the cabinets. Not only were there pots and pans, but there were cookie sheets and tin baking pans, and Rachel had laid in a decent supply of canned food.

They grabbed the lot and commenced building precarious piles of stuff in front of the bedroom and living room windows. It was trickier building a pile in front of the door. They had to build the pile and then use rope to carefully pull the whole pile close to the door behind them after they slipped outside.

He was impressed by Rachel's patience and delicate touch as she maneuvered the tower of pots and canned goods into place. Gently she slipped the rope free and eased the door shut. She locked it from the outside and then nodded at him in satisfaction.

He grabbed her duffel bag, winced as his right shoulder gave a shout of protest and switched the bag to his left hand.

Without comment, she lifted the bag out of his hands. He opened his mouth to argue, but she gestured for him to lead the way down the stairs, and he realized that if he didn't move out, she was going to head on down without him.

Pushy, that woman was.

Although, as he moved swiftly and quietly down the stairs, he amended the adjective from *pushy* to *confident*. He also admitted to himself that he liked her confidence. He just had to remember to stop thinking of her as a civilian and remember to think of her for now as a fellow operator. Which was a big shift and not easy to grasp.

He reached the bottom of the stairs and paused, gazing around the parking lot intently. Rachel's hand landed lightly in the middle of his back—just a touch to let him know exactly where she was and that she, too, was scanning the area for hostile activity.

Given that she was a photo intelligence analyst, he was glad to have her eyeballs on the job. Those folks were known to be able to see and identify details most mere mortals didn't even notice.

She gave his right shoulder a single tap. They were good to go. He concurred, and they moved out, hugging the base of her building until they were directly in front of his truck. They raced across the patch of grass, jumped into the truck and pulled out of the parking lot in a matter of seconds.

It had been a smooth operation. In quiet, out fast. No fuss, no muss.

"Any chance we could swing by Sharon-Dippity while we're breaking and entering tonight?" she asked lightly.

"What's at the sal— Oh. Do you need to get something out of your car?"

"I know better than to leave my stuff someplace so obvious," she replied scornfully. "I need to get into the salon. More specifically, into the storeroom."

He headed toward downtown Sunny Creek. It would be deserted at this time of night with all the shops closed hours ago. As he approached the salon, he pondered whether to go in the front or the back. The alley would be quieter, but it also would be tightly confining if it came to a firefight.

Although, if it turned into a gun battle, anyplace in town would be problematic. The best option would be to flee the scene and not engage.

He drove past the salon and turned down a side street and then into the alley behind the shop.

"Point out the back door when we get close," he murmured to Rachel.

"Fifty feet ahead. Second door on the right." She rummaged in her purse for something as he pulled up to the door she'd pointed out.

He parked the truck right up next to the building, leaving only about twenty-four inches of clearance to open the passenger door. As he recalled, the storeroom door opened inward, so it wouldn't be an issue to open.

Rachel opened her door, slipped out between the truck and the brick wall, and crouched in front of the door. He slid across the front seat to follow her—and stared as he realized she was picking the lock.

"Alarm?" he murmured.

"None," she replied absently.

It took her a few more seconds, but the knob turned under her hand and she slipped inside the storeroom just as he drew breath to tell her to let him go first. Irritated, he slipped out of the truck and followed her into the dark space.

She'd gone right, moving quickly behind the row of shelves that took up the center of the room. He slid left, clearing the other side of the shelves. They met at the door that led into the salon.

"Next time, don't barge into an uncleared space without telling me and without letting me help," he muttered low.

She rolled her eyes at him but didn't argue the point. Which was good because he was right. She murmured, "Guard the door while I get my stuff…please and thank you."

It was his turn to roll his eyes at her. But he moved to the back door and peered left and right down the alley. All clear.

Behind him, he heard a faint scrape, and he glanced over his shoulder to see Rachel pulling a chair over in front of the sink. He checked the alley once more and glanced back just in time to see her reach up to the ceiling, push aside a ceiling panel, grab a pipe inside the hole and do a pull-up that brought her head almost to the ceiling.

Whoa. That was a no-kidding, lift-her-whole-body-weight-with-her-arms pull-up. Not many women could do even one of those. And she made it look easy. As if that wasn't impressive enough, holding the pulled-up position, she pulled her knees up to her chest and flipped her feet over her head, into the ceiling crawl space, as neatly as any gymnast could've done it.

He realized he was staring, open-mouthed, at the hole in the ceiling where she'd disappeared. Quickly, he scanned the alley outside. Still clear.

Rachel's voice was muffled behind him. "A little help, please?"

He turned around and saw her lowering a large black nylon bag through the hole in the ceiling. He moved over beneath it and reached up, taking the weight of the bag.

Holy cow. This sucker was heavy. And metallic sounds came from inside it. For all the world, it sounded just like the weapons bag in his personal equipment kit. Surely not.

It was one thing for her to know how to move around like an operator and do the correct hand signals. But she didn't have any business hauling around the weapons of an operator. This stuff was dangerous as heck in the hands of an amateur.

Frowning, he set the bag on the floor and looked up at the pale oval of her face staring down at him. "Need any help getting down?"

"Nope. Just move aside and I'll be right down."

He went back to the door to check the alley quickly and then turned his head to watch her reverse the movement from before. She started on her belly, grabbed the edge of the hole, and flipped herself down and out of the opening as slick as a whistle.

"Were you a gymnast at some point in your life?" he blurted.

"No. Why?"

"You're pretty good at moving around your body weight."

"Um, yeah. I do work out a fair bit."

He frowned. Working out a fair bit and being able to do what she'd just done were two entirely different things.

She picked up the weapons bag, moved over to the door beside him and murmured, "Are we going or not?"

He lurched into motion, poking his head out one last time to clear the alley in both directions. "Clear," he muttered, disgruntled.

He slid across the seat of the truck as she hoisted the bag in behind him. She locked the salon door and closed it behind herself and then climbed in beside her gear.

"Let's roll," she murmured.

She even talked like an operator. And the questions just kept on piling up.

"Anything else you need to pick up while we're in town?" he asked dryly.

"Nope. I'm good," she answered jauntily.

He just shook his head and pointed the truck back toward the ranch. He couldn't *wait* to put his list of questions to her. And this time he was getting some answers.

Chapter 11

Rachel spent the drive back to the ranch mentally preparing herself for the interrogation to come. It would be so much easier just to tell Marcus about the Medusas and that she was one of them, except the team's existence was absolutely classified. She would need her boss's permission to say anything to him about the Medusas. She pondered calling her boss to ask, but it was nearly 2:00 a.m. and he wouldn't appreciate being woken at this hour. Tomorrow would be soon enough to ask.

Meanwhile, she just had to get through tonight.

A distraction. That was the key. If she could just derail Marcus and his questions for one night, that would buy her the time to talk with Major Torsten.

But what? Like all operators, Marcus was a single-minded kind of guy. Once he had his teeth sunk into a bone, he wasn't about to let go of it.

They parked in front of his cabin, and she climbed out, pushing her duffel of clothes across the seat to him while she took the heavy weapons bag herself. She'd caught Marcus wincing several times this evening. His shoulder wasn't anywhere near close to healed.

She followed him into the cabin in silence and set her bag down. And then she braced herself for the onslaught.

Except when it came, it wasn't what she'd expected. He turned and closed the distance between them until she had to step back. Her shoulder blades touched the back of the door.

He loomed over her in the dark, standing still and silent. He would probably be intimidating as all get-out to a civilian woman if he loomed like that over her. But she'd been loomed over—a lot—by men just like him. Some had been drill instructors yelling at her, some had been hand-to-hand combat instructors about to attack her. Either way, she knew how to handle them. She girded herself for the verbal or physical assault to come, relaxing her knees, balancing her weight evenly on her feet, clearing her mind.

Marcus spoke quietly. Gently, even. "Why don't you trust me?"

Okay. Not what she'd expected. It took her a moment to shift gear from expecting an attack to answering an insightful question. "I do trust you."

If only he wasn't standing so close to her, and if only he didn't smell like crushed leaves and rain and a hint of pinesap. And if only he wasn't so good-looking and so smart…and funny and kind and noble…

Oh, who was she kidding? She was ridiculously attracted to him, and her breath was coming in short, fast little gasps that had nothing to do with preparing to be attacked and everything to do with wanting to lean into him, lift her chin and capture his generous mouth in a smoking hot kiss.

"If you trust me, why are you lying to me?" His voice was a low, sexy rumble that made her toes curl inside her shoes. And the note of disappointment in it was her undoing.

A wild impulse to tell him the truth flowed through her. What the heck. Why not? She answered, "Because the truth is classified and I need permission before I can be honest with you."

Crap. She shouldn't have said that. He was a smart guy and could infer all kinds of things from even that much information. Regret speared through her. Dang it. Why did she have to be so attracted to him? It was making her do stupid things like tell the truth!

"While we're on a roll and you're answering my questions, please explain to me how you knew how to do all the things you knew how to do on our little surveillance mission tonight."

She winced and backtracked hastily. "I told you already that I'm a real-time photo intelligence analyst. Surely you've worked with people like me before. You know what we do. I've watched dozens, maybe hundreds, of special operations missions up close and personal. I see everything you guys do during a mission. I watch how you move. And, yes, I practice moving the same way."

He continued to stare at her, his expression unreadable. If only he would take a step or two back. He was so close she could practically kiss him, even without standing on tiptoe and wrapping her arms around his muscular neck. An urge to do just that hovered on the edge of her mind. Would he taste the same way he smelled, earthy and outdoorsy? She would bet he'd take over the kiss and not let her control the thing. At least, not entirely.

She continued talking—or rather, babbling. Which she knew to be the point of him looming over her like this. He was trying to get her to say something she shouldn't, and it had already worked. All that was left for her to do now was cover her impulsive verbal tracks.

She tried. "I'm required to know spec ops hand signals so I can understand what the operators are signaling to one another to do. It helps me know what information the guys need me to relay to them next."

"How so?" Marcus murmured, using that same easy, masculine tone of his that held no threat, no pressure whatsoever...and that made him completely irresistible, dammit.

"If a team leader signals his guys to move off to the right, then I'm going to relay what threats are waiting off in that direction first. If a guy signals an abrupt halt, I can assume he's heard something, and I'm going to take a hard look at what's within about twenty-five feet of his position."

"Huh. I didn't know you folks did all that."

"It's my job to anticipate exactly what the guys on the ground need to know and when they need to know it. I'm not officially part of the team, but I am their eyes, sometimes. Surely you've had intel analysts feed you valuable information out in the field before?"

"All the time. It's just that none of them told me they were practically operators themselves."

She shrugged and said in as light a tone as she could muster, "Live and learn."

He eased a few inches closer to her. The fabric of his T-shirt—which was not loose—rubbed ever so slightly against the fabric of her shirt. She plastered her back against the door, but that tantalizingly light contact invited her to do something...something dangerous. Injudicious. Disastrous. But oh, so delicious.

He breathed, a bare whisper of sound, "Why are you still lying to me?"

"I'm not! I am a live photo analyst! Give me a live feed from a drone, and I'll show you."

"Oh, I believe that. But there's something else you're not telling me."

She swore silently to herself. He was leaving her with no choice but to brazen it out. "Of course there are things I'm not telling you. Lots of things. I'm not about to reveal to you my secret passion for rocky road ice cream, or that I can't stand asparagus, or that I binge-watch sappy movies when I'm home alone. And let's face it. You're not exactly Mr. Forthcoming yourself."

"About what?" he blurted.

"I don't know. All the important stuff about yourself that you're not telling me."

"I'm an open book," he declared.

"Ha! Tell me how you hurt your shoulder."

"It involved a helicopter and a guy almost falling out of it."

Holy cow. She could totally picture that. A hot egress, incoming enemy fire. The team diving for the open chopper door, the pilot lifting off a millisecond too soon and one of the team members rolling out the door. Marcus would have dived for the guy. Grabbed him. Hauled the guy and close to a hundred pounds of gear back inside against the g-forces of a hard, climbing turn. Yep. That would've been plenty to tear up Marcus's shoulder.

"Where did it happen?" she challenged.

"Classified."

"What's your primary theater of operations?" she demanded.

"Classified."

"Why haven't you ever been married?"

That silenced him.

"Yeah. Like I said," she said dryly. "Not exactly forthcoming yourself."

He moved fast, planting his left hand on the door beside her right ear. He leaned in more slowly, giving her time to move…or slug him, she supposed.

He paused, his mouth only a few inches from hers. "You talk too much."

"Can I quote you on—"

His mouth claimed hers, cutting off the rest of her question, which admittedly was rather smart-ass.

And then he really kissed her. Or maybe she kissed him. She wasn't sure. But his mouth was warm against hers, confident and gentle, and hers was moving hungrily against his. As she'd suspected, it wasn't clear who was in charge of this kiss. He was busy holding back, and she was busy charging full speed ahead, and they met somewhere in the middle.

As it became clear this was not a momentary blip of absurdity and that he was prepared to really kiss her, some of her urgency relented. She got to know his mouth, noting that he did indeed taste like a forest after a rainstorm. Or maybe it was just that the scent rising from his clothing and skin flavored the kiss. Either way, it was intoxicating. She loved the outdoors more than anyplace else, and forests in particular.

He, too, seemed to settle into the kiss, exploring her mouth slowly. She loved that he seemed in no hurry to go anywhere with this embrace. He was just enjoying it and staying fully in the moment, which allowed her to let down her guard and do the same. So many men got in an all-fired hurry and pushed for too much, too fast. But not Marcus. In fact, he seemed to relish waiting for her to get a little impatient before taking anything to the next level.

His free hand slipped lightly around her waist and came to rest in the middle of her back. He didn't pull her against his body. Rather, he waited for her to arch up against him of her own volition. Which she both appreciated and resented. She appreciated having the freedom to make her own choices in how far this kiss went, but it also took away any pretense of her not being a willing participant. Which she supposed was the point.

Aw, heck. Why was she fighting this? She liked him. He liked her. This felt great, and nobody else ever had to know they'd scratched this particular itch. Of all people who could keep a secret to the grave, two Special Operators like them were a pretty good bet to succeed.

As she made her peace with her conscience, her lips softened, then her mouth softened, then her whole body softened. Tentatively, she put her hands on his waist. No surprise: it was as sinewy and hard as it looked.

He leaned in a little closer, kissing her a little more firmly. Their bodies came together, and they fit to perfection. He lifted his mouth away from hers, adjusted slightly, and then the angle was just right and he was really kissing her now. One of them groaned in the back of a throat, or maybe it was both of them.

She loved the smooth warmth of his lips, the sexy slide of his tongue across her teeth, the wet heat as her tongue tentatively touched his.

He lightened the kiss, then deepened it, then lightened it again. She couldn't tell if he was trying to decide how he liked kissing her best or just experimenting. But, finally, she looped her right hand around the back of his neck and pulled him in closer for a good long kiss.

That was definitely him groaning that time. Triumph surged through her. Heat and pressure began to build low in her belly and she lurched, startled.

"Everything okay?" he murmured immediately, his lips moving against hers.

"Fine. More than fine. Kiss me again."

"Your wish is my command." He swept both arms around her then and drew her up against his gloriously wonderful body. His arms were strong but didn't crush her. He was being careful with his power, but she wanted him to cut loose. She was no fragile creature that would shatter if he flexed his muscles. She could meet him halfway in that regard.

She tightened her arms around the muscular column of his neck, relishing the corded tendons there. But still, it wasn't enough. She lifted her right leg off the floor and wrapped it around his hips, using her considerable strength to pull him closer.

He laughed a little against her mouth, a gust of heat between her lips. "Got it," he murmured. "You like it a little rough."

"Not rough. Just not so careful."

"Fair enough." His head slanted to one side and his tongue swept into her mouth, claiming her thoroughly as his arms tightened and he lifted her completely off the ground.

Oh, yes. That was more like it.

She heard a sound and lurched against him. She'd moaned. She never moaned.

She froze, and he did the same.

"What's wrong?" he mumbled against her lips.

"I never moan," she mumbled against his mouth.

"You just did." A definite hint of humor laced his words.

"I know."

"Is that good?" he asked, his lips brushing lightly against hers.

"Depends."

"On what?"

"On where you're planning to go with this."

That did make him lift his mouth all the way off hers. He stared down at her in the dark, his gaze boring into her at close range. "I wasn't planning to kiss you in the first place, let alone go anywhere with it."

"Oh." Disappointment coursed through her. Wait. What? Disappointment? Surely she didn't want to jump into the sack with this guy…?

Why, yes. Yes, she totally did want to do exactly that.

Marcus broke her disjointed train of thought, murmuring, "What in the hell is going on in that devious mind of yours? Expressions are passing over your face too fast for me to register, let alone comprehend."

She laughed a little. "I wish I knew."

"Guess."

"I like you. A lot more than I ought to. And it's making all of this...complicated," she confessed.

"I know the feeling."

"Really?" She looked up at him hopefully.

"Really."

"Why's that?"

To her vast disappointment, he pushed away from the wall and spun to take a lap around the tiny living room. He stopped in front of her once more, but safely at arm's reach from her. She briefly contemplated closing the gap but was certain he would back away. And she had no desire to literally chase the man around the sofa like the sex-starved female she apparently was.

Marcus spoke, a note of desperation in his voice. "I'm only here for a few more months. I have no idea what my future holds. I don't know where I'll be or what I'll be doing a year from now."

Stomping down hard on her desire for him, she focused on her words and managed to respond evenly, "I know the feeling."

He shoved his right hand through his hair and visibly winced, stopping the movement abruptly and carefully lowering his right arm to his side. He took a spin around the kitchen table and ended up back in front of her, safely on the other side of the sofa, though. "Given the uncertainty over my future, I have no business getting involved with anyone, let alone you."

"What do you mean? Let alone me? What's wrong with me?" she demanded.

"Nothing. And that's the problem. You're freaking perfect."

"Aw, that's so sweet of you to say. But I assure you, I'm far from perfect."

"That's not what I meant," he blurted. "You're perfect for me. You're exactly the kind of woman I picture when I think of the woman I'd like to settle down with someday—" He stopped, looking horrified. "I didn't mean that the way it sounded. It's not a proposal or anything. I'm not pressing for a long-term relation—"

She stepped around the sofa swiftly and reached up to press her fingers against his lips. "It's okay. I know what you meant. You're exactly the kind of man I picture myself settling down with after I'm done running around the—" She broke off before she could say "world" and said instead, "—military system, doing my intel-analyst thing."

He nodded, apparently not catching her near slip.

He reached up to his mouth to grasp her wrist and slid his lips down the length of her fingers to press a kiss lightly in the center of her palm. It was such a simple thing, but the intimacy of it staggered her.

Real fear that she was getting in over her head with this man, and fast, speared through her.

"It's late," he said quietly, "and you've had a big night. Perhaps we should go to bed." He added hastily, "In separate beds, of course."

She laughed under her breath. "Of course. You're hot and all, but I'm not a casual-fling kind of girl."

"I'm hot? You think so?" He didn't sound the slightest bit surprised. Ah, the egos of Special Operators. They knew they were irresistible to women and weren't afraid to use it to get laid. Except in Marcus's case, he was using it to torture her and not take her to bed.

She planted her hands on her hips and glared at him. "You know you're hot. All operators know it. You guys have way too much self-confidence for your own good."

He grinned and shrugged. "But it's still nice to hear an attractive woman say so."

She rolled her eyes. "Lord save me from SEALs and their egos."

He merely laughed. "You love us and our egos. Admit it."

"I do have a soft spot for supremely confident operators, but I can do without their egos."

"Fair enough. So can I, sometimes. It's a pain in the butt to have ten or twelve guys all strutting around like roosters trying to display their tail feathers to any female who'll look at them."

"I wouldn't know," she said dryly. Thankfully, the Medusas mostly checked their egos at the door and focused on teamwork and mutual support. There was very little competition among the women. But then, the only way they succeeded in special operations was by being masters of cooperation. By working smart and working together, they got the same jobs done that the men did.

"How do you feel about going for a trail ride tomorrow?" Marcus asked as he unfolded a blanket over the sofa.

"Like on a horse?"

"Yes."

"Sounds fun. I love riding."

"Perfect. A few of the boys are riding out to the back acreage tomorrow and I thought we could go along, it being Sunday and all and the salon being closed."

"How did you know that?" she asked, startled.

"I saw the salon's hours painted on its front window. It says they're closed on Sundays."

"Fair enough." She headed for the bedroom, exhausted all of a sudden. "Sweet dreams, Marcus."

"You too, Rachel."

She dearly hoped Gunnar gave her permission to tell Marcus about the Medusas. She was tired of not being called by her real name, particularly by the guy kissing her socks off these days.

Chapter 12

Marcus was up early the next morning, and he felt great. Surely, kissing Rachel wasn't what had put him in this great mood? The woman could really kiss, though. She threw herself into it with enthusiasm and didn't seem encumbered by self-esteem issues or self-doubt. It was one of the things he liked best about her. She threw herself into everything she did. Hesitation was not in her nature.

He still didn't fully buy her story about watching special operations on video and learning how to do them. But she'd let slip that her job was classified and she couldn't talk about it. He figured she was involved in helping to train operators in some way. Maybe she played hostage or observed training runs and critiqued them. He'd never heard of field instructors who weren't active or former spec ops guys, but maybe she had some special expertise from her time as an intel analyst that she brought to the table.

Ah, well. Give him a few more days to seduce her, and she'd tell him everything—

Except something in his gut revolted at the idea of using sex to get information from her. He genuinely liked her. Enough to hate the idea of playing her like that. He really hoped he could convince her to be honest with him—fully honest—without resorting to such tactics.

He made a big skillet of chopped meat and vegetables, and scrambled in a bunch of eggs to make a breakfast out of it. Somewhere in the middle of bacon frying, Rachel wandered out of the bedroom, looking cute in a pair of pink striped short pajamas with bunnies all over them. They showed off her biceps and muscular thighs to perfection. The incongruity of bunnies and badass made him smile.

"Smells good. But isn't it kind of early?" she mumbled, looking and sounding half-awake.

He held out a mug of coffee to her, already doctored with a bit of cream and sugar the way he'd seen her drink it before.

"Bless you," she murmured.

"We aim to please," he replied.

Her gaze warmed over the rim of her mug as she sipped the coffee. She seemed several degrees more alert when she brought the mug down.

"May I help with anything you're cooking?" she asked.

"You can help me eat all this. I made us a big breakfast. I find that being outdoors all day seems to double my appetite."

"Agreed—" Her gaze snapped up to his, looking alarmed for an instant.

Why did she keep doing that? She would say something seemingly innocuous and then freeze up as if she'd just given away a national secret. She might have sworn up, down and sideways last night that she trusted him, but she still was withholding a lot from him. He really wished she would just let down her guard and be herself for once.

She wasn't talkative over breakfast, but then, it took a while for caffeine to properly kick in. Besides, he was playing the long game with her. Rather than jump all over her this morning and demand information, he planned to spend a pleasant day with her, get her out in the wilderness, where she could let down her guard, and really relax, maybe feed her a nice supper, and only then see if she was willing to tell him more about herself.

They ate breakfast quickly. She ate as efficiently as he did, not gulping food, but working through it as if she had places to go and things to do. They did the dishes together, working as a team. It was almost as if both of them were trying to learn each other's rhythms, to get into sync with each other. It was exactly what he did whenever a new guy joined his SEAL team. Before finally going out on live missions, newbie SEALs trained with their teammates for months to find that effortless synchronicity that all SEALs had with one another.

As she put away the last plate and turned to face him, he commented lightly, "If there's a rifle in that bag we got out of the salon's ceiling last night, you might want to take it along."

"Why's that?" Rachel asked with quick caution.

"We're in bear country. You should always carry a decent-sized weapon with you if you're going to head into the backcountry. I can call Brett and have him grab a spare shotgun, but if you have your own weapon you're comfortable with, I figure you'd be better off with that."

She shrugged, not responding. At least she didn't try to deny that the bag she'd pulled out of the storeroom's ceiling had been full of weapons and ammo.

He ducked into the bathroom to shower and shave, and when he emerged, Rachel was finishing cleaning what looked for all the world like a prototype Textron assault rifle. They'd recently competed to build the next squad assault weapon for the army and continued to improve upon their design. It also appeared to be sporting a scope he'd not seen before—another prototype, perhaps? Where in the world did she get a hold of a weapon like that? If he wasn't mistaken, her weapon had look-around-corner capability, some sort of modified cartridge feed, and a few other bells and whistles he didn't recognize on sight.

"How did you get a hold of that rifle?" he blurted.

"It was a gift. I helped out a group that was in a bind, and I was the only eyes on scene. I found them an exit route and saved a bunch of lives. They sent me this as a thanks."

What group? Only military units and a few other elite government units tested prototype weapons in the field. It was on the tip of his tongue to ask the question aloud, but he bit it back. *Patience, young grasshopper.*

Instead he said, "Nice. Any chance I could give it a try sometime?"

She smiled. "Sure. But it's sized for me. You might find it a little cramped to fire."

Still. He was interested to see how it handled. "Does your interest in assault weapons also come from your work with special operations teams?" he asked casually.

"I figure they're the folks who know the best weapons. I pay attention to what they're using and try to gain proficiency on similar or same weapons."

It was a reasonable explanation, but it was also a strange way of being a groupie. The Special Forces had legions of fans and wannabes, both male and female. He just hadn't pegged her as the type. She seemed too confident in her own abilities to play copycat to guys like him.

Perplexed, he picked up his own rifle, a couple of boxes of ammunition and a rucksack stuffed with bottles of water, snacks and a few survival essentials he felt naked without.

He was startled when Rachel shouldered her own rucksack, slung the Textron casually over her shoulder and followed him outside. She looked just like one of his guys, casually toting a forty-pound rucksack and rifle as if they weighed nothing and were an everyday part of her life, no more unusual to her than carrying a purse might be.

They drove to the main barn, where Brett Morgan and his brother Wes were already saddling up horses for the day's outing.

Marcus made introductions all around, and then Brett asked Rachel, "On a scale of one to ten, how experienced a horsewoman are you? There's no need to impress me. I just want to put you on the right horse."

She smiled pleasantly. "I can ride anything in this stable as long as it'll take the weight of a human without trying to buck me off."

Brett grinned. "Okay, then. I've got a couple of young horses I'm looking to put some miles on. I'll put you and Marcus up on them."

Rachel insisted on grooming and saddling her own horse, a big red gelding Brett called Rick. Rachel laughed when he told her the horse's registered name was Rickety Split. While Marcus brushed and tacked up his own horse down the aisle from her, he kept an eye on Rachel to make sure she wasn't getting in over her head. But she moved around Rick like a pro, talking quietly to the horse and generally making friends with the gelding as she brushed him, cleaned his feet, detangled his mane and tail, and finally saddled and bridled the horse.

Outside, she swung into the saddle easily and settled lightly on Rick's back. The horse's expression was relaxed and happy, and Marcus mentally sighed in relief. The two of them were getting along just fine.

Wes led the group away from the barns, heading across a big pasture and turning to parallel the line of mountains forming the north rim of the valley. It was a cool morning with bright blue skies and the promise of warm sunshine later in the day. The air smelled of freshly cut grass from the hayfield they were skirting around, and the horses walked calmly in a single-file line.

In front of him, Rachel looked around at the scenery, smiling. It was the most relaxed he'd ever seen her, and she wore it well. She was a strikingly attractive woman and rocked the whole natural healthy-pretty without a lot of makeup.

He had two ulterior reasons for bringing her out here on this trail ride today. One was to see how good she was with a horse. Most Special Operators were accomplished riders because many of the places in the world they went were only accessible by four-legged transportation. The other reason was to see how good she was with a rifle.

He'd failed to mention last night that where he and the boys were riding to this morning was the shooting range built at the back end of the valley, well away from the houses and barns. He had every intention of seeing if she actually knew her way around that Textron.

It was one thing to own a fancy rifle, and even to know how to shoot it. But Special Operators were in another class altogether when it came to marksmanship. Moreover, she couldn't learn how to be a sharpshooter by watching operators shoot weapons. That could only be learned by thousands of hours of practice.

Sure, she had a shooter's callus. But then, lots of amateurs did. A trip to the firing range was the best way he could think of to figure out what her training really was.

They'd been riding about a half hour when the silence was broken by a cell phone ringing. Both Rachel and her horse started, and she hastily dug out the device.

He listened shamelessly to her end of the call. "Thanks for calling. I'm going to text you a question and I need the answer now, if possible."

Well, that wasn't helpful. She typed into her phone for a few seconds and then put it back to her ear. It was almost as if she didn't want him to hear the question she was asking whoever was on the other end of that call. Suspicion exploded in his gut. Who was she talking to? And about what?

While she was listening to her answer, another question popped into his head. How was she getting cell service out here, anyway?

He pulled out his own phone to check it, and he had to switch it to satellite mode to get a signal. His access to a satellite communications system was strictly a government thing, reserved for Special Operators in remote locations. So how did *she* have that kind of phone service? Didn't intel analysts do their jobs from high-tech communications facilities with plenty of built-in satellite phones? Why would she have one out here? And while she was on vacation, no less?

In front of him, she listened for a moment more and then said merely, "Thanks." A brief pause, then "Any updates?" Another pause. "Let me know when you learn more."

She listened for a moment more and then let out a long-suffering sigh. "I think someone's here. I'm hoping he's just scouting me out and isn't here to kill me. He acts like an operator, though."

That made both Brett's and Wes's heads whip around.

Brett sent him a questioning look past Rachel, and Marcus shrugged back to indicate he didn't know what was going on, either.

Rachel ended the call and pocketed the phone. Seconds later, Brett's cell phone rang. Marcus frowned. That sure didn't sound coincidental. He eavesdropped again, this time on Brett, who said, "Hey, buddy. What's up?"

Brett listened for a long time, and the more he heard, the darker his expression got. By the time he said merely, "Got it. I'm on it," and hung up, he looked as if he were about to head into a spec ops mission smack in the middle of more bad guys than he could shake a stick at.

Brett didn't volunteer who his call had been from or what the problem was, and Marcus was too stubborn to ask. But the relaxed enjoyment had gone out of their little trail ride, and both Brett and Rachel were palpably tense. In fact, Rachel's horse, Rick, started acting up, prancing and sidestepping nervously.

To her credit, Rachel reached down to scratch the

horse's neck. She murmured, "Aren't you a smart boy, picking up on my mood so fast? How about you and I both take a deep breath and relax? I did get the answer I wanted, after all."

To what question? Marcus was dying to know. But no way was he going to ask if she didn't offer up the information freely.

They rode for perhaps ten more minutes, and then Wes turned away from the valley and headed up a trail that led over a small ridge into a long, narrow valley that made for a perfect natural firing range. The depression was perhaps a hundred feet wide and a thousand yards long. And the hills on both sides of it and across the far end would protect livestock from catching a stray bullet.

Wes said, "I'm gonna take a quick ride down to the other end to make sure no cattle have strayed in here and to set up a few targets while you guys get ready to shoot."

Rachel looked over at Marcus quickly. "We're shooting today?"

"You said you liked target shooting," he tossed at her.

"I do. I'm just glad I grabbed an extra box of ammo."

They dismounted and untacked the horses. They put grazing hobbles on the animals' front legs and then turned them all loose.

"Gunfire won't make them bolt?" Rachel asked Brett doubtfully.

"Nope. We bulletproof all the horses early and well," he replied.

She nodded and checked over her rifle quickly.

"Is that a Textron?" Brett asked, sounding about as surprised as Marcus had been back at the cabin. "I don't recognize the model."

She glanced up casually. "Yes. It's a prototype."

"Good thing your boss just told me who you are, or I'd have a few pointed questions for you about how you got your hands on that," Brett commented.

Marcus rounded on Rachel angrily. "You let Brett know who you are but you won't tell me?"

She pulled out her cell phone. "Read what I texted my boss in the middle of my call with him just now."

Royally ticked off, he snatched the phone out of her hand and read, "'There's a SEAL staying with the Morgans. Name's Marcus Tate. Do you know him? He's a good guy and has been looking out for me. Can I tell him about the Medusas? Please?'"

Marcus looked up and met Rachel's stare. "Who are the Medusas?"

"Are we here to shoot or to talk?" she retorted.

"You tell me."

"Let's shoot first. We can talk later."

"Yeah. All of us are going to talk," Brett said from behind her.

Marcus looked over at his old SEAL teammate. "What the hell is going on around here?"

"Let's just say your girl's got quite a story to tell us."

About what? What was up with all this swirling mystery? And what did it have to do with some guy trying to kill her?

Frustrated beyond all reason, he huffed and picked up his rifle. He was good and ready to blow something up. It might as well be those targets Wes had just nailed to a wooden wall at the other end of the valley.

And then he and Rachel were going to talk, indeed.

Chapter 13

Gia watched with interest as Marcus set up his rifle to attempt shooting left-handed. He was stretched on the ground on her left, and Brett and Wes were set up on her right. The Morgans might both be retired from the military, but they were excellent shots and casually putting holes in the center of the target some two hundred yards downrange.

She had yet to break out her Textron and start shooting. There was no need to embarrass the boys just yet.

Marcus went still and relaxed beside her. He exhaled, held his breath for a moment and squeezed the trigger.

Using her spotter's scope, she looked at his target. "You pulled left three centimeters, but your elevation is perfect. Try again before you make a correction."

He said nothing but went through his breath control exercise and took another shot. The second hole in his target was practically on top of the previous one.

"Dial in the correction," she murmured, "and you should be dead center."

Sure enough, his next half dozen shots formed a tight cluster in the middle of the target.

He sat up, looking intrigued. "It's a good exercise to shoot offhanded. Forced me to go through all the steps of setting up a shot mechanically and deliberately. It's a good reminder of the basics."

She smiled at him. "I'll take your word for it. I'm still working on perfecting shooting with my primary hand."

"Let's see what you've got, kid."

She grinned cheekily at him and picked up her rifle. Finding a level spot in the grass, she sprawled on her belly beside her weapon, blocked out everything around her and repeated the familiar shooting litany in her head. It was just her, her weapon and her target, connected by an invisible thread. She envisioned her rounds following the thread to exactly where she wanted them to go.

Then, as Marcus loomed vulture-like over her, she went still, exhaled, made her final targeting adjustment and gently squeezed through the trigger. Before he could check her first shot to call out any adjustments, she fired off four more shots in quick succession. She didn't take more than ten seconds between shots. One of the beauties of this prototype weapon was it barely recoiled after each shot. It settled back into stillness so quickly that a decent sniper could recover, aim and fire it again at light speed compared to most other weapons.

When she finished firing her group, Marcus lifted the spotter's scope from its lanyard around his neck and gazed downrange at the target they'd been shooting at. He announced with a certain smugness, "You missed the target."

"I was aiming at the five-hundred-yard target," she replied dryly. "Check that one."

He was silent for a moment. Then he merely muttered, "Show-off."

Her lips twitched. She would take that as confirmation that her weapon was still properly sighted and that she'd put her shots in their usual tight, neat cluster… and dead center. To her right, Brett and Wes chuckled. Wes said, "Wanna give my sniper rig a go? I've got a target set at a thousand yards."

"Sure." She crawled over on her hands and knees to the bipod stand with a hefty Barrett .50-caliber weapon pointing toward the horizon.

"Smooth bore or rifled bore?" she asked.

"Rifled," Wes replied, sounding surprised.

"Someone give me windage," she murmured.

She felt the men grin over her head, and Wes said, "Two right."

Without even looking at it, she put the correction into the very complicated German scope—that practically no civilians and very few military members would have any idea how to use—and gently squeezed off the shot.

"In the kill zone," Wes announced.

With long-range shots, the rounds picked up a spiraling wobble that increased the longer the shot was. No sniper expected to hit their target dead center. They only hoped to put that spiral in the target's center of mass and let the large, heavy round do the work of killing the hostile.

She put three more shots in the kill zone and called it good. As she sat up and stretched her shoulders, Brett walked over to his horse and pulled out another hefty rifle. But this one, he plugged into a tablet computer, which he handed to Marcus.

"Here you go, old man. A weapon you can fire without hurting your shoulder."

Gia jumped up eagerly and went over to Marcus's side to peer down at the tablet with him. "Oooh. We played with some of these computer-targeted systems a few months ago. They're spectacular. Once the computer locks on its target, it'll track movement, windage, atmospheric conditions—the works—and make all of its own corrections. Takes all the fun out of shooting."

Marcus grinned at her. "But if it takes the bad guys out, think how much more fun the overall missions will be."

"True."

They took turns shooting the computer-targeted system, and Brett and Wes both tried the look-around-corners function of her Textron. Marcus had to regretfully decline to try her weapon due to his shoulder not being healed.

"When your shoulder's recovered, consider yourself invited to give my baby a try," she told him as she commenced disassembling the weapon.

Wes gathered wood and built a small campfire. The four of them sat around it, cleaning and oiling all the weapons in companionable silence.

"So, Rachel," Marcus said quietly. "The Medusas."

"I'll need all of you to turn off your phones," she replied, pulling out hers and powering it down, as well.

Marcus turned off and pocketed his, then leaned forward, elbows planted on his knees, staring at her with every bit of his formidable focus.

She smiled at his aggressive curiosity. She expected after the past several days with her he had a whole lot of questions stacked up in his noggin. She said lightly, "The cocktail-party version is that the Medusas are an all-female Special Forces team."

Marcus snorted. "I'm going to need a longer answer than that."

She shrugged. "It's not that complicated. I belong to a special unit currently comprised completely of female Special Operators. We run missions specially designed and profiled for female operators. In particular, we run in places where women blend in, or are best suited to get in and get out, or where women are most likely to be completely ignored."

"How many of you are there?" Marcus blurted.

"Six. We're integrating three more to the team right now and have several more in the training pipeline. There have been two groups before the current one, and there's talk of expanding the team into a second platoon."

"How come I haven't heard of you before now?" Marcus asked.

She shrugged. "The program is highly classified. The fewer people who know about us, the higher our effectiveness in theaters of operation. If the bad guys don't know to look for a woman, we stand a much better chance of slipping past them. Unless we've actually run with a team of our male counterparts, nobody in the male spec ops community would have any reason to know we exist."

"Who trained you?"

"Gunnar Torsten is our commander."

"Gun?" Marcus exclaimed. "Did you know he ran with Brett and me on the teams?"

"I knew he ran with Brett. I didn't know if you and he had crossed paths or not."

Marcus grinned. "We go way back."

"I'd love to pick your and Brett's brains about that.

My teammates and I could seriously use some dirt on the man to hold over his head."

Marcus grinned knowingly. "So you can get out of four a.m. surf runs now and then?"

She smiled back. "Something like that."

Marcus turned to Brett. "Did you know who she was this whole time?"

"Gunnar told me he was sending a woman to the area and that she would be given my name as an emergency contact. But the name he gave me was Gia Rykhof."

"That's me. Rachel is my middle name, and Boyd is a cover name."

"Wait. You're Gia, not Rachel?" Marcus blurted.

"Technically, I'm both. But given that everybody in town knows me as Rachel, it would probably be best if you continued using that name for me."

Marcus looked at her intently. "Now that we're having true confession hour, who, exactly, is trying to kill you?"

"I told you the truth about that," she replied a shade defensively.

Wes piped up. "I'd like to hear the story. If we're going to be protecting you, I'd like to know who we're up against."

"I haven't asked any of you for protection!"

"And yet here we all are," Brett said quietly.

She sighed. "Here's the thing. I left the Medusa training facility because I don't want to put any of my teammates in danger when these jerks come after me. Why would I come here and do that exact thing to you guys? I need to be completely alone so there are no collateral deaths if whoever's trying to kill me succeeds in hitting me."

She looked around the fire, and all three men were frowning. Heavily. It was Marcus who finally spoke up, though. "That's not team thinking."

"Yes, it is. I love my teammates and have no intention of getting them killed. And I have no intention of getting any of you killed, either."

"And they love you and want to protect you, too," Marcus replied. "You ought to let them have your back."

She picked up a stick and poked it at the fire. A shower of sparks flew up and spiraled away into the sky. "Yeah, well. My Medusa sisters aren't here."

"But we are," Marcus replied firmly.

"Agreed," Brett replied.

"What he said," Wes chimed in.

She looked around at the three men. "I appreciate the offer. Really. But I have to respectfully decline."

"Small problem with that," Marcus murmured. "We know where you live. We can set up a protection detail on you whether you want us to or not."

She scowled at him. "I know evasive tactics. I can leave town and make sure none of you follow me—"

"Or you can stay and let us help you. This is us volunteering to protect you," Marcus said with quiet urgency.

"But—"

He cut her off. "No buts. And don't answer right now. I'm telling you, as a guy who's been on the teams for nearly twenty years, you're making a mistake if you don't let us help you. I don't know who you're up against, but that guy in the bushes at the high school was a skilled operator. You need us. Particularly if Bushes Guy or Baldy or whoever he is brings in reinforcements of his own."

She had no argument against that because Marcus was right.

"Who is this Bushes Guy?" Wes asked.

"Are you going to tell the whole story from the beginning, or am I?" Marcus asked her.

She sighed. "I'll do it." She relayed having been the real-time intel analyst, watching the four men carry the crate away from the operation, and she described in detail how the anonymous man had barged into the surveillance facility, stolen her computer and threatened her. Then, in technical detail, she described the two attempts on her life.

"And that's how I ended up in Sunny Creek. Gunnar suggested this would be a good place to hide while he works on figuring out what I witnessed and who's trying to kill me."

Brett asked, "What does he know so far?"

"Not much. We know Alpha Platoon is still in the Middle East, we know the crate was not part of their official mission brief, and we know they had help stateside with whatever they stole. That's it."

Marcus added, "And we know they've got resources with access to surveillance and tracking. How else did Bushes Guy find you here? Sunny Creek is not the first place anyone would go looking for a female Special Operator. And yet he's here."

"And you're sure the guy in the bushes was looking for Gi—Rachel?" Brett asked.

"Why else would some dude be hiding in the bushes with binoculars outside a school dance?" he replied.

Wes said, "Maybe he's a private investigator someone hired to see if their spouse is cheating on them."

Brett retorted, "Are you kidding? The gossip network

in this town is so good nobody could possibly cheat without every lady in town hearing about it."

Gia smiled. "I can attest to the accuracy of that after having worked in the beauty salon for a few weeks. Not to mention, female information networks are the bread and butter of the Medusas. They're a real thing and they're very, very good."

Marcus leaned back against a boulder. "So, what's next?"

She sighed. "I'd love to catch that guy from the bushes and find out who he's working for and why his people are so fixated on killing me."

Brett asked, "Do you think he's still in the area?"

She shrugged. "Given that he chased me in the alley and staked out the dance, I'm going to say yes. He'll make another run at me as soon as he figures out where I am."

Marcus said, "Then you have to stay here at Runaway Ranch, where he can't find you."

"I can't hide forever."

"Just until Gunnar figures out who these guys are."

She shrugged. "Personally, I would rather take the initiative and go find them before they find me."

"If we knew more, maybe," Marcus replied doubtfully. "I don't like running any operation without full intel."

She snorted. "No operator does."

"I keep forgetting you're one of us," he admitted.

Wes commented, "It does take a little getting used to. I ran with some women specialists a few years back—they went into villages and made friends with the local women. Gave kids vaccines and vitamin shots and birthed babies. They used to pick up good nuggets of intel now and then and pass them to us."

Gia nodded. "Those women were the precursors of today's Medusas. They had as close to full Special Forces training as the brass thought women were capable of at the time."

"How close to SEAL training is the Medusas' training?" Marcus blurted.

"As close as Gunnar and our other instructors can make it," she replied dryly. "It's horrible."

All three men laughed.

They packed up after that, putting out the fire carefully, packing up their weapons, and policing shells. They went after the horses who had wandered away a bit, saddled them and mounted up.

She had to admit it felt good to have finally come clean with Marcus. She could tell he still had a lot of questions about the Medusas and her capabilities, but they had time for that later. Assuming he forgave her for not being honest with him from the start. But that was a conversation for when Brett and Wes weren't around. And, to be honest, she dreaded it. She liked Marcus. Heck, it was probably more accurate to say she'd fallen for the guy. She desperately hoped he would forgive her for holding out on him the way she had.

While one half of her brain warned her that she was getting too close to him and they still would go their separate ways when this mess was over, the other half of her brain cautioned her direly that she was falling for the guy harder than she'd begun to admit to herself.

She wasn't sure which prospect scared her worse.

Chapter 14

It was midafternoon before they got back to the cabin. They both took naps and then busied themselves with small chores around the place and cooking dinner. It was nearly dark and the night growing chilly when Marcus built a fire in the fireplace, opened a bottle of wine and carried it and two glasses to the sofa in front of the fledgling fire.

He waited patiently for Rachel—Gia—Rachel to quit fussing around in the kitchen and join him. She did so cautiously, perching on the other end of the sofa as if ready to bolt at a moment's notice.

"Thanks for telling me who you really are," he said, pouring wine into the glasses. He held one out to her and took an appreciative sip of the golden, honey-sweet wine.

She sipped hers and then nodded in approval of the vintage. "I'm sorry I couldn't do it earlier."

He smiled a little. "It does explain so many things about you. Like how you defended yourself so well the night I mistook you for the bad guy, and how you know how to breach an apartment. Oh, and how you knew how to navigate in the dark without making a sound. I have to admit, you blew my mind coming down the mountain behind the school. I thought you were the most talented scout I've ever encountered."

She smiled over the rim of her glass. "I was as clumsy as it was possible to be when I first started training in tactical movement. Gunnar nearly gave up on me more times than I can count."

"He's a fine operator."

"He's a fine instructor, too. I owe most of my skills to him. What he didn't teach the Medusas himself, he chose the very best instructors in the world to teach us."

"Tell me more about your training. And, yes, I turned my phone off before I sat down here."

She checked her phone as well, then leaned back against the cushions, the tension appearing to leave her body. Thank goodness. He didn't want this conversation to turn into an argument. Especially now that he knew she could probably kill him as easily as he could kill her.

She said, "We have all the same training you SEALs have. Weapons, explosives, tactics, movement, surveillance, body language, breaching, offensive driving, emergency medicine, lock picking, you name it. Gunnar is always thinking up new things to teach us when we go into training rotations."

"Fascinating. Do you ladies ever train with men?"

"We train with Norwegian Special Forces every winter in arctic conditions, and the past two summers, we've run with Korean spec ops guys for jungle training."

"How do you ladies compare to the men by way of physical capabilities?"

She shrugged. "About middle of the pack. We're not as fast at the fastest or as strong as the strongest, but we get the job done. We specialize in using teamwork to overcome any physical challenges we encounter."

"Interesting. I wonder how good a male SEAL team would be if it utilized your team's tactics."

"I don't know that we're better than any other Special Operators. We're just different. Our first approach is to try to outthink a mission. Our last resort is to brute-force it."

"Tell me about your missions."

She talked for a long time, describing various missions she and her teammates had worked on over the past few years. He listened with rapt attention, fascinated by how Gunnar Torsten and his superiors brought the special talents of the Medusas to bear.

It grew dark around them, and only the flickering light of the fire illuminated the cabin. Rachel relaxed more and more the longer she talked with him, as if unburdening herself of this giant secret of hers was a relief to her. He supposed there weren't many people on earth she could talk to about this stuff, not only because it was all classified but also because who would believe her?

Had he not seen her skills in action himself, he'd have been deeply skeptical of the idea of full-combat female operators.

He shifted position and his shoulder gave a sharp twang, reminding him that he'd used it hard today, riding and shooting. He must have winced, because Rachel said, "Turn around."

"I beg your pardon?"

"Turn sideways and give me your back." She scooted over toward him and reached her hands out. He gave her his back, and her hands landed gently on his right shoulder. She massaged his upper back, his neck, his deltoid, and very carefully, she started to work on his shoulder itself.

"Let me know if I do anything that hurts," she murmured.

He was already past speech and merely groaned in deep pleasure.

She added, "One of the oddball skills Gunnar had us instructed in was sports recovery massage. I can't tell you how often we use that to help one another after a hard day in the field. We line up in a row and do a big group back rub."

That sounded sexy as hell. But right now, he was too engrossed in how good her hands felt on him and how—weird—his shoulder felt to comment on what that must look like. He let his head fall to one side, away from his injured shoulder.

"What are you doing? It feels as if you're just jabbing it with your thumbs."

"I'm breaking up scar tissue and excess fascia. That's the white connective tissue between muscle fibers. As it turns out, that stuff gets all crinkled up—think like a piece of aluminum foil that's been squished into a ball and then unfolded. But I can use my thumb to physically smooth out the little wrinkles in the fascia."

"Huh. I learn something new every day," he commented.

"Now that I've worked the fascia in your muscles some, I'm going to break up some scar tissue for you.

I feel a lot of it built up in and around your shoulder. This may hurt a little."

"I'm a SEAL," he replied dryly. She, of all people, should know what that meant about his pain tolerance.

She snorted. "I just didn't want to sneak up on you with something that might make you yelp. We wouldn't want you to appear less than completely macho, now, would we?"

He rolled his eyes at her as she started running her thumb along various sore spots in his shoulder. The pressure she exerted was right at the edge of being painful. But in the wake of her deep massage, the areas she'd worked on did feel at least somewhat better. All of that was scar tissue? Huh. No wonder his shoulder was still stiff and sore after a month of rehabbing it. How was it supposed to go back to normal with all that scarring inside and around the joint?

"It's going to take a few more treatments to break up all the scar tissue," she murmured. "But this first treatment will make the biggest difference. Move your shoulder for me and tell me where it still hurts."

He rotated the shoulder and was shocked to realize how much of the pain had already dissipated in just a few minutes of her working on it.

"How did you do that?" he exclaimed.

"It's the latest and greatest in sports medicine. Gunnar brought a team of doctors and chiropractors in to teach us how to do it. I can't tell you how often it has kept one of us up and running after a minor injury in the field. And it speeds up recovery time after a major soft-tissue injury, or even just recovery from a hard workout, like nobody's business."

"You've got to give me the name of these doctors. The SEAL teams need this training, too."

He pointed out several spots that were still tight and found the direction in which his shoulder was still stiff and painful to move, and she went back to work on it, silently now. She worked for perhaps another ten minutes, her lower lip caught between her teeth as she concentrated on the task.

Finally, she lifted her hands away from his shoulder. "There. Try that."

He lifted his elbow and rotated his shoulder experimentally. "Whoa. It feels like a whole new joint."

"Don't go wild with it. You still have to finish healing from your surgery. But I've cleaned up a lot of the secondary scarring around the joint. If you'll let me do that to your shoulder a few more times, I should be able to clear out most, if not all, of the scar tissue built up in there."

He turned to face her, and their knees came into contact. He didn't pull away, but then, neither did she. Aloud, he said, "Wow. Thanks for the help with my shoulder."

She smiled at him, but then her gaze slid away from his. Now, why would she go all shy on him, when she didn't have anything to hide from him…or did she? He reached forward and hooked his index finger gently under her chin, asking her to turn her face back to him. He felt her ribs lift in a sigh before she looked back at him reluctantly.

"What's a brave, strong woman like you doing turning away from me? I'm just a guy. Nobody to be put off by."

She laughed a little. "To quote you from several days

ago, have you looked at yourself in a mirror? You're a wee bit intimidating in the best of circumstances. And when you put your mind to it, you're downright scary."

"Aren't you used to running around with guys like me?"

"Yes. But that's work. This…" she finished lamely, "…isn't."

He leaned forward slowly, closing the gap between them inch by careful inch. "I'm glad you see me as more than some jerk from work."

"It's not that simple," she groused.

"Nothing worth having ever is," he replied.

She made a frustrated sound and grabbed the front of his shirt, dragging him over to her. He smiled a little, loving her unabashed desire for him and how she wasn't coy about what she wanted. She was in a hurry, though, and he was not. He planned to take his sweet time getting to know this woman and enjoying every minute of it.

But then she kissed him with an enthusiasm he wholly approved of, and he abruptly found himself reconsidering his timetable. His entire body tightened in response to her sweet mouth moving hungrily against his. She looped her arm around his neck and plunged her fingers into his hair, tugging him deeper into the kiss.

Not that he needed any urging. He loved kissing her. She tasted like sunshine and something sweet and tart—maybe the strawberries they'd eaten for dessert. She opened her mouth against his, and he kissed her more deeply, sweeping his tongue inside the softness of her mouth. She sucked on his tongue and he about leaped up off the sofa in his surprise. Oh, man. That felt good.

Experimentally, he sucked on her tongue, and she

groaned as she flung herself against him. Good thing he was a strong guy, because she was an athletic woman. He caught her up against his chest tight and then half turned, dragging her across his body and into his lap.

She came along entirely willingly, snuggling against him as she kissed him again. He kind of loved knowing there wasn't much of anything he could force her to do. She could stand up to him like few women could. And that excited him. A lot.

But right now, she was wiggling on his crotch in her eagerness to find exactly the best position to plaster herself the most completely against him, and he was starting to have a little trouble breathing normally. But then, breathing normally was highly overrated, he supposed. And, after all, she was breathing erratically, too, in little gasps that were starting to drive him out of his right mind. For they were making him think seriously of carrying her into the other room, laying her down on the bed and making love to her until neither of them could barely breathe at all.

He lifted his mouth away from hers and squeezed his eyes shut hard.

"What's wrong?" she asked.

"I'm trying to control myself. Let's just say you're more tempting than most women."

"Aw, thank you!" A pause, then "But why are you trying to control yourself? I'm trying very hard here to make you lose control."

His eyes snapped open. She stared back at him, her expression entirely earnest. He laughed in spite of the throbbing pain his groin was currently experiencing.

"I'm serious," she declared. "I want you. You want me. This may be the last time we're together that we're not fighting for our lives. Nobody else can see us. If you don't want anyone ever to know this happened, I'm fully capable of keeping it just between us."

But that was the problem. He wasn't at all sure he wanted to keep this secret. "You deserve better than a one-night stand," he said.

"Then don't make it a one-night stand. Stay in touch with me after we both leave Montana and let's figure out a way to make it more."

"Easy to say. Harder to do," he mumbled.

"But not impossible," she pointed out.

She was not wrong. Which was a problem for him. He wanted an equal partner if and when he ever settled down, and she might very well be that rare woman. Most of the women he met were overwhelmed by the force of his personality. They accused him of being too intense, and in truth, he ended up steamrolling over them.

Some of the guys solved that problem by marrying women who were exceptionally patient and willing to go along with their operator husband's program. His plan was to wait until he left the teams. He would unwind his personal intensity a whole lot and then see how dating went. He'd find a nice, normal woman and settle down, have a few kids and live a quiet life.

But in his heart of hearts, he wanted more. He wanted fireworks and friction. A woman who liked him just the way he was now, who would say no to him and stand her ground. A woman he could respect and admire. One who would call him out when he was wrong or pigheaded or acting stupid.

A woman like Gia Rachel Rykhof.

He sank into their kiss, realizing it felt like coming

home to kiss this woman, who was so much like him, but so much unlike him, as well. Yes, she was hard and fit, but she was also soft in places he was not. Like her lips. He loved how they felt like velvet against his. And her skin. It slid beneath his fingertips like fine satin. Relaxed in his arms like this, she felt delicate—fragile, even. But he knew for a fact she was made of finely tempered steel beneath that feminine exterior.

The contrast of tough and tender, sweet and feisty, thoughtful companion and hard-as-nails operator, was intoxicating. He'd long joked with his teammates that as soon as one of them became a woman, he'd marry her.

The funny bit was he'd been wildly attracted to Rachel long before he'd known she was finally the female Special Operator he'd joked about falling in love with.

Welp. At least he had a type and he'd been true to it with this woman.

"What are you thinking about so hard?" she surprised him by lifting her mouth to ask. "I can hear your mental wheels turning. And, if I do say so myself, it sounds as if they could use a little grease."

He grinned at her. "Are you calling me rusty at thinking?"

"I'm saying that whatever you're grinding on is gunking up your mental gears."

He laughed aloud. "I was thinking about you."

"Indeed? What has you so stuck, then, about me?"

"I was thinking about how perfect you are. I've never been attracted to women I could bowl over."

"I'm stubborn, huh?" she murmured.

"In a good way. You stand up to me when you disagree with me and you call me out when I'm being an idiot. I like that."

She made a face. "Most men say I'm too pushy. Aggressive, even. They call me bossy or a bitch."

"They don't know what they're missing. And their own insecurities are showing if they can't handle being with a strong, independent woman. I find you exhilarating."

She stared at him in the flickering golden firelight. Very slowly, she leaned forward and kissed him again. But this time was different. The playfulness from before was completely gone, replaced by a serious intensity that frankly knocked his socks off.

Abruptly, their kissing was intimate. Personal. And from her, maybe laced with a little gratitude. Which he surely didn't deserve for simply accepting and liking her the way she was.

Against her mouth, he murmured, "You've dated some real jerks, haven't you?"

"How did you know?"

"Because you shouldn't be so abjectly relieved to have any man think you're great just the way you are. Obviously, some real losers have done their best to tear you down because they can't measure up to your exceptional standards."

"Wow. And the man is a psychologist, too. Did they teach you that on the teams?" she asked, laughing a little and kissing him again.

Thank goodness. He'd broken through whatever baggage she brought to the table. She was back to her usual confident, relaxed self, all of a sudden.

He bent his head and kissed his way down her neck and across her collarbone. "Nope. All the amateur psychology is pure Marcus Tate. Observer of human behavior and connoisseur of fine women."

"I see your ego didn't get bruised when you busted up your shoulder."

He laughed against her shoulder. "That. Right there. That's why I find you irresistible. How many women would say something like that to a guy like me?"

"I honestly don't know. I always got along better with boys than girls growing up, and I tended to hang out with the jocks when I wasn't studying up a storm. My family didn't have much money, and I wanted to go to a topflight university. I had to get serious scholarships to make it happen."

"And did you?"

"Yale undergrad. Major electrical engineering and a minor in military history. Master's from Harvard in satellite optics."

"Whoa."

"What's your educational background?" she asked.

"Economics at Michigan. Master's in public policy from Georgetown."

"My goodness. That's not a bad résumé, Mr. Tate." A pause. "What's your military rank?"

"Lieutenant commander. You?"

"Captain. I'm up for Major below the zone next year. All the Medusa have pinned on Major as soon as they're eligible. I hope not to break that streak."

He grinned. "You won't. Overachiever is your other middle name."

She sighed. "Yeah. I get that a lot from men."

"It's because you make them feel so inadequate when they compare what they've done with their lives to what you've done with yours."

She sighed again. "Sometimes I wonder if being a workaholic has cost me too much."

"Like what?"

"Like any chance at a normal relationship, for one."

He shrugged and kissed his way from her earlobe to her temple. "Who wants normal, anyway? Why not aim for an exceptional relationship with an outstanding person?"

"Like you?"

"I was speaking in general terms. I'm not qualified to comment on whether or not I'm exceptional."

She snorted. "Trust me. You are. Extremely."

He pulled back enough to gaze down into her eyes, which were touched by gold as the firelight danced off her irises. "Pot, meet kettle." He pushed a stray strand of hair back from her face gently. "You are the most extraordinary woman I've ever met."

"That's because you haven't met the rest of the Medusas."

"Stop putting yourself down. I gave you a compliment, and the correct response is to say 'thank you.'"

She stared up at him searchingly, as if measuring whether or not he was being honest with her when he declared her exceptional. At length, she finally said on the breath of a sigh, "Thank you. Truly. It means the world, coming from a man like you."

"What does that mean? A man like me?"

"You're the kind of operator I aspire to become."

"Honey, from what I've seen of your skills, you can already hold your own with me just fine, right now."

She laid her palm lightly on the side of his face, and he felt both the softness of her hand and the hardness of her shooter's callus lying against his jaw. That, right there, was her in a nutshell. Hard and soft. Sweet and tough.

He leaned forward slowly, his gaze never leaving hers. Her chin tipped up and she met his mouth with hers. He kissed her gently, and she kissed him back. Who knew that mutual respect was such a turn-on?

"Just think," she mumbled against his mouth. "If we ever went on an op together, during our downtime, we could do this in full combat gear."

He groaned. "I'll never sit by a campfire on an op again without thinking of this moment."

"I hope it puts a smile on your face."

"Oh, it will," he assured her. "And it'll make me homesick as hell."

"The married Medusas always say having a guy to go home to helps motivate them to make it through the hard spots in missions."

"They let you ladies get married?"

"Of course. They let SEALs get married, don't they? We're Special Operators, not nuns."

"Sorry. I'm still getting used to the idea of women operators."

She laid her head on his shoulder and stared into the fireplace, and it was almost more intimate than kissing him. She said quietly, "The hard part is when a Medusa falls in love with one of the men we work with or who trains us. That gets messy, sometimes."

"That hadn't even occurred to me. You don't send couples out together on missions, do you?"

"We've discovered over the years that it's not a great idea. The operators worry too much about their significant other and it causes problems in high-risk situations. They try too hard to protect each other from harm, and they don't focus one hundred percent on the mission."

"I could see that." He added slowly, "Don't get me

wrong. I love my teammates. I'm closer to them than to my own brothers. But we all understand we're out there to do a job, and that it's a dangerous job. We all take the risk together."

She nodded. "I feel that way about my Medusa sisters, but I know what you mean. We all expect to risk our lives and we don't fear other members of the team risking theirs."

He nodded, clocking that this was the only woman he'd ever talked to about this kind of stuff who fully understood what he meant. It was exceedingly strange having any woman instantly grasp and accept the intense camaraderie between SEALs who stood side by side, with their acceptance of watching one another die if necessary, to get the job done. He didn't even have to mention the part to her where every single operator went on every op believing that they would come home alive and unhurt. She already knew.

She was speaking again. "…not to mention, if one was in charge of the other, how would he or she send their significant other into a situation where they might get killed? And how bad would it mess that person up if their lover did die? If one of them dies, you inevitably lose both operators."

He imagined being on a mission with her and losing her, and it made his arms tighten convulsively around her.

"Yeah. That," she said softly.

He kissed her again, but with more urgency. The thought of losing her that way sent a frisson of desperation through him that he didn't like. Not one bit.

"It's okay, Marcus. I'm right here, and I'm not dying anytime soon."

Damn, she read him like an open book. And double damn if he didn't love that about her. Most women found him completely inscrutable and incomprehensible. But she got him. Knew what made him tick. Would that translate to knowing what he liked in bed, too—

Nope. Not going there.

"I'd love to sleep with you, too," she murmured, plucking the thought right out of his head.

Marcus stared, stunned. And choked a little. Then blinked down at her. "You'd…what?"

She pulled back enough to look up at him. Her gaze was direct. Open. "You and I both know better than most people that life is short. Too short for beating around the bush. I want you, and I'm pretty sure you want me. After all, I am sitting on your lap."

He had to chuckle. How many women would point out so frankly that his erection was poking them in the hip? She was right, of course. Life was too short to pussyfoot around, not doing the things he wanted to do.

"Yes," he admitted. "I want to take you to bed and make love with you all night long. But at what cost to both of us? If we're being baldly honest here—and that does appear to be what we're doing—I don't think walking away from you is going to be easy, and I don't think walking away from me is going to be easy for you."

"Why do you think we're going to walk away from each other? Sure, I get that we both have things to do for the next few years. But we both get time off. We can see each other now and then. And when we both finish running with our teams, there's a whole lot of life left to live." She added hastily, "I'm not asking for nor expecting any long-term commitment from you. I'm just saying this doesn't have to be a dead-end relationship."

He frowned. "It'll be hard."

She lowered her chin and glared up at him from under her soft eyebrows. "Are you afraid of a little suffering, sailor?"

He guffawed. Both of them thrived on suffering or they wouldn't be Special Operators.

She complained, "I can't believe I'm having to talk you into sleeping with me. It's usually the guys in the bar trying to convince me to go home with them."

"Oh, believe me. I want to. But I'm trying to be responsible here."

"I'll be responsible for myself, thanks," she retorted dryly.

He just shook his head. "You are one of a kind."

"And don't you forget it," she purred. "Nor that I choose you."

Well, hell. That might just be one of the sexiest things a woman had ever said to him.

"You're killing me," he muttered.

"You haven't seen anything yet," she chuckled.

"Are you planning to torture me until I sleep with you?"

"Certainly not! That would be sexual harassment," she replied quickly, looking alarmed.

"Relax. I was just teasing. I don't feel pressured here."

She squirmed a little, rubbing her posterior against his deeply uncomfortable man parts. "I don't know. Feels to me like you're experiencing a significant buildup of pressure."

He threw his head back and laughed heartily. Oh, she was *so* not like most women. Totally enjoying her frank honesty, he slipped his hand under the warm, silky length of her hair and drew her close to him for a deep kiss. Their smiles mingled and became one.

And then the kiss took an abrupt turn for the serious as their smiles faded and their tongues tangled sexily. He groaned in the back of his throat. Was he being an idiot for resisting her? She was warm and willing and knew the score. Heck, she was as likely to walk out of his life on no notice as he was to disappear from hers. He had to admit, it added a desperate urgency to the moment that he found irresistible. No wonder women found SEALs to be impossibly romantic. He was finding her to be the exact same for him.

"Are you sure about this?" he murmured against her lips between the hot little love nips they were trading.

"Dead certain," she answered breathily.

"It could be dangerous," he warned.

"It could be spectacular," she countered.

"Which is the exact danger I'm talking about."

"Afraid of falling for me, are you?" she challenged.

"What if I am?" he allowed.

"I promise not to walk away from you and never look back," she murmured. "I'll give you a shot at more if you'll give me a shot at more."

The weight of the moment struck him forcefully. But it didn't scare him in the least. He answered with a single word. "Deal."

And then he stood up and carried her into the bedroom.

Chapter 15

Gia loved how he carried her so effortlessly. She was a muscular woman and not featherlight, but Marcus seemed to barely notice. She also loved how his eyes blazed with desire when he looked at her. And how he'd promised her more than a meaningless one-night stand before he finally agreed to take her to bed. He respected her, and that made all the difference. It was sexier than just about anything any man had ever tried as a way to seduce her.

Although, she was fairly sure she was the one who'd seduced him into bed here. Which was also incredibly sexy. She could be aggressive with Marcus and he wasn't the least bit intimidated by it. In fact, he enjoyed her forwardness and met it with his own.

Yes, indeed. They were a great match for each other.

He leaned down for her to grab the covers and toss

them back. Then he laid her down gently on the bed, putting his knee beside her and following her down. She welcomed him eagerly, loving his weight and muscular density as he kissed her with his whole body. Their legs tangled together, and then got tangled in the sheets, and they laughed as they kicked together, trying to free themselves from the cotton top sheet. She noted the way his hard, flat abs contracted as he laughed, the quick flex of his biceps as he pressed up and away from her to reach down and push the pesky sheet to the bottom of the bed.

She commented drolly, "In a while, we're going to get cold and have to go looking for that sheet, and it'll be nowhere to be found."

Propped on one elbow, he grinned down at her. "I don't know about you, but I get warm whenever I exercise, and I'm not planning to be cold for a good long time."

"Big words, Marcus. Let's see you put your money where your mouth is."

He threw his head back and laughed. "You did not just challenge my fitness and stamina!"

Grinning back, she retorted, "Why, I believe I did. I'll pit my training against yours any day, big guy."

They took off their clothes in a rush, shirts and jeans going flying, socks and underwear stripped off and chucked across the room. She had faith they were going to end up on their hands and knees naked, hunting down bits and pieces of clothing in the morning. But that was a problem for tomorrow.

Still grinning at her bold challenge, Marcus gathered her against his delicious body, and her smile faded as wonder took over. She loved his hardness, the way his muscles bulged and flexed beneath her palms, the way his jaw went tight when she reached between them to grasp his erection in her fist.

She guided him into her body, but as soon as his velvet-sheathed hardness penetrated her warmth and heat, Marcus took over. He rolled fully on top of her, his elbows planted on either side of her head, and sheathed himself to the hilt inside her. *Oh my.* That was nice. Very nice, indeed. She loved the stretching fullness, the way her internal muscles gripped at him, the way the slick heat of their bodies felt as his flesh glided against hers.

But then he surprised her by going completely still.

"Is something wrong?" she ventured to ask.

"Not at all. I'm making a memory for those hard times when I'm exhausted and hungry and freezing cold or burning hot and I ask myself what I'm fighting for."

She knew the moments well. She stared up at him, memorizing his face, memorizing that slightly glazed look of utter pleasure in his eyes, memorizing the glorious feeling of his body against hers. She, too, would reach for this memory when the going got tough and she needed a moment's respite from the stress of a mission.

This was what made life worth living. These moments of pure joy, of relaxation and pleasure, of sharing the warmth of another human being, of intimate and emotional connection to Marcus.

She stared up at him, and he stared back at her. Then, ever so slowly, he began to move inside her. Her hips rose gently to meet his and they found a rhythm, slow and easy, taking their time and savoring each thrust, each slide of flesh on flesh, each shimmer of pleasure racing through her body from her core to her extremities.

She really shouldn't have challenged his stamina. He was going slower—much slower—than she wanted, as hunger built impatiently in her belly. She wanted more from him. More energy, more power, more friction.

But, infuriatingly, he kept up that slow, steady pace as pleasure built and built inside her. When the pressure of it grew so great she didn't think she could stand it, she arched her back and thrust up against him impatiently, silently demanding more from him.

All of a sudden, an orgasm burst over her, like a great dam exploding and unleashing all the pleasure pent up behind it. She cried out, shocked as it ripped through her. She opened her eyes, dazed, and stared up at Marcus in the deep shadows. In the faint firelight coming through the open bedroom door, she caught the silhouette of his smile, and then he resumed moving inside her, in that maddening, unhurried pace of his.

No surprise, her highly sensitized body responded immediately to his steady, piston-like thrusts, building to another orgasm quickly. This one broke over her without warning, taking her by surprise. Where the first had been slow and big, this one was sharp and fast, like an electric shock bursting through her entire body and exiting from her fingertips and toes.

"Oh!" she cried.

"Everything okay?" Marcus asked, amusement rich in his voice.

"Uh-huh," she panted.

And he just kept on driving into her slowly and steadily, never stopping, never speeding up. And a third and a fourth orgasm ripped through her, and she was starting to feel a little overwhelmed by all this pleasure.

"Are you sure you're enjoying yourself?" she asked

breathlessly after her fifth orgasm. "I feel as if I'm getting all the benefits of this interaction."

Marcus smiled. "Ah, but I get to watch. You can't imagine what it's like to see—and feel—you come apart around me."

"And I suppose you're memorizing it all?"

"Every second of it," he replied with maddening calm.

"But I want to drive you wild, too," she declared.

"Oh, you are. I'm just exercising restraint and not showing it to you."

"Let me rephrase," she said darkly. "I want you to lose control, too."

And how do you plan to make me do that?" he asked lightly.

She braced one elbow at her side, hooked her leg around his ankle, and heaved upward and to the side, hooking his leg and using it for leverage to push him off her.

He fell onto his back, laughing as she pounced on top of him. He said, "Welp. I can't say as I've ever had anyone use that move on me in bed before. Nice move. Where'd you learn it?"

"A jujitsu instructor taught it to me."

"Remind me to thank him if you ever introduce him to me," Marcus replied, laughing.

But then she threw her leg across his hips and impaled herself on his erect flesh, sliding down the hard shaft until it touched her womb. She couldn't help herself. She gasped with pleasure.

Abruptly, the laughter left Marcus's face, and he gripped her hips with his hands. She lifted up a little, but Marcus pulled her back down strongly onto him. She moaned a little, and he groaned.

"Again," he panted.

She found a new rhythm with him, this time with her pumping his flesh steadily, all the while gripping his hips with her thighs and daring him to throw her off him. But he didn't seem inclined to return the favor of the wrestling move and was content to let her ride him like this.

She threw her head back and he reached up, running his fingertips down the taut column of her throat and trailing them between and across her breasts. His thumbs flicked at her erect nipples and she gasped as pleasure speared sharply through her.

She brought her head forward and her long hair fell in a curtain around her face, and she put her hands on his shoulders and smiled down at him. He stared up at her, his gaze intense as he anchored her hips with his hands and drove up into her forcefully.

"Oh, yes," she breathed. "Again."

He repeated the maneuver and she cried out, loving his power and loving absorbing it into herself. She met each of his upward thrusts with a downward one of her own. It wasn't elegant, and it was raw and physical, but it felt glorious.

Perspiration broke out on his forehead, and he bit his lip as he visibly fought to hold back his orgasm.

As if.

She clenched her internal muscles tightly around him and rode him like she was breaking a wild bronco. He bucked and twisted beneath her, but nothing he did could unseat her. He pounded up into her and she slammed down onto him.

And then, all at once, Marcus reached up, wrapped his left arm around her shoulders and dragged her down to him. Off balance, she was not able to do anything but roll with him as he flung himself sideways and landed on top of her.

She wrapped her legs around his hips and hung on for dear life as they rode the storm together toward its crashing, lightning-and-thunder conclusion. Finally, he cut loose completely, slamming into her with all his formidable strength, and she met him with hers. Their bodies were slick with sweat and slapped together wetly as their limbs slid across each other's skin.

She reached forward and grabbed his glutes in both hands, pulling him even deeper as her entire body quivered. He paused for one endless moment at the edge of the precipice, and then he slammed forward with a shout, seating himself so deep she wasn't sure where she ended and he began. The orgasm ripping through him ripped through her, and they strained together, frozen in time as pleasure so intense it nearly made her pass out roared through her and over her. Marcus seemed gripped in the same wave of paralyzing pleasure as he froze, his back arched, buried in her as deep as it was possible to go.

Then, all of a sudden, he sagged against her and she sagged back to the damp mattress. She was breathing as hard as if she'd just run full out for a few miles while wearing a hundred-pound pack. But, thankfully, he was sucking wind like a race horse, as well.

He collapsed on top of her, his face resting beside hers on the pillow.

"I can't move," he groaned. "You've killed me."

"Same," she panted. "Except I think you've killed me."

"I'm not crushing you, am I?" he mumbled.

"Nope. Don't move. You feel perfect where you are."

They were silent for a while, each waiting for their bodies to recover, and filing away last memories for later recall when they were in the field and their situations totally sucked.

He murmured, "When I've recovered—in about a year—let's do that again."

She chuckled a little. "Only a year? I don't think I'm ever recovering from that."

"Touché. I yield the point to you." Marcus sighed. "I will never be the same after that."

"Do you want to sleep now?" she asked.

"One of us has to go fishing for that damned sheet first," he grumbled.

She slipped partially out from under him and reached down to one side. "Or we could just pull up the quilt and call it good."

He kissed her jaw and neck below her ear lazily. "I like the way you improvise."

"I like the way you make love," she whispered back.

She felt him smile against her shoulder, and then relax against her body as he drifted off to sleep. She followed him quickly, a smile on her own lips as she, too, drifted off to dreams of making love with Marcus Tate for the rest of her life.

She woke up sharply like she always did, sometime before dawn. It was dark outside, but she thought maybe the first light of dawn was creeping around the curtains. Marcus's arm was thrown across her middle, and she relished its weight and the safety it represented. She might be capable of protecting herself, but it was nice having him there and looking out for her, too.

One thing she knew for sure, though. She wasn't dragging him into some dangerous confrontation with her pursuers. She was no more interested in seeing him get killed in the name of protecting her than she was of seeing her Medusa teammates die for her.

Which meant, of course, that last night had been a massive mistake.

She lay there for a long time, listening to his quiet breaths. Last night was… She struggled for a word grand enough to describe what making love with him had been like. She'd never ever had sex with any man who fit her so perfectly in every way. They had perfect simpatico in the sack. As in *perfect.*

And that would make it all the harder to do what she had to do next. She had to break it off with him. Her feelings of protectiveness toward him would be as problematic in a dangerous situation as the personal feelings of Medusas for men they loved were. She might not love him, per se, but she was definitely headed down that road. Which meant she had to stop this thing between them right now, right here.

It figured that this mess would cost her a chance with the one man she'd ever met whom she could see herself spending a long, long time with. It had cost her everything else in her life. What not Marcus, too?

She checked her bitter thoughts. She could hear Gunnar's voice in her head, admonishing her that defeatist thinking was a fast way to get herself killed.

Marcus had the right of it. They would get through this mess and catch her would-be killers, and then the two of them would figure out how to hang on to a long-distance relationship until they could be together again.

But she didn't like it. She wanted Marcus now. And she wanted Baldy and his buddies to go away and leave her alone. But that wasn't how life worked. She was going to have to earn her life back and earn a shot at a future with Marcus.

Carefully, she swung her feet out of bed and slipped out of the bedroom. The fire had died completely overnight since neither of them had banked the coals. They might have been a wee bit distracted last night when he carried her into the bedroom.

Once the fire took hold and started putting out a little heat, she moved over to the stove and put on a pot of water to boil. She hunted down the jar of instant coffee and restrained an urge to swallow a mouthful of dry crystals straight from it.

She managed to wait until the water was properly hot and made herself a cup of coffee and carried it over to the fireplace. She'd sipped most of the way through it when Marcus appeared in the bedroom door with a bedsheet wrapped around his hips.

"I see you finally found the sheet," she commented dryly.

He grinned. "Want me to lose it again?"

"I think we need to talk."

Chapter 16

Uh-oh. He didn't like the sound of that. Rachel's voice had the tone of a Dear John speech about to be delivered.

"Let me pull on some clothes before we get all serious," he said quickly. In truth, he wanted to give himself a minute to find his equilibrium. He'd never woken up this giddy from a night with a woman, and that grim tone of voice she'd hit him with had knocked him off balance hard.

He dressed and even shaved before he emerged from the bathroom. When he did, she was fully dressed, too, and had made him a cup of coffee to go with the one she was sipping.

He sat down on the hearth, facing her directly. "Okay. I have some caffeine in my system and I'm fully awake. Talk to me, Rachel."

"Last night was wonderful. Beyond wonderful…"

She trailed off as if searching for more words to describe it.

"I was there," he said gently. "You don't need to hunt for superlatives to impress me with. I know precisely how incredible it was."

She smiled a little, but the expression didn't reach her eyes. "Then maybe you also know already why we can't do that again."

He exhaled heavily. "Yeah. I do. The connection we formed, the closeness, it's going to be a problem if we end up in a firefight with your bald guy, won't it?"

"You tell me," she said in a low voice.

"It's a problem," he admitted. "I'll throw myself on a grenade for you at this point and not think twice about it."

"Same for me."

"So, now what?" he asked. "We pretend last night never happened and do our damnedest to erase it from our memories?"

"I couldn't forget last night if I tried," she replied.

"Good. Me neither. But I'm out of my depth here. How do we move forward?"

She sighed. "A few of my teammates have met men on the job. Mostly, they've struggled through to the end of that mission and then they've immediately figured out how to spend their off-duty time with their guy and never work with them operationally again."

He leaned forward and took both of her hands, which were ice-cold, in his. "I get it. But this sucks."

She nodded miserably.

He continued, "But we're both adults, we both know the stresses of a dangerous mission, and we both have to do the responsible thing here."

She disengaged her hands from his and laid her palms on his cheeks. Then she leaned forward and touched her forehead to his. "Thank you for not fighting me on this."

"I would never do anything to endanger your life, Rachel."

"I hate this," she breathed so low he nearly didn't hear her.

"Me, too."

"When this is over, Marcus, if you're still interested, I'll still be interested."

He groaned deep in his chest as more desire than ever for this woman welled up in him. She was right here. Right now. And they were all alone. He could still smell last night's sex on them both and it made him want her so badly he could hardly see straight. Nobody would ever know—

The two of them would know. And it would negatively impact their performance if her problem went south and got violent.

"This is killing me a little," he muttered. "But, of course, you're right."

Her hands fell away from his face and he looked up at her as she rose to her feet. He reached forward and wrapped his arms around her waist, burying his face against her belly. "For the record, I'm going to miss making love to you something fierce until we do it again."

She ran her fingers lightly through his hair. "Me, too."

He squeezed his eyes shut hard for a moment and then opened them. He released her, turned to one side and stood up. He took a careful step back from her to put her out of arm's reach and of temptation. Although, truth be told, just being in the same room with her presented a nearly unbearable temptation.

She said formally, "Thanks for understanding and being a gentleman about this. I'll try to keep my hands off you going forward."

"Same," he ground out, hating the word with all his heart.

It was just his luck. He'd found the perfect woman, she liked him, he liked her, and they were mind-blowing in bed together. Worse, she was right here in front of him…and he couldn't have her. Sometimes the universe had a really freaking rotten sense of humor.

Without warning, a cell phone rang, and they both jumped.

"Mine," she bit out, digging in her jeans pocket. "Hello?"

Gia put her phone to her ear. Only a handful of people had her number, and none of them were likely to call her with good news.

It was Gunnar Torsten.

"Hey, boss. What've you got for me?" she asked, hoping she sounded more focused than she actually was. Having Marcus stand there in all his brawny hotness was distracting at a level she'd never experienced before with a man.

"I just got off the horn with the boots-on-the-ground leader of Alpha Platoon."

That got her attention, and all of it. "Well?" she demanded. "What did he say?"

"He asked me to pass you a message—thank you for your outstanding real-time intel support. He said you made a big difference in how the operation went down, and you saved lives. He's grateful."

"Aw, thanks. But I was just doing my job."

"You and I both know that. But still. Take the compliment."

"Fine," she huffed. "So, what did he have to say about the guys who hauled out that crate? Was it a last-minute mission add-on?"

"Nope. Those weren't his guys. They weren't even from the forward operating base. He went back through all the unit roll calls for that day and where every soldier at the FOB was assigned that night. Everyone… *everyone…*has been accounted for."

"He's sure about that?"

"Positive. Every person at the FOB was present and accounted for in the time frame when you saw those men hauling out the crate. Even the cooks and drivers."

"What about his own men? Did four of them sneak off and steal something in the middle of the mission?"

"Negative. He'd called the whole platoon together in the middle of the compound to hand over the operation to the marine support team by the time you saw those men go out the back gate. Oh, and the three marines in that Humvee behind the compound? They were found dead in their vehicle the next day, over a hundred miles away from that compound."

She gasped. "How did they die?"

"Single gunshots to the head, execution-style."

"What rounds were used to kill them?" she bit out, horrified.

"Russian issue."

She frowned. "The guy who stole the computer from me in the surveillance facility was American by voice accent. And the men who stole the crate wore American tactical gear. I'm sure of it. I mean, I wear that gear all the time. I recognize it on sight."

"I believe you, Gia."

"So, who did I see? Russians in disguise? Or Americans trying to leave an evidence trail pointing at Russia? And what was in that crate?"

"The Alpha Platoon leader said there was an extensive underground network of tunnels and there were exits from the tunnels all over the compound. His guess is your crate came from down there. Alpha Platoon did find a large weapon stash in the tunnels and seized a bunch of low-grade explosives. Maybe it was part of that."

"Maybe," she said doubtfully. "Did the platoon leader have any idea who the men I saw might be?"

"Nope. My guess is they jumped the mission. They must've heard the raid was happening that night and positioned themselves just outside the compound. They would've slipped in—maybe in the back gate—before the marines surrounded the compound and Alpha Platoon went in."

"I accounted for all the bodies I saw on the ground, though," she disagreed. "I had accurate head counts of both hostiles and soldiers from Alpha Platoon."

"Not down in the tunnels. Your imagery couldn't show you anyone underground. They could've hidden down there," Gunnar pointed out.

"True."

"If any of our guys stumbled upon them down there, they would've signaled that they were friendlies and nobody would've questioned them. Like you said, they were in American gear, were squawking American identification signals, and were most likely American and had access to American intel and ops planning to know exactly when the raid was going to happen."

She nodded. "It *was* a joint task force of operators from several different units. It wouldn't have been a red flag for guys from Alpha Platoon not to recognize some of the operators on the raid."

"I would agree with that assessment," Gunnar murmured.

"Great. So we still don't know who I saw, nor what they took, nor why they're trying to kill me."

"We do know they killed three marines to haul their booty out of there, though. I've got a guy in the Pentagon pulling air traffic tapes from that night in the vicinity of where the Humvee was found. Maybe we can pick up a lead based on how they flew out of there and where they went."

She sighed. "If they're as good as they seem to be, they used a helicopter and a pilot who terrain followed and stayed below any radar."

"If that's the case, that'll tell us something about them, too."

"I suppose. I'm just getting sick of having to look over my shoulder all the time."

"I'm glad you hooked up with Brett and Marcus, Gia. They're both outstanding guys and will keep you safe."

Outstanding enough for him not to mind her sleeping with one of them? Aloud, she said, "I don't want anyone keeping me safe and catching collateral damage from an attack on me."

"We've been through that before. You have to learn to let your teammates look out for you, even if it puts them in harm's way."

"It's one thing to do that in combat, but it's another thing entirely to endanger my teammates when they're off duty and supposed to be resting and unwinding."

"Remind me to ask Marcus and Brett to have a conversation with you about accepting assistance from your teammates. It has always been your Achilles' heel. You don't take help well."

She sighed. She'd heard the refrain a hundred times in her Medusa training. Her various instructors consistently called her independence her worst character trait. "I'm working on it," she groused.

"Work on it faster," Gunnar said sternly.

Marcus, who was making no secret of eavesdropping on the call, shifted weight in front of her, looking grim.

"Call me if you learn anything more," she told her boss.

"Will do. And you keep your head down."

"Yeah, yeah." She hung up, smiling at her phone.

"Well?" Marcus demanded.

She filled him in quickly. He was no more amused than she was at the idea of some rogue soldiers jumping a spec ops mission to steal something in the confusion of combat.

"I'll give these bad guys of yours one thing," he said as they moved around the tiny kitchen making breakfast. "They're smart and well organized. It takes good timing and real nerve to jump a raid like that and get away with it."

She turned from the refrigerator with milk in hand and bumped into him turning toward the table with a box of cereal. As they collided, chest to chest, her gaze snapped up to his, and the sexual tension abruptly hung in the air between them, so thick she could scoop it up with a spoon.

"Um, coffee?" he mumbled.

"Sure." She spun back toward the refrigerator and stuck her head inside. She prayed the cold air inside cooled the heat in her cheeks and erased the blush she felt coming on. Head inside it, she asked, "Orange juice?"

"Yes, please."

If she wasn't mistaken, his voice sounded a little hoarse all of a sudden. She knew the feeling. Her throat felt unreasonably tight at the moment, too.

They sat down at the tiny table, and darned if their knees didn't bump. They both jerked away sharply.

Marcus audibly exhaled. "Look. I'm extremely attracted to you and you seem about as attracted to me. We both get that. And we're going to have to touch each other from time to time. Can we both just relax about it and not act like we both have cooties?"

"Cooties?" She couldn't help laughing. "I haven't heard that word since about the third grade."

He scowled at her, and she said in a conciliating tone, "You're right, of course. We can touch each other without acting as if we've been electrocuted." To that end, she reached across the table and laid her palm on top of his hand.

But her breath still hitched in her chest, and he must've heard it, for he raised an eyebrow at her.

"It's a work in progress," she allowed.

"Speaking of works in progress, you need to work on this lone-wolf attitude of yours—"

She rolled her eyes at him. "Did you hear Gunnar tell me he was going to ask you and Brett to give me a lecture on being less independent and letting my teammates help me more?"

"No. But he's completely right."

She sighed. "I am working on it. But I care about my Medusa sisters and you so much—"

He cut her off. "And we all care that much about you. We're all trained Special Operators. It's okay if we volunteer to put ourselves in harm's way on your behalf. You'd do the same for us. Hell, your teammates do that for you on every mission you go on."

"But those are missions. This is the real world," she objected.

"Missions are the real world. And when dangers come to us, we need to respond to it the exact same way as we would on a sanctioned military mission."

"I guess I just separate missions from my regularly scheduled life when I think about the two."

"They're one and the same," he said quietly.

Which was exactly why they couldn't sleep together again until her mess was sorted out and they weren't going to end up in a firefight side by side.

She sighed hard. "I'll try to wrap my brain around that and keep my hands off you."

He smiled a little. "Right. Good luck with that. I'm resigned to reacting to you every time we touch, whether I like it or not."

"I'm sorry. I'll try to be more respectful of your space."

"Don't you dare. You keep right on doing you. It's my problem—I'll deal with it."

"It's our problem. I react the same way to you."

They met gazes, commiserating for their shared misery.

"Soon," he said low, his voice charged.

"Soon," she replied hoarsely.

They finished their meal in uncomfortable, highly charged silence.

"Speaking of soon," she said as she carried her dishes over to the sink, "how do you feel about setting a trap for Baldy?"

"Interesting. How do you plan to lure him into it?"

"With bait, of course."

"And what bait would that be?"

He sounded skeptical enough to suspect where she was going with this.

"Me. I'll be the bait," she declared.

"No. No way!" he burst out.

"I knew you would say that. But set aside your feelings for me and think about it. It's the logical thing to do. And, honestly, the sooner we do it, the better. I don't want his homicidal buddies to join him before we try this."

Marcus scowled ferociously and nearly scrubbed the flower pattern off the dishes.

"Can we get together with Brett and Wes and at least talk about it? If we can come up with something that we all agree would work and minimize risk, I think we should go for it."

He scowled down at the soapy dish in his hand.

"Just talk with us about it." She knew not to lean on a SEAL too hard, for no male human on earth was more stubborn than a SEAL when one dug his heels in. Marcus would resist her to the death, if necessary, if he decided it was a bad idea for her to act as bait in a trap. She added, "I value your opinion and experience greatly. I really want your input."

"Oh, you'll get it, all right," he promised darkly, drying his hands with quick, angry jerks of the dish towel.

She couldn't help it. She moved over to him and put her arms on his waist. "Don't be mad. We're just going to talk it over. Nothing more for now."

He stood rigid, as if her merest touch might burn the flesh off his bones. All of a sudden, he turned around sharply to face her. "I thought we weren't going to do this."

"I was just trying to placate you."

"Don't. I never respond well to people fussing over me in an effort to calm me down."

Her hands fell away. "I'm sorry I touched you. I thought it was a reasonable, onetime exception to the rule to help you calm down and not be so angry."

"I'm not angry. I'm just deeply opposed to your idea."

"Please withhold judgment until we all talk it through."

She looked up at him pleadingly, and he stared down at her in frustration. The tension between them broke all of a sudden and they both stepped forward into each other's arms.

She whispered, "Just this once. It's only a kiss."

He sighed, and as his lips captured hers, he murmured, "This is a bad idea."

Chapter 17

But, as bad ideas went, this one was a great deal more enjoyable than most.

Her mouth tasted like Frosted Flakes and orange juice, and he couldn't get enough of either. There was a lightness about her, a joy that permeated her whole being and washed over him anytime they kissed like this.

With a groan, he swept his arms around her and drew her up tight against him, loving the way her body molded to his without going soft or hard. She was just right, warm, vibrant and as eager for more as he was.

She murmured against his lips, "We already broke the rules once. Would one more time be so bad?"

Her words were a bucket of cold water on his libido. "You know the answer to that already."

She sighed and came down off her tiptoes, stepping back from him. "Yes. I do. But..."

She trailed off.

"Yeah. I know," he replied regretfully. "Soon. That's got to be our mantra for now."

She closed her eyes tightly for a moment, seemed to gather herself and opened her eyes. "Right. Soon. And speaking of which—"

He groaned. "I know that look. You've had an idea, and I'm not going to like it."

"Really? You already know me so well?"

He raised an eyebrow at her. They'd spent a good chunk of the night making love to each other. He would say they'd gotten to know each other quite well. For example, now he knew exactly how generous and fun-loving and adventurous she really was. Truly, the more he learned of her, the crazier he was about her.

In a long-suffering tone, he said, "Fine. Tell me how you plan to lure Baldy into a trap. That is what you're planning, is it not?"

She smiled a little. "Well…yeah."

He sighed. "Lay it on me."

"What do you think of me going fly-fishing? I'd be outdoors, well away from any civilians. It would limit the approaches to me because the river would be in front of me. You guys could hide behind me and catch him when he comes in toward me."

"What if he stands off a half mile or so and just blows your head off?" he asked bluntly.

She frowned. "He's had a clear shot at me before. Why didn't he take it?"

Marcus frowned back. He hated the idea of a killer having had a clear run at her before now. "Maybe he was still waiting for a positive ID on you or on orders to proceed with the kill."

"Maybe. Or maybe he has other orders. Maybe he's supposed to kidnap me and find out what I know about what I saw that night. Maybe he wants a list of other people who know about the theft."

"Speaking of which," he asked, "who all does know about it?"

"Everybody. I made a full written report that will have gone to the various internal crime-solving agencies of the military, the FBI, customs officials, and even the CIA. Hundreds of people are aware of the theft and are keeping an eye out for something big and heavy to be smuggled into the US."

"And now the SEALs know about it, too," he said. "I left a voice mail for myself at my office, detailing everything we know. In the message, I told my teammates that if I die while on leave from the teams, they should find Baldy and his buddies because they're my probable killers."

When she looked alarmed, he added, "Nobody will mess with my phone unless I die. Then they'll find the message."

"Okay. Whew." A pause. "So what do you think of my fishing idea?"

He grinned at her. "I can personally attest that you're lethal with a fly rod."

She swatted him on the upper arm and then went in for a tickle. They ended up wrestling briefly and he ultimately pinned her to the wall beside the back door, using his larger, heavier body to basically crush her. It was the only way to subdue her, for she was a highly proficient martial artist.

"Uncle?" he murmured against her temple.

"Uncle," she grumbled.

"No need to be cranky about me beating you. I outweigh you by something like eighty pounds and I've got a good six inches on you in height and reach." She still looked grumpy, so he added, "You forced me to work hard for it. Most SEALs can't do that."

"You're just saying that to make me feel better."

"No. I'm not. You're good. Really good."

"Then you'll agree to my plan?"

"I'll agree to talk it over with Brett and Wes and see what they think."

She huffed, but he shrugged. The Morgan boys knew the lay of the land around here a lot better than he did, and he would need both of them on board to help protect Rachel if they went ahead with using her as bait to draw out Baldy and capture the guy.

They met with Brett and Wes at Wes's place, Outlaw Ranch. The two men were stacking bales of hay in a loft, and he and Rachel donned gloves and pitched in. This was exactly the sort of high-repetition, low-weight work his physical therapist wanted him to do. Granted, the bales each weighed around seventy pounds, but using his left hand to grab the baling twine and his right hand holding a hay hook, that worked out to less than forty pounds that his right shoulder had to lift.

And they put him to work unloading hay from a stacked wagon and dropping it down onto an elevator—a long conveyor belt that carried the bales up to the hayloft over the horse stalls in Wes's new barn. Up in the loft, Wes, Brett and Rachel took turns grabbing the bales off the end of the elevator and building tall stacks out of the bales.

They talked as they worked. Rachel outlined her idea

to go fishing by herself while the guys set up a perimeter around her and caught Baldy as he approached her.

Marcus called up to the loft, "Yeah, but what if he brings reinforcements and we're outnumbered?"

She called down, "Then I'm going for a swim downriver while you guys back off and don't engage the larger force."

Brett asked her, "Do you, by any chance, have some scuba training?"

"I'm a certified dive instructor."

Of course she is. Was there *anything* Gunnar hadn't taught his female operators? Marcus rolled his eyes because he knew where Brett was going with the line of questioning. They could tuck a small rebreather pack in her fishing gear, and if Baldy and his buddies came in too hot, she could pop underwater and swim away. In point of fact, it wasn't a bad escape plan. He just hated the whole idea of her exposing herself to danger of any kind.

This was exactly why they shouldn't have slept together last night. Although, no matter how hard he tried, he couldn't make himself regret spending the best night of his life with her.

"Hey! You gonna send some hay up here or what?" Wes shouted down.

Marcus lurched into motion and tossed a bunch of hay bales onto the elevator. Sheesh. He'd zoned out there for a minute, reminiscing about sex with Rachel. He couldn't do that out in the field, especially not if her life depended on him being on his A-game.

Brett said, "What do you say, as soon as we finish stacking this hay, we take a look at your gear, Gia? We'll sync up radio frequencies, make sure everything is shipshape and drive into town. I figure you should buy a fishing rod and walk down the street with it before you head down to Sunny Creek."

Wes added, "What if she goes down by the cliffs to fish?"

Rachel said, "I don't want to get pushed off a cliff if this thing goes south."

Brett laughed. "Nah. The creek runs past a rock wall. The cliffs form the south bank of the creek for about a half mile. Wes has the right idea. Nobody will be able to approach you from the far side of the river. Which means Wes, Marcus and I would only have to worry about someone approaching you from the north bank. That will halve the number of approaches we have to cover."

Wes and Brett were pleased with the prospect, and they were right to be happy about reducing the area they had to cover, but he still didn't like any of this. Irritated, he sent up the hay fast enough that the three people in the loft had to stop talking and focus solely on catching bales as they came off the conveyor and hoisting them up into stacks.

Unfortunately, they only had this one wagon to unload, and with the four of them working together, the job took barely twenty minutes. Far too soon for his taste, Wes, Brett and Rachel were jogging down the stairs from the loft, looking chipper.

She said brightly, "Shall we go catch ourselves a bad guy?"

He merely scowled at her and followed the others from the barn. They drove back to Runaway Ranch, where he fetched his gear and Rachel fetched hers from the cabin. Then they met Brett and Wes at the main barn, where Brett unlocked a storage room that held his old operational gear and an impressive array of weapons and ammunition.

"You expecting a war?" Marcus asked dryly as he gazed at the arsenal.

"This is Montana. The law is often a long distance away, and it falls to the individual rancher to maintain order and keep his herd—and his family—safe."

Wes teased, "Plus, it's fun to shoot stuff and play with cool weapons."

Brett grinned. "That, too."

All four of them pulled out their equipment and gave it a thorough going-over to make sure it was all in good repair and perfect working order. Wes unfolded a pair of rubber wader pants, and they all fooled around with how best to stow an oxygen tank down one leg of the big, loose overalls. Rachel tried them on, and Marcus examined her critically. The bulge of the tank was visible along her right thigh, where it hung from a concealed shoulder strap under the waders' suspender strap.

Brett commented, "Once she's in the water, nobody will notice the bulge. And even if they do, they'll have no reason to believe it's scuba gear."

"Can we shift the tank to my left side so I can stick a weapon down the right leg?" she asked.

It took them a few minutes to make the shift, but then everyone was satisfied.

"Ready to go do this?" Brett asked jauntily.

No! Marcus shouted inside his head. "Can you wear your Kevlar vest under your shirt and fishing vest?" he asked.

"I don't see why not," she commented. "If I can shoot and fight in it, I should be able to fly cast in it."

Brett and Wes grinned, and Brett commented, "A woman after my own heart."

A quick surge of possessiveness in his gut startled Marcus. She was *his* woman. Of course, Brett was deliriously happy with his new bride and meant nothing by the remark. Still. An urge to put his arm around Rachel and drag her tight against his side persisted.

Rachel stripped off her shirt casually, completely unaffected by the men seeing her in her sports bra. But then, he supposed she dressed and undressed in front of male operators a lot. His molars ground loudly against one another, and his jaw felt as hard as concrete.

It was her job. She'd made it clear she'd never had any romantic interest in any other male operators she'd worked with before. He trusted her. She was honorable and honest, and seemed completely smitten with him, dammit. But still. His inner caveman lurked very close to the surface of his mind.

The drive to town was far too short for him, and before he knew it, she'd hopped out of his truck and strolled into the hardware store, which doubled as the local sporting goods store. An urge to go inside and make sure the smart-mouthed clerk didn't flirt with her nearly overcame him. But the plan was for him to lie here in the back seat of his truck and stay completely out of sight.

He hated this, he hated this, he hated this.

The truck's front door opened and Rachel put her fishing rod in the truck. Its long tip poked over the seat and loomed over his head.

She closed the door and backed out of her parking space. Brett and Wes had gone ahead to the area where she would fish and would already be in position when she got there. He would sneak away from the truck after they parked the vehicle, and he would be responsible for watching her as she made her way down to the creek.

"Did you make sure to get seen?" he asked from the back seat.

"Sure did. Strolled right down Main Street with that pole over my shoulder and my fishing vest on."

"Did the kid behind the counter at the hardware store keep a civil tongue in his head with you?" The question was out of his mouth before he could stop it.

Rachel laughed. "Why, yes. Yes, he did. After I told him exactly how I would remove his naughty bits and shove them down his throat if he ever spoke to me that way again."

"I'll go back there when this is all over and have a talk with him—" Marcus started.

"Really. It's okay. I took care of it. The kid didn't have any blood left in his face by the time I was done with him. He's scared to death of me now."

Good. Marcus subsided against the bench seat. He spent the remainder of the short drive down to the creek reminding himself over and over that she could take care of herself. She was a Special Forces operator and fully capable of taking out anyone who messed with her. She didn't need him to be her personal Neanderthal. She only needed him and the Morgans to help her catch the guy trying to kill her so they could all have a nice long chat.

She parked near the river and said into her throat microphone hidden under the collar of her shirt, "Check in, please."

He smirked. SEALs never said "please" when they called for a radio check. Brett reported in and then Wes, both of them speaking so quietly that only microphones plastered against their throats would pick up the sound.

From the back seat, Marcus said, "I got everyone five by five." Meaning, he heard everyone loud and clear.

"All right, then," Rachel said calmly. "I'm heading out."

She sounded as chill as an ice cube. As if she was going out for a casual stroll, and nothing more. He listened as her footsteps crunched on gravel. She moved around to the rear of the truck, where she pulled out the rubber waders. She would carry them in a casual-looking wad down to the creek, disguising the oxygen tank inside them.

The truck's rear gate slammed shut, and her footsteps moved away from the vehicle.

"Parking lot is clear." Her voice came, low. "You're clear to exit the truck, Marcus. Nearest trees are at the truck's twelve o'clock, ten yards away."

"Roger," he murmured.

He didn't question her call. If she said it was clear, then he could safely get out of the vehicle and not worry about Baldy or anyone else spotting him. Huh. This was the first time he'd ever operated with a woman. And it wasn't weird at all. She was as competent and trustworthy as any male SEAL he'd ever worked with.

Quietly, he opened the back door and eased out of the truck, staying low and using its bulk for cover. He clicked the door shut as quietly as he could and knelt to scan underneath the truck and look for any movement across the parking area. All was still.

He moved out fast then, staying low and heading for the trees she'd called out to him. Once he reached their cover, he turned around and took his own hard, long look around the parking area. It was completely still, with only an occasional puff of breeze ruffling the knee-high grass and making the leaves overhead flutter just a little.

He picked up twigs off the ground and stuffed a few of them into his clothing, and then he eased off to his right, toward the creek.

Within a minute, Brett murmured, "I've got you in sight, Blue. I'm almost directly between you and the creek. Turn thirty degrees right and go about a hundred paces, and you'll be in position to cover Gia's western quadrant."

"Got it," he murmured, making the course correction and counting his steps in his head. A hundred paces put him perhaps fifty feet from the creek. He looked around for a good hiding place and spotted a nice stand of brush and weeds a few yards away. He crawled into the middle of the thicket on his hands and knees and quickly built himself a nest. Then he cleared away enough grass and weeds to give himself clear sight lines in all directions.

And then he lay down on his stomach to wait.

Normally, he settled into a zen state where time passed without meaning and all that registered were the sounds and smells and movements around him. A yellow moth flitted from flower to flower in the grassy area in front of him. A fish jumped in the river off to his right, a quicksilver flash and a small splash in the background gurgle of the water slipping past.

But his zen completely evaporated the moment Rachel came into sight in front of him. Nervous as heck, he watched her walk to the riverbank and make a big production of putting on her waders. She fooled with her line and reel and then scanned up and down the creek, as if looking for the perfect hiding post.

Of course, she was checking for any sign of Baldy or other hostiles. And given her eye for detail, the bastards had better be hidden, and well, or she'd pick them out in a minute.

"Clear," she muttered without moving her lips. This spot had a shallow, almost beach-like bank, and she walked down it and into the creek. Knee-deep, then thigh-deep. She moved away from the bank perhaps thirty feet.

Wes murmured, "Slide west about twenty feet, Gia, and then you'll be centered up between the three of us."

Casually, she made the move.

Marcus watched as she threw out her line. She'd remembered his lesson and made a nice cast. She reeled in her fly and cast again. Over the next fifteen minutes or so, her casting got even smoother and more confident.

But he couldn't resist saying low, "Reel your fly in slower, and do it in fits and starts. Bugs move more jerkily than that."

"Thanks for the tip," she muttered, sounding a bit annoyed. "But I'm not out here to catch a fish. At least, not one with scales."

Grinning to himself, he scanned the area once more. All quiet. *C'mon, Baldy. She walked down Main Street practically with a neon sign over her head announcing what she was about to do. Come and get her.*

"Anything?" Rachel murmured.

Marcus waited his turn and reported a negative after the other men.

"I can't stand out here all afternoon pretending to fish. I mean, I physically could, but it would start to look weird eventually."

Brett replied, "We can still give it a while. Just keep fishing."

"By the way," she murmured, "what do I do if I actually catch a fish?"

"Reel it in, take the hook out of its mouth and release it," Wes answered. If Marcus wasn't mistaken, Wes was laughing a little. "Unless you know how to scale a trout and feel like making a production of building a fire and cooking it."

She replied dryly, "You don't scale a trout. You skin it. And, yes, I know how to do it. Not only have I been to survival school, but I've caught plenty of fish on missions to supplement my diet with fresh protein."

Brett chuckled. "Score one for Gia. She passed your little test, Wes."

They settled back into waiting silence, and Marcus had to remind himself to keep scanning around. It was easy to get mesmerized by the graceful flight of the fishing line and the glittering droplets of water it threw skyward in rainbow arcs.

Rachel moved downstream slightly, facing him. Was she going to tease him by throwing her line at him? A subtle reminder of the day they'd met? A smile curved his mouth—

She gave a shout and went down face-first into the water as if she'd fallen. She disappeared under the rippling surface of the creek.

His impulse was to bolt for her, but Brett said tersely, "Hold your positions. Scan for hostiles."

Rachel was flailing around under the water. The creek's surface churned and splashes went up, but he didn't see her come up for air. Frantically, he scanned the area in his quadrant, as his gaze kept straying back to her in the water. What in the hell was she doing? The river wasn't more than waist-deep where she'd gone down. All she had to do was regain her footing and stand up.

But the seconds ticked past, and still she didn't surface.

What on earth was going on?

Chapter 18

Something big and powerful grabbed Gia's ankle and yanked it out from under her, tipping her right off her feet. She went down face-first and just had time to grab a breath before her face went under the frigid water. Her waders filled with water, and she flailed in the thick rubber as it impeded her movement. She kicked her trapped ankle hard, but whatever had it was hanging on tightly.

Had she tangled it in a submerged tree branch? Except she hadn't been moving when it grabbed her.

A snapping turtle, maybe? Except if it was big enough to put its mouth all the way around her ankle like this, it was probably strong enough to bite through the joint completely. And the vise around her ankle wasn't getting any tighter.

A catfish? Except they had teeth, and nothing was piercing her skin. At least, not that she could feel.

A trap of some kind? It didn't feel like metal around her ankle. She kicked again and reached for her ankle, but whatever had it jerked her ankle away from her reaching fingers hard and fast. But her fingertips did graze something—

That felt like canvas.

She opened her eyes, but all she saw were bubbles and churning water. A bunch of silt had kicked up from the creek bed, and the water was green and murky, with visibility near zero. Her vision started to narrow as her brain got low on oxygen. She guessed she'd been underwater for over a minute now, and she'd been flailing hard the whole time.

She kicked again, as hard as she could, and thought she heard a grunt. What on earth? She was getting low on oxygen and tried to stand up but was off balance and could hardly tell which way was up at this point. She curled her body into a ball and reached for her foot to feel what was trapping it, and abruptly something hard hit her.

That felt like a fist. Slowed down by water as it impacted her jaw, but a fist nonetheless.

Sonofagun. A human being was hanging on to her ankle.

Where did *he* come from?

She had no more time to think about it because she was running perilously low on oxygen. Spots were dancing in front of her eyes and she felt light-headed. Her chest felt as if it was about to explode from the inside out.

Frantically, she reversed her tuck, stretching out at full length in the water and arching her body backward, away from her assailant—and his fist. At the same time, she plunged her left hand inside the top of her waders. As she kicked both feet for all she was worth, using up the last of her air, her hand bumped into the regulator attached to her oxygen tank. She grabbed it, yanked it frantically to her face and jammed it into her mouth.

She dragged in a gasping breath of air. Her vision cleared—as much as it could in stirred-up creek water that was so cold it made her eyeballs ache—and she saw a diver, dressed in a black wet suit. He had a hold of her foot.

But now she had air, too, and that evened the odds. A lot.

Using her leg for leverage, she yanked the diver toward her as she bent down toward him. He had a mask protecting his eyes, so she went for his throat instead, wrapping her hands around it and pressing as hard as she could on his carotid artery with her thumbs.

He flailed hard, trying to jerk his head away from her, but he would have to let go of her ankle to succeed. He hesitated, and then let go of her foot.

She surged upward, breaking through the surface of the water and spitting out the regulator to shout, "Diver!"

Then he had his hands on her throat, too, and she thrashed violently to one side in an effort to escape him, all the while keeping her thumbs jammed against his neck. He pushed her away from him, using his longer arms and superior upper body strength, and she felt her grasp slipping. But still, he had a hold of her throat and was pressing on her airway so hard she could barely breathe.

At the last second before she lost her hold, she let go and grabbed fast at his mouth regulator. She caught the hose and gave it a hard yank. It popped free of his mouth. There. Now they both had no air.

They must be drifting downstream, for her feet bumped into a boulder sticking up from the creek bed a good foot or more. It was big and heavy enough for her to brace her feet on it and give a mighty shove upward.

She ripped free of her attacker's grip on her neck and burst free of the surface once more. She inhaled a big, desperate lungful of air. She barely had time to glimpse a large black shape charging toward the creek, and she prayed it was Marcus, not this jerk's buddies.

In an effort to distract the diver, she kicked at him with both feet, fending off kicks of her own with blocks using her forearms. The water took most of the power out of their kicks and punches, transforming it into a weird slow-motion version of a fight.

She heard something hit the water, and then more hands were there. Marcus had dived in, knifing through the water behind her attacker and coming up behind him fast, using the momentum of his running dive.

She saw an arm go around the diver's neck from behind, and she helped along the situation from the front by burying her fist as hard as she could in the guy's solar plexus. Even with the water impeding her blow, she heard his grunt.

She stood up and was in shoulder-deep water. Marcus stood up in front of her, dragging the diver up with him. "Move toward shore!" she called to him.

To the diver she snarled, "Stop fighting, or I'll slug you again, this time in the throat. I'll break your larynx and kill your sorry ass."

The diver's glare was visible even through the glass of his mask. She drew her fist back, and when he was staring intently at it, she kicked upward with her foot as hard as she could, nailing him solidly between the legs with the toe of her hiking boot.

He cried out and curled into a ball with Marcus's arm still around his neck. But all the fight had gone out of him. Marcus hauled the guy to shallow water, and when they could stand and walk out of the creek, Marcus goose-stepped the guy ashore, to the extent that the diver was able to walk after her crotch shot. He mostly stumbled bent over, his hands cupped around his privates. When he and Marcus had fully cleared the water, the diver sank down to his knees, moaning.

She noted with distant approval that Brett and Wes had not shown themselves and were still scanning for incoming hostiles, no doubt. Good discipline, that. Smart. This guy could've attacked her with the intent to sacrifice himself to get her entire team to show itself to his team.

She pulled her sidearm out of her waders and gave it a good shake to make sure the barrel was free of water. Then she pointed it at her attacker.

She said calmly to Marcus, "Blue, how about you fetch some rope from the truck and tie up our friend, here?" No sense using real names in front of this jerk.

Marcus nodded and jogged out of sight while she kept her gaze and her weapon trained on her prisoner. She said nothing and noted that neither did he. An amateur tended to babble and plead for mercy when a gun was pointed at his or her face. But this guy seemed cool as a cucumber. It was not his first rodeo with being on the receiving end of a lethal weapon.

But then, it wasn't her first rodeo being on the business end of a lethal weapon, either. She held the weapon steadily, staring down the short barrel at her prisoner, never wavering in her certainty that if this guy even twitched the wrong way, she was emptying her weapon into him.

Marcus returned with rope and quickly trussed the guy's hands behind his back and tied his ankles together. Only then did Marcus pull the guy's diving mask off his face and pull back the rubber hood of the man's wet suit.

"Baldy," Gia said pleasantly. "We meet at last."

Except the guy wasn't bald. He had blond hair cut very close to his head on the sides and slightly longer on the top. It was a cooler and slicker style than a crew cut, though. More ultramodern punk than military short.

She studied his face carefully. He had clean-cut features and blue eyes. Definitely not the man from the surveillance facility. This man was younger, too, maybe in his early thirties as opposed to the early fifties she guessed her computer thief's age to be.

"Baldy?" he muttered in disgust.

"What's your name, then?" she asked him.

"Kane. Nicholas Kane."

She doubted it was his real name, but it would do for now. "Care to explain why you tried to drown me just now, Nicholas Kane?"

"I wasn't trying to drown you. I needed to talk with you. Still do."

"Hell of a way to invite me to have a conversation with you," she retorted.

"I saw your guys along the riverbank staking you

out. I just wanted to swim you downriver far enough so we could be alone."

"That's not gonna happen," Marcus snapped.

"I'm complimented that you went to such lengths to get a little privacy with me," she murmured. "But you could've just introduced yourself to me where I work and asked to speak with me."

"It's not that simple," he ground out.

"Are you alone out here this afternoon, Mr. Kane?" she asked.

"Yes."

He didn't hesitate. Didn't look away guiltily, but neither did he make excessive eye contact with her. Which all meant nothing. He was probably as well trained as she was in knowing the tells of a lie and how to disguise one.

"Are you by yourself in Montana, or do you have teammates here with you?"

"An interesting choice of word—*teammates*," he muttered. "And in answer to your question, yes, I'm in Montana by myself. None of my *teammates* knows I'm here."

She thought she caught a note of bitterness in his voice as he emphasized the word. What was up with that?

"How about I take you somewhere private so the three of us can have a little conversation?" she said lightly.

For the first time, his gaze flickered. He didn't like the idea of being their prisoner somewhere where they could…enhance…the interrogation to their heart's content. Too bad. He shouldn't have followed her and attacked her if he didn't want to face the consequences.

Into her throat mike, she murmured, "The tango says he's alone out here. Blue and I are gonna load him into the truck and drive him out of here. Hold position until we're gone and make sure he's telling the truth."

"Will do," Brett replied.

To Kane, she said, "You know the drill. On your feet and don't try anything stupid. We're heading for my truck."

Marcus hauled the prisoner to his feet and took a firm grip of his elbow. He had tied the guy's feet so that Kane could only shuffle along, taking baby steps toward the truck.

She fell in behind the two men, never taking her weapon's aim off the prisoner. But she did notice his arms and elbows were tightly tied behind his back. It actually looked deeply uncomfortable. She made a mental note to have Marcus show her how to do that someday. One thing the Medusas had not been trained to do was restrain prisoners in anything more than basic fashion.

They loaded Kane into the back seat of the truck and she climbed into the front passenger seat, turned around and pointed her gun at him. Marcus drove.

They'd been on the road about ten minutes and were about halfway back to the ranch when Marcus's cell phone vibrated.

He held it to his ear while he drove with the other hand. "Go ahead," he murmured.

He listened for about twenty seconds and then said merely, "Got it."

He hung up. At the next intersection, where he would usually turn right to head for Runaway Ranch, he turned left. She was curious as to where he was going. She would lay odds one of the Morgans had made that call and told Marcus an isolated place he could go to question Kane.

They drove for about a half hour and turned onto a tarmac road. They passed a sign announcing a state park with another sign below it announcing that the park was closed.

Perfect.

They drove for another ten minutes or so, catching glimpses of a gorgeous lake they appeared to be circling around. Finally, Marcus turned where a park sign pointed toward the lakeside cabins.

Nice.

They pulled to a stop in front of the first sturdy log cabin they came to. The lake wasn't more than a hundred feet from the front door. The pine trees ringing the lake and mountains at the far end of the lake were reflected on its glassy surface with mirrorlike clarity. Wow. Beautiful.

Marcus opened the truck's rear door and Kane said, "Look. I don't want any trouble. I really do just want to talk with you, Ms. Rykhof."

The use of her real name made her go cold inside. "Who are you?" she blurted.

"That's part of what I want to talk with you about." He paused, then added significantly, "Alone."

"Nope. Not happening," Marcus said bluntly.

"Then, regretfully, I can't say anything." Kane looked over his shoulder at her as she followed him toward the cabin. "I need to speak with you about something classified, and I won't do it in front of a civilian."

"Lucky for you, then, he's military," she commented, lifting her chin toward Marcus.

Kane's gaze snapped to Marcus. "I'll need some proof of that."

"You're the guy trussed up like a roast. I'm not showing you anything," Marcus snapped.

Marcus moved to the door of the cabin and pulled out his wallet. From inside it, he extracted several lock picks and went to work on the padlock above the doorknob. Once he had the padlock open, he picked the lock in the knob itself. She knew the second lock to be kid stuff after that double-action, heavy-duty padlock, and sure enough, Marcus blasted through the second lock in a matter of seconds.

He opened the door, and she followed him and Kane inside. The plain interior was dim. Marcus pulled up the slatted wood blinds and light poured inside, illuminating the thick layer of gray dust on everything. Marcus pulled out one of the wooden kitchen chairs.

"Have a seat, Kane," he said pleasantly.

Kane sat down, sitting on the forward edge of the seat while his arms hit the chair's tall back. Marcus moved across the main room to lean against the closed front door. He pulled his own sidearm and nodded at her, silently taking over guard duty. She holstered her damp weapon in her sodden leather thigh holster. Both were going to need a good cleaning and oiling when she got a chance.

As for her, she pulled out a second chair and dragged it around to face the prisoner.

"You're going to have to take me at my word when I say my friend has most of the same security clearances I do. The only way you're walking out of here alive is to start talking…and to convince me there's a darned good reason for me not to tie a bag of rocks around your feet and toss you into the middle of the lake."

The prisoner shot her a rather withering look as if to say, "Duh."

"How about you start with your name and job title?" she said.

"I already told you my name. And I'm—" he glanced over at Marcus and then continued "—I'm a Special Operator with a classified government team."

She laughed. "You're going to have to be a little more specific than that, Sparky."

Kane huffed. "I'm an employee of the US government. I work off the books—very off the books—doing the jobs amateurs like you two wouldn't get near."

She shrugged. "If I'm supposed to be impressed, I'm not."

"You should be," he replied quietly. "Guys like me don't get caught unless they want to be."

"And why did you want us to catch you, then?" she asked.

"I didn't want *him* to catch me. I wanted *you* to. And I already told you the reason. I want to talk with you."

"About what?" she asked in growing frustration.

He exhaled hard. "Here's the thing. I work on a team. Much like the team you work on, Captain Rykhof. Special operations. Way under the radar."

She managed not to gape, but it was a close thing. Nobody outside a very small, very tight chain of command knew the Medusas existed, let alone that she was one of them.

Kane continued. "A few weeks back, my team did a job, and I think you witnessed it. I want to know what they did on that job."

She frowned. Was he talking about the theft of the crate? Or maybe about the guy who stole her computer? She replied, "If you're part of this alleged team, you tell me what the job was."

"I wasn't on it. Through what I now know to be a series of lies, I was diverted to another operation and wasn't with my teammates on a certain trip they took."

"Where to?"

"Zagastan," he replied promptly.

Again, she spotted no hesitation or signs of a lie from Kane. Interesting. That was where Alpha Platoon's raid had taken place.

"The date?" she asked.

He rattled off two dates a week apart that included the raid on night five of that week. The timing was right for his guys to have been the crate thieves.

"Describe your team to me," she said, tension mounting in her gut.

"Four men. Probably in tactical gear. They'd have moved around quietly. Undetected."

"In and out of where?" How much did he actually know about that highly classified mission?

He described in concise detail the raid, the location of it and the target of the raid itself.

Well, okay, then. This guy definitely had access to very high-level intelligence, if nothing else.

"What did your team want with that particular target?" she asked.

"That's what I'm hoping you can tell me."

She stared at him. "I beg your pardon?"

"My team did something that night. They've been evasive with me about it, and ever since that trip to Zagastan, they've been acting weird around me."

"Weird how?" she prompted.

"Secretive. Furtive. They're having conversations behind my back. When I walk into a room, they fall silent a little too quickly. They suddenly act as if they don't trust me."

"Did you do something to make them suspicious of you?" she shot at him.

"Let's just say it was not easy for me to integrate with all teams. The fact that I formed a great working relationship with this one is notable. The fact that they abruptly withdrew that hard-earned trust from me is more notable."

She leaned forward, propping her elbows on her knees, genuinely interested now. "What do you think happened?"

"I think they did something on that mission that they don't want me to find out about. They all know what happened, but they're keeping it from me."

Her gut said he was telling her the truth.

"You wanted to talk. So, let's talk. It's my turn to tell you a story," she said.

Marcus interrupted instantly. "Are you sure? Maybe we should wait till the guys run his ID."

She snorted. "If this man is who he says he is, there's no ID on him anywhere. Or, at least, no accurate ID."

Kane met her gaze and nodded slightly as if to agree.

To Marcus she said, "It's not as if what I saw is any big secret at this point. Dozens or hundreds of people know about it. Why not tell him? Maybe he can shed some light on it."

Marcus scowled, but shrugged.

She turned to Kane. "As you undoubtedly know, I'm a real-time photo intelligence analyst."

He nodded. "I'm aware."

Of course he was.

She described in generalities the mission that Alpha Platoon had run. After all, this guy already had a fairly complete working knowledge of what the raid's mission had been, who'd carried it out and what the outcome had been.

But when she got to the part about seeing four men haul a large, heavy crate out the back exit of the compound, Kane stared at her intently. "Full tactical gear, you say? And squawking American identifier codes?" he asked her tersely.

"Correct."

"What did they do with the box?"

"I watched them approach the marines in the Humvee guarding the back gate. They appeared to identify themselves to the crew. My video glitched, and when I got back the feed, they were finishing loading the crate into the vehicle. I watched them drive away in the vehicle with the crew."

Kane nodded slowly. "That sounds like my team."

Marcus snapped. "Does it also sound like your team that the three marines in the Humvee were found dead in their vehicle over a hundred miles away the next morning?"

Kane's head whipped around and he stared at Marcus. "They killed the Humvee crew?"

"Execution-style. With Russian bullets."

Kane swore under his breath.

She said quietly, "I gather that also sounds like your team's MO?"

He looked up at her miserably. "It does. And it also explains their odd behavior."

He seemed genuinely distressed.

"Any idea what your team took?" she asked.

"No."

She didn't know whether or not to believe him. He'd bit out that answer a little quickly, a little abruptly. But it was also possible he was just upset over his teammates murdering American soldiers.

"Any idea why your team cut you out of their theft?" Marcus asked.

Kane said succinctly, "Besides the fact that I wouldn't have gone along with it? I'm known for being a straight arrow. Incorruptible."

"How about your teammates?" she asked.

"Let's just say the four who went to Zagastan were known to have a somewhat more transactional view of morality than me."

"Have your teammates ever stolen stuff before?"

"We steal stuff all the time, but at the behest of the government."

"Any idea what was in that crate?" she asked.

"No. But I'm bloody well going to ask a few pointed questions—"

"Don't," Marcus bit out. "Asking questions will raise red flags. And if your buddies are as smart as you say they are, they'll be watching for you to get nosy."

Kane wilted in the chair a little. Marcus was right, and they all knew it.

She jumped in. "There's one last bit to my story." She described the man invading her surveillance facility and stealing the computer tower.

By the time she was done, Kane was staring at her, openly aghast.

"Do you know who he is?" she asked.

"Yeah. My boss."

"What's his name?" she demanded.

Kane shook his head. "He doesn't exist in any database. He's a ghost."

"Here's the thing," she said heavily. "Your boss threatened to kill me if I told anyone what I saw that night, either from the mission on my monitors or from when he busted in and stole the computer."

"You told, didn't you?" Kane asked grimly.

"I did. And shortly thereafter, two attempts were made on my life."

"No wonder you were so jumpy when I tried to approach you to talk."

"You were trying to approach me?" she blurted.

"I was trying to catch you when you were totally alone and nobody would see me." Kane added, "But I have to admit, you're good. Honestly, if you're alive after my team tried to kill you twice, I'm impressed."

"Gee. Thanks," she replied dryly. "Speaking of being impressed, how did you know to bring diving gear down to the creek to go after me?"

Kane rolled his eyes. "You've been in hiding for days, and then suddenly you stroll through the middle of town, practically shouting, 'I'm going fishing.' Of course it was a trap. I figured by water was the only way to reach you safely."

Fair.

He continued, "I didn't expect that oxygen tank in your waders. That was smart."

"Thanks." She might be a Medusa, but it was still nice to get a compliment from a man like him. If, as she suspected, he was CIA special operations group or the like, they were the absolute best of the best of the Special Forces world.

She asked quietly, “Not to put too fine a point on it, Nicholas, but what do you plan to do about your team now that you know, more or less, what they’ve been up to?”

Chapter 19

Marcus looked up sharply as he heard a vehicle approaching. He took up a defensive position beside the front window and only relaxed when Brett's pickup truck came into sight. The Morgans joined them in the cabin, and Kane nodded at the brothers, who frowned and looked over at him.

Marcus gave them a quick recap, and Brett asked Kane, "So, how do you know your teammates weren't carrying out a mission you simply weren't briefed in on?"

"Because I know my teammates. Same way you know yours. I can tell when they're hiding something from me and sneaking around behind my back."

Rachel added, "He identified the guy who broke into the surveillance facility and stole my computer. It's his boss."

Wes sprawled on the small sofa to one side of the

main room and Brett perched on its arm. It was Brett who asked, "So, Kane's whole team is corrupt. What's the plan now? Turn this guy loose, hope he's telling us the truth, and pray he doesn't go back to his team and finger all of us to be killed?"

"Actually..." Rachel said thoughtfully.

Marcus's gut clenched in apprehension. He recognized that tone of voice. She'd had an idea. A bold, even ridiculous one, and he was going to hate every second of hearing it. Girding himself to do battle against her wilder impulses, he said grimly, "Actually what?"

"What if we do exactly that? What if we have Nicholas call his team and tell them where to find me? He may not be trying to kill me, but his teammates certainly are."

"You want me to lead my team into a trap?" Kane squawked.

Marcus stared hard at the guy. "You said you're a straight arrow. Are you going to put your money where your mouth is and do the right thing now?"

Kane met his stare long enough for Marcus to see the pain of betrayal in the man's eyes. He could imagine how Kane must feel. His team had cut him out, left him behind, and was now keeping secrets from him. No way could Kane work with those men again. The trust that was the core of any special operations team was broken and could never be fixed.

Rachel said soberly, "It's a hard thing I'm asking you to do. But you're not the one betraying them. Your team betrayed you."

Kane's head bowed. He closed his eyes and was silent for a long time. Marcus could feel the conflict pouring off the guy as he wrestled with his decision. Honestly,

Marcus didn't know what he would do in the same situation. Every cell in his body would yell at him never ever to betray his brothers. But then, he would never ever expect his brothers to turn on him the way they'd turned on Kane, either.

He felt sorry for the man. It was a terrible choice, either way.

Finally, Kane raised his head. "I'm willing to make the call. But you're going to need more help than these three guys. And I won't participate in taking down my teammates. I just…can't."

Rachel nodded in understanding, and Marcus realized he was, as well. Yeah. He might be able to set up his brothers, but to mow them down in cold blood? That would be too much for him, too.

Rachel said, "I know where to get backup. Let me make a phone call."

Marcus pivoted as she walked past him, and he followed her outside. "Walk with me, Rachel."

She fell in beside him as he headed down to the lakeshore and turned to follow the beach.

"Are you sure about this?" he asked. "We could also ask Kane to tell his team he killed you. You might have to change your appearance. Live under an assumed name for a while, but these guys would go away, eventually."

She laughed a little. "My hair is naturally brunette and I never wear flannel shirts or jeans. And I traveled to Montana under an assumed name. Not to mention, I haven't used a credit card since I left home. I do everything in cash. I don't get on social media. I don't even get on the internet. And yet Kane's here. If he can find me that easily, so can his teammates."

He sighed. She was not wrong. "How good are the Medusas? If Kane's who I think he is, his teammates will be incredibly dangerous."

She kicked at a pebble. "We're very good. But we've never run up against a bunch like this. Any chance you could call in a few SEALs to help us out?"

He glared at her under his eyebrows. "Does the sun rise in the east?"

She smiled a little. "Okay. I'll call the Medusas. You call all the SEALs you can scrape together."

"Brett and Wes have volunteered to pitch in, too."

She looked up at him in concern. "Do you really think it's going to take an entire army to take these guys down?"

"Yes. I do."

She looked back over her shoulder and he did the same. The cabin was out of sight behind a stand of trees. Which was probably why she stepped forward and hugged him. He wrapped his arms around her and rested his chin lightly on top of her head as she laid her ear against his heart.

They stood like that for a long time, silently sharing their worry. Like it or not, the best option—really, the only option—was to draw in Kane's black ops team and eliminate them once and for all. Marcus had gone up against some very bad people in his day, but he suspected these guys would be among the worst he'd ever encountered.

If only his shoulder was at full strength. Not that he was going to let it stop him for a minute from going out in the field with Rachel. He planned to personally protect her in the upcoming operation, whether she liked it or not.

To that end, he wasn't going to admit to her how bad his shoulder was aching right now. Choking out Kane in the creek had strained it badly, and he could barely move it. He was hugging Rachel gently because it was all he could manage, not because he was choosing to treat her as if she was made of glass.

She sighed and lifted her head. "Thanks for not fighting me on this."

"Trust me. I would fight you tooth and nail if I could think of any better plan. Unfortunately, I think it's the only play we've got."

She took a deep breath and stepped back. His arms felt empty and his body felt cold where she'd been pressed against him. An urge to pull her into his arms again nearly overcame him. But the time for getting cuddly was over. It was time to go to war.

He listened grimly as she called Gunnar Torsten and explained what she needed. No surprise, her boss replied without hesitation that he would gear up the gang and be on the next plane to Montana.

He pulled out his own cell phone and called some of his teammates. Not only did they agree to come to Montana, but they offered to reach out to a few more guys who were in downtime rotations and available to come to the Rocky Mountains on a short-notice hunting expedition.

He was startled when they stepped back inside the cabin to see Wes and Brett leaning over the kitchen table. Kane, his arms still tied behind his back, was also leaning forward, studying what looked like an elevation map of the state park. The map covered most of the table, and someone had fetched fist-sized rocks from outside to weigh down the four corners of the unrolled map.

He and Rachel joined the other men at the table.

Brett murmured without looking up, "We're scouting the best possible ambush site. We're going to need every tactical advantage we can get to lick these jerks. Nick was telling us about the backgrounds of the men we're luring here."

"Like what?" Marcus asked quickly.

"Nick is a former ranger gone Delta Force, and he's the least experienced guy on this kill team. Every one of them is a trained sniper with dozens or hundreds of confirmed kills. They're fast, quiet and stealthy, and are out-of-the-box thinkers. They'll anticipate anything even remotely conventional that we try and will turn it against us."

Beside him, Rachel shrugged. "Then we'll have to make sure to be highly unconventional every step of the way."

"Easier said than done," Kane warned. "When we plan a mission, we anticipate everything we can think of—and we're pretty creative—and we prepare a counterattack for every eventuality."

Rachel smiled. "Have you guys ever planned for women operators?"

Kane frowned. "Not that I recall."

"Then they won't be ready for us."

Darkness fell as the five of them brainstormed various options for how to capture or kill Kane's teammates. He was strongly in favor of a capture-only mission. But, privately, Marcus didn't think Kane's buddies would go down that easily. He expected they would choose to die rather than let themselves be caught.

And one thing he knew from long years of experience: an enemy willing to die was a very, very dangerous enemy, indeed.

Brett called a national forest service ranger in Apple Pie Creek, Cal Sutter, who agreed to reach out to his counterpart managing this park and inform him that classified military exercises were going to be held here over the next few days and to keep all of his staff out while the park was shut down.

The next day at noon, a large helicopter landed on the beach outside the cabin, and the Medusas and four men—one of whom he recognized as his former SEAL teammate Gunnar Torsten—jogged out from under the twin rotor blades. The pilot lifted off and Rachel ran forward to hug her teammates, who looked, to the untrained eye, like just a group of more-fit-than-average women in their late twenties.

They'd already unlocked the other dozen cabins and cleaned them out, and Rachel led the Medusa entourage to their temporary quarters. Over the course of the afternoon, a half dozen of Marcus's SEAL teammates, who were on leave and able to get to Montana on short notice, arrived.

They convened in the largest of the cabins, a two-bedroom affair with a large main room. Rachel filled everyone in on how she'd ended up here, and who they were here to apprehend or take down.

Then Kane filled in everyone on the capabilities of his teammates. Clearly, it pained him to rat out his teammates this way, but the sentiment in the room was clear: his brothers had stolen something and murdered three marines. They had to face justice or be killed.

Then one of Marcus's SEAL buddies asked the obvious question. "I get that Gia is the bait we'll use to catch these guys, but who are these other women? No offense, ladies, but given how dangerous our targets are, you'd best leave this to us SEALs."

He caught the glints of humor in the women's gazes as Gunnar Torsten said, "I'd probably better answer that one. Gentlemen, allow me to introduce you to the Medusas. They're an all-female Special Forces team, fully trained to SEAL standards. This group has been operational for about three years. They're combat-tested and battle-hardened. And they'll keep up with you step for step in the operation."

The silence was deafening. Marcus couldn't read the SEALs. Were they simply shocked? Or was that utter skepticism? Either way, he spoke up. "I've been working with Rach—Gia—for the past couple of weeks. I can attest that these women are the real deal."

Rachel—he would probably think of her by that name forever—looked over at him gratefully, and he nodded back at her infinitesimally.

Brett added, "Marcus isn't kidding. She shot circles around me a couple days back."

Then Kane surprised Marcus by adding, "She fought me off when I attacked her underwater. I've never been so shocked in my life."

That made the men chuckle briefly.

The dark-haired man named Avi, who'd arrived with the Medusas, said, "I'm Israeli Special Forces, on loan to the US to help train these women. And I'd bet my life they can hold their own against any SEAL team."

A man who introduced himself as Beau Lambert nodded. "I'm an ex-BUD/S instructor. We run the Medusas through everything the men go through."

The last man who'd shown up with the Medusas, who introduced himself merely as Zane, said quietly, "I come out of CIA special operations. I've been working with the Medusas for a year now. They're topflight operators."

"All right, then," Gunnar said. "That's probably enough testimonials. Now we just have to get all of you to run around together so you can see the Medusas in action for yourselves. I'm happy to be the point person on deploying the Medusas. Who's going to call the shots for the SEAL contingent?"

Marcus looked over at Brett, who'd been a team leader in the field.

Brett said, "You're the active-duty guy, Marcus. And they're your men."

He nodded. "Looks like I'm up to bat, then. First order of business—let's get all our gear and radios synced up."

Everyone adjourned and in short order returned with their kits. There was hardly an inch of open floor left as the five Medusas and eight SEALs spread out their equipment. It was loud as they chatted back and forth, comparing notes on their equipment and weapons. He had no doubt the SEALs were testing the Medusas on their knowledge of firearms, as well. But they would settle down and get to business once they realized the Medusas were legit.

Once the radios were all tested and the weapons all cleaned, oiled and inspected, Marcus said, "Tomorrow, let's scout the area and run some exercises. For now, everyone sleep while you can. Kane's boys are going to be no joke to take down."

Everyone departed to their cabins, leaving him and

Rachel to share a bedroom in this cabin, along with her teammate Rebel and the tall Israeli, Avi, in the other bedroom. They were obviously a couple.

Marcus asked Rachel quietly as she closed the bedroom door, “Am I imagining it, or are those three guys who came with Torsten all, um, involved with members of your team?”

She smiled a little. “You’re not imagining it. Lambo—Beau Lambert—wrecked his knee and was rehabbing it when he was assigned to train Tessa up to SEAL standards. They went to the swamps of south Louisiana to do it in secret.”

She sat down on the bed beside him and began unlacing her boots. “Piper was kidnapped about a year ago by a terror cell that mistook her for the wife of a guy they were trying to kill. Zane was undercover, embedded with the terrorists. He rescued Piper, and then the two of them escaped the terrorists together.”

She kicked off her boots and lay back on the bed with a sigh of pleasure. “Rebel and Avi met when we pulled security duty at last summer’s Olympic Games. They’ve been together ever since. Gunnar pulled strings to get him assigned to help train the Medusas. He’s been really interesting to work with. The Israelis have a ton of real-world special operations experience with terror organizations.”

Marcus dropped his boots to the floor and stretched out beside her in the dark. “I’m not going to get a wink of sleep tonight,” he confessed. Not lying beside her like this, he wasn’t.

“Want me to make a bed on the floor?” she offered.

“No way. I’ll sleep on the floor if it comes to that.”

“Your shoulder needs the soft mattress. I’ll take the floor,” she argued.

"How about we both just be adults and go to sleep without worrying about who else is in the bed with us?" he suggested.

He heard her quiet gust of laughter. "Easier said than done, my good sir."

He groaned under his breath and resigned himself to a long, *long* night in purgatory.

Chapter 20

Gia woke up slowly, gradually becoming aware of being sprawled across Marcus's chest. She rolled away carefully, but he murmured a good morning alertly enough that it was obvious he'd been awake for a while and letting her sleep on him.

"Ready to go play with the Medusas?" she asked him.

"I am. I don't know if my guys are."

She smiled and sat up. "We find that male spec ops teams take about one day to forget we're women and start treating us like one-each operators."

"Good. I think that's about as long as we've got to prepare. We need Kane to call his team before they start to get suspicious about where he's been and what he's up to."

She rolled out of bed, dressed and followed Marcus outside to where a bunch of the guys were standing around a charcoal grill eating scrambled eggs and sausages someone had cooked. Thankfully, the cook had prepared enough food for a marching band because the group polished it all off.

They spent the morning playing tag in the woods using the laser designators on their weapons to tag one another. It was fun, but it was also serious work. The Medusas won the first round of capture the flag easily because the SEALs violently underestimated them. The second round was closer because the SEALs were a little embarrassed by their first loss, but still not going full out.

Gia and her sisters had seen it enough times before to know how this went. Now that the boys had actually tried a little, but unconsciously held back, taken it easy on the girls and lost a second time, they would come the whole hog at the Medusas the third time around.

The third round of capture the flag was hotly fought and most of both teams had been shot with laser designators before Gia was able to sneak past the SEAL defenses and snatch the SEAL flag just as Marcus shot her, laughing.

"Dang, you're good," he murmured, holding a hand down to help her up from where she'd dramatically fallen down "dead."

"As an actress or as a soldier?"

"Both."

She smiled up at him privately while the Medusas and SEALs gathered around.

"Lunch?" Gunnar asked.

A loud chorus of hoo-yahs rang out.

They came together in the main building to talk. Everyone agreed the terrain was terrible for tracking

Kane's kill team. It had way too much cover and way too many hiding spots for bad guys to operate out of.

Marcus asked the group as a whole, "If not the woods, then where do we ambush the team?"

She was the first one to answer. "What if, instead of hiding, we wait for the team right out in the open?"

Marcus frowned at her...along with the rest of the SEALs.

"What if we sit right here on the beach? Maybe some guys go out fishing in a boat. Some of us sit around a campfire. A few people go swimming. Let's act like regular people camping at a state park. The kill team may guess that I'm with an operator or two, but they won't suspect that everybody in the whole camping area is an operator."

Kane commented, "If I saw a bunch of couples camping, it would never occur to me that the women were dangerous. I would discount them as decoys. Covers, if you will."

A couple of the SEALs nodded in agreement.

They spent the afternoon playing out various scenarios in and around the beach and cabins and ultimately decided that putting Gia in a cabin was the logical candidate to draw in and ambush the attackers.

They spent the evening running scenarios in various cabins and finally agreed that the best bet was to keep her in the largest cabin and pull the kill team into it. The smaller cabins were too tiny and tight for fourteen operators to crash into without facing serious cross fire and target identification problems.

The next morning, they made a series of strategic modifications to the main cabin and spent the afternoon running attack scenarios, with Kane suggesting ways that his team might choose to assault the cabin. When they'd run through every idea they all could come up with and figured out how to counter each attack, Gunnar finally said, "I think we're ready. Kane, make the call to your guys."

Nicholas pulled out his cell phone. "Hey. It's Kane. I found the target. The woman…Yeah. She's hiding out in Montana. I've got eyes on her. Head for the Clearwater Valley. It's in the northwest part of the state. The high Rockies. Call me when you get close and I'll guide you in. In the meantime, I'll keep eyes on her around the clock till you get here." A pause. "How long?…See you then."

He disconnected the call. "They'll be here tomorrow."

When she and Marcus went to bed that night, they lay side by side for hours, not sleeping. She couldn't tell which one of them was more tense. Were it not for her teammate in the next room, she totally would have jumped his bones just to release some of her stress. But as it was, she knew the tightness to be a good thing. It would make her sharp, on edge, tomorrow.

Morning dawned gray and drizzly, and they worried that their plan to act like visitors to the park was in jeopardy. But by early afternoon, the skies cleared and the sun came out.

It was midafternoon when Kane got the call. They were all lounging by the beach and froze when his phone rang.

He spoke quietly, as if working a surveillance hide. "I'm in a park at the west end of the valley. The target is here, camping with some friends. I'll send you GPS coordinates and meet you there."

He hung up and looked around. "They'll be here in an hour."

Someone was sent to the park entrance to remove the Closed sign while the others got ready to play their roles as couples, fishermen and campers. Several scouts were sent into the woods to attempt to spot the kill team, not that anyone expected Kane's men to be that sloppy. But they'd mapped out the route Kane would take to bring them in, so at least the spotters knew where to look.

The vehicles were moved and parked beside various cabins. Beach towels were laid out, fishing gear deployed, and the grill was fired up to cook a batch of hamburgers. And then they waited.

They all wore wireless earbuds and had weapons hidden nearby. They all knew where to dive for cover if a firefight started, and they all knew where Gia would run for cover and how to form a security cordon around her.

An hour passed.

Two hours.

The third hour was almost gone and the sun was starting to drop in the sky when one of the spotters finally breathed, "Contact."

Here they came.

She looked down at the tablet computer beside her, noting where the radio locator Kane was secretly wearing put the position of him and his team. She said to no one in particular, but broadcast to everyone, "They're taking the west approach like Kane thought they would."

That would put the kill team down the beach to her left.

Twenty minutes or so passed and Kane's identifier stopped about a hundred feet inside the trees down the beach.

"They're setting up surveillance right where we thought they would," she commented into her hidden microphone. She laughed aloud at a joke Tessa was telling, and Marcus went over to the grill to pull out the meat and put burgers on to cook.

Tessa and Beau and Rebel and Avi sat on the beach blanket beside her. There was a small chance that one of Kane's teammates might recognize Zane from his time at the CIA, so he was deployed in the woods as a spotter. Piper, an accomplished scout, was also out in the woods. They would be making their way in behind Kane and his team now.

She stood up and went to a picnic table to lay out the rest of the meal. Marcus carried a big platter of burgers to the table, and the three couples sat down to eat. It was weird eating in the middle of a mission, but she was glad for the calories. She might need them later.

Down the beach, three SEALs rowed their fishing boat ashore and built a fire. They commenced cleaning and cooking their catch and drinking beer from a cooler. Farther down the beach, Gunnar and Lynx got in an SUV and drove away as if going home. They would park and hike back under cover of darkness. It all looked perfectly normal and mundane.

She finished eating and helped the other women clean up after the meal while the guys built a fire. They sat around the fire and watched the sun set. Darkness fell, and they talked around the fire for a while. And then they put the fire out, collected their beach towels and headed for the cabins.

Here went nothing.

The heavy log walls of the cabin prevented visual surveillance, but not infrared surveillance, so she brushed her teeth, put on her pajamas, moisturized her face and crawled into bed. Except her "pajamas" were black pants and a black shirt. And her "moisturizer" was black greasepaint.

Marcus was "sleeping" on the couch in the main room, and she missed his reassuring presence to help pass the tense silence of waiting. It took until nearly midnight, but finally one of the scouts breathed in her earpiece, "They're on the move."

That was her cue to get out of bed quickly and put in her place the life-size decoy doll, complete with a battery-operated heater inside it to fool any infrared sensors the hostiles might use. Then Marcus helped her climb into the big stone fireplace, and she crawled up on the ledge they'd built inside the chimney.

They'd kept a fire going in the fireplace all day and had only put it out when they came inside tonight. Which meant the stones still held a lot of heat and would disguise her heat signature from Kane's men. It was quite warm in here, and she hugged her knees and her Textron assault rifle, waiting for Kane's men to attack.

Earlier, she'd threaded a small camera on a long tubular feed up the chimney and had taped its camera end just inside the corner of the fireplace, pointing into the main room. Perched in her hiding place now, she picked up the optic lens on the other end of the tube and peered through it. The view of the great room was flattened and distorted, and in black and white, but at least she could get a general idea of what was happening in the cabin.

A scout reported that the team had stopped about fifty feet from her cabin.

And then they all waited.

For hours.

No surprise: Kane's kill team was a) patient, and b)

waiting until the dead of night, when their target would be deeply asleep, to make the hit. Her guess was they would come in planning to slit her throat quietly. No sense waking up anyone else and having to kill a bunch of innocent civilians to cover their tracks.

Although, they hadn't hesitated to kill three marines. They might come in guns blazing, which was why her cabinmates were wearing bullet-resistant vests and had helmets ready at hand.

It was just after 3:00 a.m. when Piper whispered, "Incoming."

Tension shot through Gia, but she did several repetitions of patterned breathing to calm herself, and her heart rate settled down…more or less. If Marcus weren't here, she wouldn't be the least bit worried. But he was right out in the open on that couch. The odds of him getting shot were higher than she liked.

His job was to play possum and pretend to be asleep when the kill team came inside. The idea was to let them get all the way into the bedroom and then spring the whole group of SEALs and Medusas around them. The hope was that four or five laser designators on each attacker's chest would be sufficient to convince them to surrender. Barring that, they would die.

Five minutes ticked by.

Ten.

All she heard were Marcus's gentles snores. Which amused her, given that she'd slept with him before, and he didn't make a sound while sleeping.

And then Gia heard another noise, the faintest of scraping sounds. That would be the back window of the main room, facing the woods. She went perfectly still, practicing her technique of pulling in her energy and disappearing.

She listened with all her might but didn't hear a single shuffle or squeak to give away the presence of the kill team. She counted to sixty in her head. Surely they were all inside by now?

Ten more seconds. They would be at the bedroom door by now.

She listened for all she was worth but heard no sound whatsoever to indicate that the kill team had entered the house.

Without warning, she heard a low voice mutter from the bedroom, "Decoy. Get out. Go, go, go."

And then all hell broke loose. Doors and windows slammed open as SEALs and Medusas rushed inside. There was shouting in the bedroom, and it sounded as if a fight broke out.

A black shape came out into the main room low and fast. She watched in her optic lens as Marcus surged up off the couch just in time for the black shape to leap at him. The two men grappled, and she caught the dull glint of knives in each man's fist.

Should she reveal herself? Everyone on both the SEAL team and Medusas had implored her to stay hidden. Out of sight. Out of the fight. As long as there was no sign of her, the kill team had no target to sacrifice themselves in the name of killing. They would bug out rather than stick around to take a shot at her.

Marcus and the black shape broke apart for a moment and then leaped at each other once more, knives slashing.

Oh, Lord. She couldn't just sit here and watch Marcus get skewered protecting her. His shoulder wasn't at full strength, and he was trying to fight left-handed. She watched in agony.

Stay or go?

She heard Marcus grunt in pain very close to her, and that was it. She rolled off her perch and landed in a crouch inside the fireplace. The bad guy had Marcus by the throat.

Apparently, the fight in the bedroom had mostly ended, for SEALs and Medusas were pouring out into the living room. Marcus's attacker was using him as a human shield. Two other members of the kill team were cornered, one in the kitchen and the other over by the dining table. The one by the table appeared to be trying to edge over toward the front door to make a run for it. One more attacker was already down on the ground with a pile of SEALs subduing him.

The four Medusas stood in an arc, weapons pointed at the fireplace, ignoring the fights behind them, their focus intense and complete on the vignette in front of the fireplace. From this angle, Gia could see their faces—well, part of them, since they all had their right eyes pressed against their assault weapons' night scopes. They looked cool, calm and absolutely prepared to pull their triggers.

A moment's pride surged through her at the professionalism and lethal skill of her sisters in arms. She didn't for a second worry about one of the Medusas shooting her. The infrared function of their scopes would have lit her up in green relief behind Marcus and his captor. They'd all practiced shooting around hostages in close quarters, and she wouldn't even get nicked by any round one of them shot.

But the attacker kept moving, ducking and weaving

behind Marcus's big body, making the tiniest and most difficult possible target of himself.

Small flaw with his plan. He had his back to the fireplace and had no idea she was crouched inside the firebox.

She couldn't see it, but the guy probably had his knife to Marcus's neck. She knew all too well how fast and easy it was to fatally slice a person's carotid artery. Marcus would bleed out in under thirty seconds if the hostile swiped that blade under Marcus's chin.

Still crouching, she reached for her own razor-sharp field knife in her ankle sheath. She had one shot at killing the target before he killed Marcus. She eased the blade free of its sheath and rose up behind him.

On the floor beyond Marcus, one of the bad guys—now under a pile of SEALs—spotted her and his eyes opened wide in shock. But she didn't wait for him to shout a warning to his buddy.

Focusing on the attacker holding Marcus, she lunged. Knife held high, she jammed the blade with all her strength into the back of his neck, just below the base of his skull.

The guy stumbled forward into Marcus, and Marcus staggered forward. Please, God, let her target not have cut Marcus. The attacker dropped to his knees as his legs collapsed, and he pitched forward onto the floor, dragging her to her knees beside him as she kept a tight grip on the knife. She yanked the blade free and spun to face Marcus, who was pressing his hand against his neck.

"Are you all right?" she cried.

He lifted his hand away from his neck, and a thin line of red showed. "He nicked me, but that's all."

She flung herself up and forward against him. "Thank God you're safe."

"If I'm safe, it's thanks to you," he muttered against her temple. He held her tightly in his arms. Or rather, his left arm. His right arm had no strength at all in it.

She pulled back to stare up at him. "What did you do to your arm?"

"I might have gotten into a fight with that piece of trash." He glanced down at the dead man at their feet.

She looked around hastily. "Is the scene secured?"

Gunnar grunted from on top of a flailing attacker. "More or less. Someone knock this jerk out."

It took a minute, but Zane dug out a vial of something and injected it into each of the three surviving kill-team members. As soon as they were unconscious, Kane, who'd been pretending to fight, stopped and was helped to his feet by one of the SEALs who'd been holding him down. The other SEALs tied his teammates so tightly they looked almost mummified in rope.

Zane made a quick phone call, and in under an hour, a CIA team arrived to take custody of the three surviving kill-team members and the body of the fourth. The unconscious men were loaded into a black van, and it drove away into the night.

"What will happen to them?" Gia asked Zane.

"They'll be drugged and interrogated. And then they'll be put down a dark hole for a good long time somewhere that doesn't technically exist."

Marcus, who had a medic examining his shoulder, commented, "Not that they'll talk. Guys like that take their secrets to the grave."

Gia looked around. "Any sign of their boss? The gray-haired guy?"

Kane replied bitterly, “Oh, he doesn’t get his hands dirty. That’s what he has men like me for.”

She asked him quickly, “While you were skulking around with them today, did they say anything about what might have been in that crate or what they planned to do with it?”

“Nope. Not a word. They didn’t trust me enough for that.”

“Too bad.” She went over to Marcus to have a look for herself at his shoulder as the medic finished strapping a sling on his right arm.

“How bad is it?” she asked the medic.

He shrugged. “Blue undid most of the healing he’s done on the shoulder. Maybe he can rehab it again, maybe not.”

She looked at Marcus, stricken. “I’m so sorry.”

Surprisingly, he didn’t look too broken up over it. “If I make it back, great. If not, I’ve got other things to do with my life.”

As the medic moved away and general conversation hummed around them, she lowered her voice to speak beneath it. “Oh, really? Like what?”

“I was thinking about retiring. Moving to Louisiana. I hear there’s great fishing down that way. Maybe I’ll buy myself a house. Build a picket fence. Maybe start a family in a few years.”

She smiled at him as something warm and wonderful swelled in her chest until she couldn’t contain it. “Is that so? Sounds nice.”

“Care to join me in picking out that house?”

“I just might.”

He stood up and put his good arm around her, drawing her close against him. She wrapped her arms around his waist carefully.

"You'd better heal fast," she murmured to him. "We have a date to, you know, make love again."

He grinned down at her. "Honey, I plan to do that on a regular basis until the day I die."

"We haven't even said we love each other or anything. Isn't it a bit premature to be talking about the rest of our lives?"

He shot her a withering look. "You know how I feel about you without me having to say it aloud, don't you?"

"Well…yes. But it would still be nice to hear it."

He raised his voice. "May I have your attention, everyone?"

"Marcus," she hissed.

He grinned down at her. "I would like everybody here to know that I love this woman and intend to marry her if she'll have me."

She rolled her eyes at him as cheering and whistles erupted.

"Well?" Gunnar called. "Is another one of my Medusas off the market for good or not?"

She scowled at her boss and then looked up at Marcus. "Yes, I'll marry you. But I'm getting even with you for proposing like this. I don't know how yet, but I'll think of something dastardly."

"I can't wait to see what you come up with," he said warmly.

She looped her arms around his neck, being careful of his shoulder. "But until then, I plan to kiss you all the time."

"Maybe we can come up for air to eat now and then?" he murmured against her lips.

"Now and then," she murmured back.

And then she kissed her SEAL bodyguard and thanked her lucky stars that he was the one she'd sunk her fish hook into that day in Sunny Creek. She had landed the best man ever when she'd caught him.

"Rachel?"

"Hmm?"

"I love you."

"I love you, too, Mr. Trout."

It took him a moment, but then he figured it out. He bent down to her, and their laughter and kisses mingled together. Joy burst over her, along with the sure and certain knowledge that the rest of her life would be spent laughing with and loving this man.

"Forever," she whispered against his lips.

"Forever, my very own Medusa."

* * * * *

Don't miss other thrilling stories by Cindy Dees:

The Cowboy's Deadly Reunion
Navy SEAL's Deadly Secret
Special Forces: The Recruit
Special Forces: The Spy
Special Forces: The Operator
Her Mission with a SEAL
Navy SEAL Cop

Available from Harlequin Romantic Suspense!

COMING NEXT MONTH FROM

HARLEQUIN

ROMANTIC SUSPENSE

#2183 UNDERCOVER COLTON

The Coltons of Colorado • by Addison Fox

Sami Evans has long suspected her father may not be entirely aboveboard. So she's not surprised when her one-night stand turns out to be an FBI agent. Dom Colton needs to get closer to Sami's father, but when Dom and Sami fake an engagement, he's realizing his feelings might be more than a cover.

#2184 CAVANAUGH JUSTICE: DEADLY CHASE

Cavanaugh Justice • by Marie Ferrarella

Embittered and broken detective Gabriel Cortland is forced to pair up with an optimistic partner to take down a prolific serial killer—the one who killed Gabriel's pregnant wife. Gabriel is determined to work alone on this, but Shayla Cavanaugh knows how to break down his defenses. But with a killer on the loose, Gabriel's new lease on life may not last very long...

#2185 COLD CASE COWBOY

Cold Case Detectives • by Jennifer Morey

When she finds refuge at his ranch, Indie Deboe struggles with her feelings for Wes McCann. She's lost everything before—to the same killer who could be a threat to both of them now!

#2186 HOTSHOT HERO UNDER FIRE

Hotshot Heroes • by Lisa Childs

Hotshot firefighter/paramedic Owen James is in danger—and not from firefighting. Someone is trying to kill him, and he finds himself falling for the prime suspect!

Hotshot firefighter-paramedic Owen James is in danger—and not from firefighting. Someone is trying to kill him, and he finds himself falling for the prime suspect!

Read on for a sneak preview of Hotshot Hero Under Fire, *the latest book in Lisa Childs's thrilling Hotshot Heroes miniseries!*

He winced. "Yeah, I remember..."

A smile tugged at the corners of her mouth, pulling up her lips. "Don't go looking for any flowers from me as an apology."

"There's something else I'd rather have from you," he said, and the intensity of his blue-eyed stare had her pulse racing. Then he leaned forward and brushed his mouth across hers.

And shock gripped her so hard, her heart seemed to stop beating for a moment before resuming at a frantic pace. He'd kissed her before, but it still caught her by surprise. Not the kiss so much as the passion that coursed through her. She'd never felt so much desire from just a kiss. And why this man out of all the men she'd dated over the years?

Why Owen James, who'd hurt her in high school with his cruelty? Who hadn't saved her mother?

HRSEXP0422

Why would she be so attracted to him?

It wasn't just because of his flowers and his apology. She'd felt this passion last night before he'd come bearing the roses and his mea culpa.

She'd worried about him yesterday, but just like in high school, she didn't believe it was possible that he really cared about her, that he wanted her. Was he up to something? What did he want from her?

His mouth brushed across hers again. Then his lips nipped at hers, and a gasp escaped her. He deepened the kiss, and she tasted his passion.

He wanted her as badly as she wanted him.

And that was bad…

Very bad.

Because she had a feeling that if she let herself give in to her desire, she would be the one who wound up hurt next…

Don't miss
Hotshot Hero Under Fire *by Lisa Childs,*
available June 2022 wherever
Harlequin Romantic Suspense books and ebooks are sold.

Harlequin.com